SURROUNDED

Dake came to a quick stop as he, Stennis and Stafford reached the thrust of weathered and splintered rock lifting like a shallow hand out of the flat. The Osages fired a few desultory shots which chipped the crumbling stone.

Hugging against it, Sherrod hissed, "What in God's name is the good of this? If—"

A cry came from the thicket. A soft climbing sound of pain that became a pure wail. It could have been either of their women, but Sherrod yelled, "Alex!" and started to struggle upright.

Dake grabbed him by the arm. *"Keep down!"*

But the screaming went on. In a mad fury, Sherrod broke Dake's hold, lunged up and scrambled across the rock. Dake and Stennis moved simultaneously, each grabbing one of Sherrod's legs to haul him back. He tried to kick free.

Cut Face's rifle crashed. Sherrod's struggling ended. He flopped backward, they caught at him. His body fell bonelessly against their hands, turning as it slid down the rock between them. The ball had made a neat hole in his temple where it went in. Almost no bleeding.

An Indian's voice rose in a taunting howl.

MISSION TO THE WEST

T. V. OLSEN

LEISURE BOOKS   NEW YORK CITY

A LEISURE BOOK®

September 1997

Published by special arrangement with Golden West Literary
Agency.

Dorchester Publishing Co., Inc.
276 Fifth Avenue
New York, NY 10001

Printed in the United States of America.

MISSION TO THE WEST

PREFACE

In 1833 America was poised on the edge of its last frontier; the true and final West. The East was settled and staid; the 'Old Northwest' was conquered and occupied. To the southwest, toward Mexican Texas, lay the Great Plains and the nomadic free roaming horsemen who dominated them· the Comanche, the Kiowa, and the Pawnee Picts or Wichitas. Tribes that had never recognized U.S. authority. People who would fight to hold their ancestral lands against the westward tide of white expansion.

To deal with them on their own ground, a new branch of the military would plainly be needed· soldiers on horseback.

American cavalry had remained in virtual limbo for a half century after the War for Independence. The 'light horse' troops of the Revolution had been too small to play any significant part, and afterward they had been disbanded. Americans harbored a deep distrust of any 'man on horseback'; he stirred up memories of Attila and the Cossacks, of mounted and mailed hordes which had terrorized European peasantry for centuries. And the ear of a cost-slashing Congress had been cocked to the public voice: a horse army would be costly to train and equip, expensive to maintain.

The horse had never lost popularity with the militia or irregulars – companies of civilian volunteers who were state raised in emergencies, state-paid, and when their job was done, state-disbanded. But they were expected to provide their own weapons and animals. Mounted militia had been largely responsible for 'Mad Anthony' Wayne's spectacular coup at the Battle of Fallen Timbers in 1794 and for William' Henry Harrison's victory at Tippecanoe in 1811. The land fighting of the War of 1812 was successfully concluded by Colonel Richard Johnson's mounted volunteers at the Battle of the Thames in 1814.

The need for horse troops became increasingly apparent as America's westward thrust carried her onto the vast reaches of the Louisiana Purchase. The annexed country was more lightly wooded than the East; it boasted plenty

5

of grass and water. The opening of the Santa Fe Trail in the 1820's brought a demand for guard troops, and in 1832 the Mounted Rangers, a battalion of congressionally authorized volunteers, was organized as mounted escort for the wagon traders. In a short year, the Rangers proved that even an unruly, undisciplined gang of horse backers could patrol miles of country that would require a dozen times as many well disciplined, well trained foot soldiers to cover.

Finally, on March 2, 1833, the United States Congress authorized the young nation's first unit of regular mounted cavalry. Then designated as the 1st Regiment of U.S. Dragoons, its creation marked the birth of the United States Cavalry of fame, fact and fiction in the nineteenth century West The man chosen by President Andrew Jackson to head it was the commander of the now disbanded Rangers, Colonel Henry Dodge; he was a civilian who had also led a company of mounted volunteers with striking success during the Black Hawk War of 1832.

Within a year of their founding, the Dragoons were given their first assignment· an expedition to the plains of the Far West. Their mission was to impress the proud and fierce plains people with a show of mounted might.

This is a fictionized story of that expedition It was the first of its kind, and, in a way, the last Both heady tri umph and heartbreaking fiasco, it seemed a terrible and costly way for the nation's first horse army to earn its spurs. Yet it set the stage – for better or worse – for America's greatest drama· the conquest of its western frontier.

More than half of the people in this novel are fictitious. But the background is true; the historical facts are merely embellished.

CHAPTER ONE

Lieutenant Stennis Fry was quietly broiling to death in his thick wool uniform. But he sat his saddle with a flat backed dignity and hoped his discomfort wasn't too evident to the four troopers riding behind him. Jogging alongside him, Sergeant Bohannon gave Stennis an occasional glance that was mildly curious and possibly sympathetic. It was never easy to guess what Bohannon was thinking. He was a slight man, narrow as a plank, but tough as a twist of dry rawhide. His pale eyed saturnine face was sun darkened to the color of an old saddle.

Stennis said 'How far to this . . . what do you call it?'

' "Blind tiger," ' Bohannon said, violently working a chew in the pouch of his cheek. Stennis found a certain fascination in watching Bohannon prepare to spit You always expected him to spatter something or someone, not least of all himself. But he never did 'About five miles by the river road, sir ' Bohannon let go, arching a compact brown stream across his right arm

It was rather a nice day. Hot but pleasant. The bottomlands of the Grand River were lush and green. Marsh tules stirred to a hint of wind; here and there a cragkneed cypress rose gauntly against the sweeping sky. The Arkansas prairie was blooming like a garden in these wet warm days of early June Thousands of wildflowers splashed the grassy slopes with pastel brilliance; towhees and larks, hidden in the deep clumps, trilled out silvery runnels of song.

Pleasant. But how could you enjoy it in the woolen sweatbox called a Dragoon uniform? Stennis's neck was chafed raw; he could feel sweat puddling in his ankle boots. Well, no use blaming the weather because the Army wouldn't let you dress for it. Of course the troopers were equally uncomfortable, but at least they could fret openly, cussing their discomfort in discreet undertones.

Stennis Fry only hoped that Satterlee was worth the bother

He didn't know Dake Satterlee except by sight and reputation. He appeared to be a sly, boisterous fellow of thirty or so; garrison gossip assumed that he hadn't much on his mind except squaws and whiskey and that there was damned little to be said for his taste in either. He wasn't untypical of the border riffraff that a gentleman was supposed to look down a long nose at Yet Ben Poore swore by him, and Poore was Chief of Scouts for the regiment. Of all the Indian and mixed blood scouts under his command, Poore was counting most on Satterlee.

This morning Colonel Henry Dodge had assembled all the staff and line officers of the 1st Dragoons around a map table in the headquarters building at Fort Gibson. They had spent hours thrashing out detail of the expedition that would begin three days from now. A mission that would mark the first real thrust of United States troops onto the Great Plains of the Far West. Ben Poore had been present too. Poore was a mountain man who had trapped the upper reaches of the Missouri with General Ashley's brigade He had traded with the Spanish in Santa Fe. He was an intimate of Hugh Glass, 'Old Bill' Williams, 'Broken Hand' Fitzpatrick, the handful of buckskin men who knew the vast ranging mountains and plains between the Canadian and Mexican borders better than any other Americans did in this year of 1834. But the purpose of the expedition was to treat with Indian tribes so remote, so isolated by distance and geography, that few white men of any nationality knew them well

One of those who did, claimed Ben Poore, was Dake Satterlee He'd actually lived with the Pawnee Picts for a spell, though Poore was vague as to the circumstances. Any way Dake was the man to consult about that end of the trip. Poore allowed Dake might be hard to locate right off, he usually was, but place to look was anywhere he could swab his tonsils with panther spit and honeyfuggle a breed lady or two. Likeliest place would be the nearest 'blind tiger.'

From what Stennis could gather, a 'blind tiger' was any place in the Territory that a man could get his fill of hog swill booze and low stakes gambling Since selling liquor was strictly prohibited throughout Arkansas Territory, traders sold it on the sly, either from under the counter in otherwise legitimate posts or from hidden distilleries back in the hills. General Matthew Arbuckle, commander of the

7th Infantry at Fort Gibson, had regularly sent out patrols to break up the 'blind tigers,' but they continued to flourish everywhere that soldiers, settlers and Indians were thirsty. Which was everywhere.

'Be specific, Ben,' Colonel Dodge had said. 'You must have an idea where Satterlee hangs out.'

'Well, Cunnel—' Poore had scratched his beard 'I'd have to allow that Antoine LeBarge's upriver place holds an uncommon attraction for Dake.'

Dodge's frosty gaze had impaled Stennis. 'Lieutenant Fry, take your sergeant and a couple of men and ride straightway to Mr. LeBarge's. I fancy Bohannon knows the way; it is a sty of some repute.'

Ben Poore had cleared his throat. 'Cunnel, I think this shavetail bluejay of yourn is going to need more men'n that '

'All right Take Bohannon and four men, Lieutenant If you find Satterlee, fetch him back here. On the double, understand?'

Stennis did understand As the newest young subaltern in the regiment, fresh from special training at Jefferson Barracks and less than half a year out of West Point, his understanding was practically flawless. If any assignment appeared to be particularly dirty, petty or plain onerous, Second Lieutenant Fry could count on getting it.

What he'd never counted on, to his frequently bitter regret, was that the career of a Dragoon officer assigned to an Arkansas border post was far from what it had seemed cracked up to be He'd arrived at Fort Gibson just a couple of weeks ago, proudly anticipating service with the Army's newest and most elite regiment Which the 1st Dragoons certainly was, thanks to the spine snapping discipline im posed by Dodge's second in command, Lieutenant Colonel Stephen Kearny Men buttoned their trousers by cadence. As to the rough conditions in the Dragoon camp, he'd expected no less But many months of looking forward to the dashing life of a mounted cavalier, plenty of adventure in the field, saber charges on horseback against the painted foe, had hardly prepared Stennis for his actual duties Thus far, these had consisted almost solely of ordering details of soldiers to quarry stone, cut lumber, build barracks and stables, grade roads, herd cattle, make hay and gather wood That sort of thing. His only action against Indians had been

9

to order a pair of tame but drunken and quarrelsome Osages who'd tried to wreck the sutler's store thrown in the guardhouse...

Some dash. Some adventure.

The road wasn't much more than a broad path rutted to a chocolate mire by hoofs and an occasional wagon. It twisted up and down the corrugations of shallow hills timbered with post oak, blackjack and other scrub hardwoods. Green clouds of willow greenery banded the riverbanks, here and there breaking to a view of the Grand's crystal run. Soon the road branched onto a slight elevation A long log building squatted like a brown fungus on the muddy site. A few rickety outsheds and a rail-fenced paddock stood off beyond it.

'LeBarge's?' Stennis asked.

'Yessir.' Bohannon geared his jaws some more. 'That'd be Satterlee's horse tied in front.'

'Are you sure? There are five horses'

Bohannon spat. 'The bay mustang with a white stocking right front. Satterlee's, sir.'

Stennis's nose twitched as they rode across the yard. Animal smells were part of everyday living, but this place was unusually high even by horse army standards. No wonder, with pigs and poultry wandering all over the place. A large spotted hog grunted in annoyance as they disturbed his wallow; a mixed flock of ducks, geese and chickens bunched around their pickings scattered in squawking indignation That set off some goats in the paddock, all of them blatting at once. Men's loud voices drifted from the building's open door, and apparently they were quarreling. Altogether, it made the damnedest sounding racket Stennis had ever heard

He raised his arm for a halt, then dismounted and handed his reins to Bohannon. 'I'll go it alone, Sergeant. I'll call if I need you.'

'Yessir.'

Stennis circled the hitching rail and started toward the porchless doorway. The slick mud kept balling his boots and sloughing him off balance; his saber crossed between his long legs and nearly tripped him. It was embarrassing as hell. He wanted to cut a gallant figure in front of his troops, but nature had pretty well precluded the possibility.

Stennis was inches taller than most men and he gangled like an oversize scarecrow. He'd achieved nearly all his heft and height by the age of fifteen; nine years later he hardly looked any different. At twenty four he could pass for nineteen or so. His face was boyish and pleasant, almost apple cheeked, and he sometimes wondered if it were impervious to climate, weather and time alike. Having it season to craggy lines like Ben Poore's would please him immensely.

But no doubt his eyes would remain as mild as blue-bells, the plains sun would still blister his fair skin to an angry red. When his beard had finally sprouted at twenty, he'd cultivated it to a pair of twisty long mustachios which had never resembled anything more ferocious than corn silk. But he'd doggedly retained them. More recently he'd let his pale hair grow long over his ears and neck, hoping to promote a hirsute plainsman's look, but that had only resulted in his irrepressible barracks mate, Lieutenant Sandy MacPherson, dubbing him 'Mary Ann.'

MacPherson had a delightful sense of fun.

Stennis was almost to the doorway when a man came out at a floundering run, as if someone had flung him. Which, from the eruption of laughter that followed his exit, seemed to be the case.

The man barreled past Stennis, lost his footing and hit the mud belly down. He skidded for a half dozen feet and came to a stop beneath the hitching rail and the horses, which shuffled away from him. He lay on the ground, groaning and clutching his head. Stennis recognized him as Asa Callicutt, a teamster.

A man came to the doorway, roaring with laughter. It was Dake Satterlee. A double eared jug dangled from his right thumb; his red rimmed eyes were tough and happy as he gazed down at Asa.

'That'll larn you not to trod on your betters, boy. Well, say. How you doon, Lootenant?'

Satterlee tipped up the jug and took a deep swig. He wasn't exceptionally tall or big, but he looked brown as a nut and hard as hickory. His wide braced legs strained his tight leggings like oak trunks, his chest and shoulders swelled like a young bull's against his buckskin shirt He might have a drop of Indian blood, but he'd 'gone Indian'

11

about as completely as any white man Stennis had ever seen. His buckskins and moccasins were heavily fringed, trimmed with gaudy beads and dyed quills and claws. An enormous red feather projected from the crown of his crushed slouch hat. A tomahawk and two hunting knives were slung from his beaded belt, which also supported a powder horn and shot pouch What showed of his broad smirking face was ugly as sin, his bright rust colored hair and beard burring over and around it.

Stennis wasted no words. 'Satterlee, you're to come with me,' he said crisply.

'Dew tell?' Dake Satterlee lowered the jug, his pale blue stare sweeping the soldiers. 'Where might that be?'

'To the fort. You're wanted at a conference.'

'That so?' Satterlee swigged again and drew the back of a hairy hand across his mouth. He hiccoughed. 'Dearie me. And you brung all these nice bluejays just to gimme an escort? Am purely favored all to hell, Loot, but ain't fixing to go yet. Have got me tree tall medicine to make right here. Do par'n me.'

He drained the jug, then swung it against the doorjamb, shattering it to pieces. Turning, he strode back inside.

'I say – Satterlee!'

Swearing softly, Stennis went in after him, ducking through the low doorway. The lintel knocked his tall gold-corded cap askew and he paused to straighten it, silently cursing the Army's penchant for shako headgear that failed to be a damned nuisance only when a fellow happened to stand less than five and a half feet tall. Coming out of blazing daylight, he was several moments adjusting his eyes to the taproom's sour gloom.

It was pretty much like any trader's store he'd seen. The walls were dark with smoke and age and natural dim ness, the only light being admitted by the open doorway and a pair of small windows covered with hides that had been scraped to a yellowish translucence. Shelves and counters were stacked with all kinds of goods. The orthodox odors of spices and tobacco failed to drown an all pervasive stink of blackjack rum and cheap whiskey, yet there wasn't a sign of kegged or jugged spirits on the premises LeBarge must have whisked every testimonial to booze out of sight directly someone had glimpsed the approach of soldiers.

Stennis was bleakly impressed with such efficiency, but LeBarge's traffic in illicit spirits wasn't his prime concern just now.

He pushed forward between the counters. 'Satterlee!'

He stopped short, staring in disgust. Dake Satterlee was leaning against a counter made of whipsawed boards pegged across a couple of barrels. Pressed up next to him was a dish-faced girl who was giggling like a lunatic. Satterlee had one arm snaked around her plump waist, his other hand plunged inside her calico bodice fondling her plump bosom. He nuzzled her neck and paid no attention at all to Stennis or to the three men who sat on puncheon benches flanking a puncheon table at the back of the store.

Stennis warily eyed the three They were Oshel Callicutt and two of his sons. The third son, Asa, still lay groaning outside The Callicutts were civilian teamsters who were drawing Dragoon pay, having been hired by Colonel Dodge to drive supply wagons on the forthcoming trek They looked a bit ridiculous just sitting at a completely bare table, or would have if it hadn't been for the deadly looks they were giving Satterlee. The fact that he'd beaten up and thrown out their son and brother might have something to do with it, and their moods couldn't have been improved by LeBarge suddenly snatching up and hiding the hooch they'd doubtless been quaffing

The girl giggled explosively.

Standing behind the counter and looking on with no particular concern was a portly, dirty looking, half-bald man whose features strongly resembled the girl's. 'Ah, *mon capitaine*,' he beamed at Stennis. '*Soyez le bienvenu!* Welcome to the store of Antoine LeBarge '

'Satterlee, did you hear me?' Stennis demanded. 'You're returning to the fort now.'

Satterlee tipped up a bloodshot eye, grinning. 'Aw shuckins, Loot. Just when a feller's fancy is getting nested all cozy and toasty like, you ..'

'I sha'n't argue with you,' Stennis snapped. 'While you're drawing Army pay, you are expected to obey orders as any soldier does, without question Will you stop dallying with that female and come along or must I have you trussed up and carried?'

Satterlee gently moved the girl aside and straightened

13

up, his eyes crackling with wicked glee. 'Not a bad idee. Set-to with that Asa-boy wa'n't worth a wee piddle o' sweat for working off a feller's evil humors. You just whistle up your bluejays, we'll see . . .'

'You hold on,' rumbled Oshel Callicutt.

He got slowly to his feet, a towering rawboned man whose eyes were like pewter-colored ice between his shaggy brows and great beak of a nose. His gray powdered russet beard hung almost to his waist and tobacco drippings made a dark streak down the middle of it. He wore greasy leather pantaloons and, despite the heat, a heavy buffalo coat. A coiled bullwhip was slung around his neck.

'We got a bone er two to pick with Buckskin, here,' Oshel said. 'Now we was all sitting just a-minding our own, pert as you please, and my boy Asa was a-honey-fuggling with his gel, that's her yonder, Antoine's darter. In sashays this Satterlee with a big bug up his ass, just a-spoiling to split up Asa and his squaw.'

Satterlee chuckled. 'Shouldn't wonder, seeing's I shared her hay last night. Anyways t'were her idee,'

'That don't cut no ice on the pond, son. She's a dumb Indin don't know enough to squat when she pees. What I'm saying, you don't go a honeyfuggling no woman a Calli-cutt has staked for his, not 'less you are honing to burn powder on't.' His hamlike fist closed around the handle of his bullwhip. 'You just back off, Army, and wait your turn.'

'Whooee, that do shine,' Satterlee shouted, cracking his palms together. 'Come on, you Tennessee walking jays! I'm a canebrake boar what got crossed with a bayou 'gator. I got weaned on cannon balls and I chew up a whole sty of corn raised hill hawgs like you for breakfast!'

Stennis strode to the door and shouted, 'Bohannon!'

In five seconds the troopers were off their horses and stalking smartly into the store. Stennis nodded at Satterlee. 'Sergeant,' he said curtly.

Bohannon barked an order. Two troopers, Tevis and Murphy, wheeled in at either side of Dake Satterlee and caught his arms 'Take his legs,' Stennis told the other two Instantly Kline and Brander seized Satterlee's legs at the knees, yanked them from under him and lifted Half drunk, caught by surprise, Satterlee was swung up and

14

carried toward the door. He let out a whoop of mirth, yelling·

'Well, I be a sowbelly son of a bitch!'

Oshel lifted the coiled whip off his neck. At the menacing move, Stennis swung around, his saber clearing scabbard. The curved Dragoon blade had a wicked silvery sheen.

'You Callicutts stay where you are,' he grated. 'I'll brook no interference '

'Bluejay,' growled Verl Callicutt, 'you just tore the rag clean offen the bush.'

He and his brother stood up, flanking their father. Both were raw boned copies of the old man, more or less Verl, the eldest, had blank bleached eyes and a tangled black beard He was even taller and more massive boned than Oshel. Tute, the middle son, was a younger twin of his father except for one distinguishing feature, if you could call it that. Eyes that were close set, mean, porcine, so pale they were colorless.

Both sons stirred like restive bulls, but Oshel checked them with a gesture. 'Leave it be,' he said.

LeBarge's daughter gave a squeaky giggle.

Stennis threw her a look of disgust. He turned and tramped out after his men, sheathing his saber.

He had hardly passed out the doorway when a noise brought him wheeling clumsily around. Too late. Oshel Callicut wasn't eight feet behind him, his whip whirring like a rattler as it streaked out.

The lash curled cleanly around Stennis's neck. He grabbed at it with both hands, trying to choke out an order that gurgled off in his throat. It was as if a redhot band had enclosed his neck. Oshel gave a yank and Stennis stumbled forward, falling to his knees.

'Ain't you just the pert one, though,' Oshel snorted.

He walked over and bent down, jerking Stennis's saber from the scabbard. One hand gripping the hilt, the other bracing palm flat along the blade, he contemptuously raised a huge knee, snapped the saber in two across it and dropped the pieces He swiftly unwound the whip from Stennis's neck, placed a foot against his chest and shoved, slamming him over on his back.

Verl and Tute came piling out the door.

15

'You sojers clear off,' snarled Oshel. He cracked his whip. 'I mean to whup some smarts into that sassy mountain pup.'

Stennis lay helpless for the moment, half-strangled, lights popping in his eyes. Rolling on his side, he saw his men come turning around, bracing for the attack. They were still holding Satterlee. The mountain man twisted his powerful body like a snake's, yelling, 'Leave go, you goddam fools!' They did, dropping him and scattering away as Oshel's whip snaked out in great whistling cracks.

Dake Satterlee was on the ground and Oshel came at him, his lash whirring back and forward. Dake rolled away; the tip geysered up dust where he'd been. He bounced to his feet, springy-footed as a panther.

The transformation in him was incredible. Suddenly he looked cold sober, tensely poised, mean eyed as a catamount.

'You are grabbing for fire and pizen, old man,' he said softly. 'You'd a touched me with that thing, I'd have your tripe spilled out in the dirt afore you could say "possum up a gum tree "'

Oshel threw back his head with a bray of laughter He shook out his lash and fired another savage cut at Dake. The mountain man leaped aside at the moment, so quickly you could barely follow his movements. Suddenly a long-bladed knife flashed from the beaded sheath at his belt.

'Watch out, Daddy!' Tute Callicutt yelled.

Satterlee was in and out in one lithe weaving motion. As he stepped back, grinning, Oshel let go a bellow of rage. He was holding the stump of a whip. A stroke of Dake's razorlike blade had sliced it through three feet from the stock before Oshel had realized what was happening

He rushed at Dake now, the whipstock flailing up and down like a club.

Asa Callicutt had climbed groggily to his feet, still holding his head. He was of a like size with his kin, but bonier, with a sly quick witted face and hair like dirty hemp. He grabbed the hitching rail for support and shook his head to clear it.

Satterlee had easily ducked Oshel's wild swings. One blindly caught his knuckles and made him drop the knife. Then Dake's hand closed over the whip handle and immo-

16

bilized it. For a moment they wrestled chest to chest, and now Oshel's great arms wrapped around Dake in a crushing hug. He lifted and heaved and flung Dake away. The mountain man hit the ground loose as a rag bundle and bounded back to his feet unhurt. He wheeled in on Oshel, his grin streaking white across his face as the club-hard heel of his right palm whipped up against Oshel's jaw in a shattering blow. It would have laid a lesser man out cold. Oshel merely grunted and staggered back a few steps.

Asa scowled, taking in the scene now. 'Goddammit!' he bawled at his brothers. 'Why ain't you two he'ping Daddy? Come on –'

Like Verl and Tute, the soldiers had held back. All seemed willing to let Oshel and Dake settle the matter. Bohannon alone made a move, coming over to help Stennis to his feet.

'Dammit,' Stennis managed to whisper, 'why don't you stop 'em?'

'Well, sir, in lieu of orders to the contrary,' Bohannon began to say. Then his dark glum expression changed to a fighting one. With Asa in the lead, all three sons were converging on the two battling men. And the four soldiers were promptly moving to stop them.

Bohannon sprang into the fray too, leaving Stennis to stand alone, swaying on his feet. He watched the tableau dissolve into a total brawl. The pigs and chickens added to the bedlam, grunting and screeching as they scattered off from the ruckus. LeBarge's dishfaced daughter had stepped outside, smiling imbecilically as she stood rubbing one bare foot against the other.

Verl laid Brander out with a single smashing blow, but Kline was almost as big as the largest Callicutt and he wrestled Verl to the ground. Struggling, they rolled over and over in a tempest of dust Asa had closed with Murphy and gotten him down, straddling his chest and hammering at his face. Small wry faced Tevis now leaped full onto Asa's back, small hard fists beating a savage tattoo on his head and shoulders Asa floundered away from Murphy, clawing backward in a futile effort to dislodge the leechlike Tevis Bohannon, meantime, was toe to toe with Tute Callicutt, slugging it out.

Oshel and Satterlee seemed equally matched. Both were

17

solidly powerful, Dake making up in speed what he lacke
of the older man's heft and reach. Oshel had clamped
viselike grip on Dake's head, but the mountain man kep
pummeling his ribs with short sledging blows, Oshel takin
a grunting step back with each one. His grip loosened; Dak
twisted free.

Tute had plenty of reach on the wiry, slightly built ser
geant. He slammed a chance blow to the Irishman's nec
and knocked him flat. Tute wheeled and stumbled toward
his father and Satterlee. Stennis saw his hand dip, fumbl
at his boot and yank a long dagger blade free of a hidder
sheath – one of the 'Arkansas toothpicks,' a killer's weapon.

Stennis tried to shout, at least gasp a warning to Satter
lee But all that his mortified throat could manage was
whispery wheeze.

Satterlee and Oshel were warily circling each other
arms spread, as they braced to close again. All of Dake'
attention appeared to be on Oshel, not on Tute who wa.
sidling behind and to the left of him. But as Tute lunged
knife point set for Dake's ribs, the mountain man half
pivoted suddenly. His leg swept out in a side lashing kick.

His toe met Tute's wrist Bone snapped.

Tute screamed, then sank twisting to the ground

'By God, I will deal you as good,' roared Oshel Calli
cutt, and charged at Dake again.

Driven back by the sheer rage of Oshel's rush, Satterlee
kept out of reach and waited his chance The yard wide
brawl was bogging into a stalemate that might go on til
each side had ground the other down to lathered exhaus
tion. Nothing would be solved and somebody might be
killed

Forcing his legs into rubbery motion, Stennis crossed to
the hitching rack He leaned against his horse's flank and
worked open one of his saddlebags, pulling out a heavy
pistol. He half cocked its hammer, fumbled a fulminate
cap out of his pocket and crimped it on the percussior
nipple.

Turning now, he held the pistol at arm's length and
leveled it straight at Oshel's head.

'Mr. Callicutt,' he said hoarsely 'You will desist from
fighting and will tell your sons to do so. Then you wil

mount your animals and pack out of here. Quietly. Or I will scatter your brains across this yard.'

His voice sawed like a mere thin wire through the brawling. But it reached Oshel. He came to a stop and looked at the youthful lieutenant. Stennis's left hand dragged the hammer to full cock.

'You have five minutes to decide.'

'Aw shit,' said Dake Satterlee.

'Mr. Satterlee.' Stennis swung the gun a little, his voice scraping from a raw throat. 'I will as readily put an ounce of lead into your leg, if necessary. Don't tempt me.'

Satterlee said nothing, but he started to grin. The battle was breaking off, all the combatants pulling apart and all of them watching Stennis. Oshel Callicutt's jaw worked solidly; he wiped a broad palm across his nose from which blood was leaking into his russet beard.

'I hear you, son,' he said finally. 'I am owing you too, sojer boy, but will tot up the reckoning for another day. It'll come. Boys –'

All four of the Callicutts moved to their horses, Verl and Asa supporting Tute between them. Tute gripped his arm above the broken bone, tears streaking his grimy face, gazing at the wrist in fascination.

'Christ, Christ,' he moaned. 'I will kill that buckskin bastard for this. I swear, Daddy, I will do it.'

'Set up,' said Oshel.

The four climbed onto their mounts and swung across the yard onto the Fort Gibson road. Stennis walked over to where he'd fallen, picked up his shako and adjusted it on his head, then straightened his uniform. His hands were shaking a little.

He looked at Bohannon. 'Sergeant –'

'Yessir!' Bohannon marched up to him, braced and flung a salute. The martial severity of it made Stennis blink. But he couldn't be mistaken. A genuine respect smoldered in Bohannon's moody eyes.

'See that Mr. Satterlee is mounted on his animal. If he resists, bind his hands and tie him on.'

Dake Satterlee chortled quietly. He was leaning his rump against the paddock fence, rubbing a welt on his forehead. 'Ain't no call for a hard hand, Loot,' he said affably. 'One

19

of you'll fetch my rifle from inside the store, I'll com
peaceable.'

Stennis eyed him suspiciously. 'Why – now?'

'Well, Loot –' Dake lounged away from the fence anc
ambled over to his paint horse, giving Stennis a friendl
wink. 'You just showed you are more'n a uniform with
head on its shoulders. You wa'n't a-bluffing. You'd a blowec
that old man's head clean off if need be. And he goddam
well knowed you would of. You got a man under you
fancy cloth, bluejay, and I don't mind a going with you.'

'I haven't changed my mind about you,' Stennis saic
coldly. 'You're a damned ruffian, Satterlee.'

'Ooo my, lah de lah,' Satterlee leered in a high mockin_
voice. Then laughter exploded from him. 'Goddam righ
I am,' he said happily.

They got aboard their horses and started up the rive
road to Gibson. Satterlee's appearance and behavior indi
cated that he was on the crest or off taper of a monumenta
bat, but he rode jauntily, flat backed and whistling, aheac
of Stennis Fry and his sergeant.

'I don't see what all the fuss was about,' Stennis mut
tered 'She looked like any flat faced squaw to me '

Bohannon turned his head and spat a brown gobbet
'I'd wait till I been around here a spell, sir,' he said mildly.

CHAPTER TWO

'Dammit, Satterlee!'

Colonel Henry Dodge strode to the map table and cracked his riding crop across it. Half-wheeling then, he glared at Dake Satterlee with eyes that Stennis had heard one private declare 'give a man a case of pure ice in his innards.' Dodge was six feet tall, a burly thickset man who moved with more speed than grace. He was fifty-two. His bearing was anything but military, an impression emphasized by his fringed faded buckskins and high jackboots that were old and scuffed and cracked. He never wore the uniform of his rank and you couldn't picture him in it. Yet authority crackled from him. His face was like brown iron, his hair bristling gray.

The room was General Henry Leavenworth's office at the headquarters building of the 7th Infantry, Fort Gibson, where the general had summoned the Dragoon leaders for consultation. Besides Dodge, the officers present included Lieutenant Colonel Stephen Watts Kearny, Captains David Perkins and Whit Mulady and Lieutenants Davis and MacPherson and Fry. Chief of Scouts Ben Poore was on hand too. General Leavenworth, who'd been leading the animated discussion when Stennis had left, had departed.

Stennis wondered what had occurred during his absence. Dodge seemed furious about something.

'I'll hear no more,' he barked, 'about why the mission is a "goddam foolishment" as you call it! This expedition will take the 1st Dragoons as far as the Wichita Mountains—' Dodge whacked his crop across the chart again He habitually carried it to gesture with, to emphasize a temper-taut mood or to punctuate his rapid-fire statements. 'Our orders come direct from President Jackson. Final, explicit and irrevocable orders. Give me no more negative talk about why "it cain't be done." Your job, Satterlee, is to acquaint us with the hazards, problems, general conditions facing us. That and that only.'

Standing negligently, arms crossed, Dake rubbed his rump

against Leavenworth's desk. 'Shuckins, Cunnel,' he grinned. 'That's what I been doon. Am telling you if you go abatting off across the plains middle o' June on Ole Hickory's say-so or whoever, it is a foolishment to start with. You get across the Washita and past the Cross Timbers, there's the Great Plains. Which ain't a spit'n' swaller this side o' hell. Man can see for miles, but he can't see nary a tree. Plenty room to hunt in, but hardly any game Not in the hot spell, they ain't. Same with water. Damn few waterholes and ever' small stream gone bone dry. Even without a man mentions these Dragoons o' yourn is greener'n spring grass.'

Ben Poore coughed quietly and shifted his feet. He was a tall spare man who ordinarily stood still as an Indian, looking like a single carved piece of dark gnarled oak until he moved. Then he'd move like a panther Poore must have been fifty or more, but had the worn and yet preserved look that made you discount his years. Quite a spectacular figure in his own right, Poore wore the regalia of a full chief in the Creek tribe into which he'd married · beaded white doeskin shirt, leggings of gaudily decorated yellow leather and a colorful silk turban.

After winking at his old friend to show he had gotten his message, Satterlee shrugged. 'All I'm saying, Cunnel, be better we'd got this fandango on the trail two month ago, even a month ago. . . .'

'I know that,' Dodge snapped. 'Hell's fire, I wanted to get underway by first good grass. May first at the latest. But it was impossible, what with general confusion about orders, a shift in command, the new recruits arriving late –' He paused, snapping a glance at Lieutenant Colonel Kearny. 'Sorry, Steve. Not blaming you. It's just, dammit, that everything has conspired to hold us up.'

Kearny merely gave a curt nod.

Through last summer, the new regiment had mustered at Jefferson Barracks near St. Louis, training headquarters for the Western Department of the Army. Their officers, drawn from the cream of the U.S. Infantry, had been sent out to beat the recruiting drums across every state and territory. After training, the first batch of recruits had been ordered to Fort Gibson While Dodge had jauntily marched the three undersize companies off to Arkansas, Kearny

22

had headed up another recruiting mission to bring the regiment up to size. With six companies that still didn't swell the Dragoons to full strength, he had arrived at Fort Gibson two weeks ago. Among his new officers was Stennis Fry, happy and proud to be the first West Pointer assigned to the Dragoons without having put in prior service in another branch.

Jaw jutting, Dodge strode up and down the general's office. 'Once,' he muttered, 'just once, by God, I wish things would go smoothly with this outfit.' He halted and shook his crop at the west wall of the room and the plains beyond it. 'Think I don't know what that country's like in high summer? My Mounted Rangers escorted trade wagons on the Santa Fe Trail; I know much of the country beyond the Washita and past the Cross Timbers as well as any of you high-prairie *hivernants*. Worst stretch of wilderness this side of hell after mid June. No timber. Damned little grass and water and almost none in a hot spell. Water holes few and far between and all small streams gone dry. And the Santa Fe trip is a pleasant promenade next to the territory we'll be crossing!'

Dake Satterlee took a blackened strip of jerky from a pocket, tore off a piece with his teeth and chewed ruminatively. 'Yeh. You name it sweet 'n' straight, Cunnel. You shoulda tol' them big brassheads in Washington City you wasn't gonna go gadding across the high plains in the dead o' summer.'

'It's hardly that simple, Satterlee,' the colonel snapped. 'We've a job to do – at all costs. You're aware that the Kiowas and Osages are warring among themselves across that region. A highly combustible situation that could endanger our settlers and emigrants. Also the Comanches have been restive of late. Small bands of their braves have made actual strikes against settlements to the south. A full-scale war party attacked the only caravan that put out for Santa Fe this spring, though two companies of Dragoons commanded by Captain Wharton were riding escort. Maybe they were merely testing our patience with the small raids, but that one on the wagon train was something else. Clear defiance of United States authority. An open challenge to the mettle of the Dragoons.'

'Yeh, well –' Dake paused, ripping off another twist of

the jerky. 'How you allow this here expedition gonna make 'em all come t' taw?'

'We discussed that earlier.' Dodge resumed his angry pacing. 'If you'd been here when you should have been, you'd —' He came abreast of Dake and wheeled to a stop, nostrils twitching. 'Thunderation, man! Don't you ever take a bath?'

'What for?' Dake said amiably. 'T'ain't New Year's.'

Lieutenant Sandy MacPherson didn't quite suppress a snicker He was twenty-six, stocky and strong, and too cheerfully and cynically ebullient to be fully believable as a career officer. He had copious freckles, a thatch of blazing hair and baby-fair skin that never stopped blistering and peeling under the Arkansas sun. The young officer standing with folded arms by the door only grinned a little. Lieutenant Jefferson Davis, regimental adjutant for the Dragoons, was a slender, robust Mississippian whose handsome and aristocratic features held a streak of mischief. He was of an age with MacPherson, but unlike Sandy, Davis had a cool rein on his emotions. Except, occasionally, for his temper.

'Pay attention,' Dodge said irritably. 'Our purpose is to impress the savages of the Great Plains that the Grand father has a long arm. This won't be a punitive expedition, but we do mean to impress the Kiowa, the Comanches, the Pawnee, with a show of mounted power on their own terms on their own territory. God willing, that'll be sufficient.'

Dake gazed dourly at the jerky in his hand. 'Dandy, Cunnel. Just dandy. How many sojers you got to show 'em with?'

'Well, roughly five hundred, but of course our companies aren't up to strength —'

'Wagh!' Dake shuttled a lazy glance at the older scout. 'Ben, you tell these bleeding bluejays how much show they gonna stand out there?' Poore gave the faintest of shrugs, indicating he'd said all he could. Dake, with an ex pression of bored disgust, pointed a thumb at Dodge's chest. 'I will give it to you sweet 'n' straight. Five hundred sojers or five thousand, you won't stand no show out there. You're talking about facing the best hossmen in the world on their own ground That's Comanch' country They run ever'thing south o' the Arkansas and east o' the Pecos.

24

The Kiowa are their brothers, but there's Pawnee, Osage, Tonks and Navajo out there too. Betimes the 'Paches come up from the south and the Sioux come down from the north. Comanch' have taken a stick to all their red hides one time or t'other.'

'I know that, Satterlee. May I finish? We intend to demonstrate good faith by taking along two Indian girls, one Kiowa and one Pawnee.'

Dake showed a flicker of interest. 'Squawmeat, huh?'

'Both were lost to their people years ago. The Kiowa was captured by Osages when she was ten and they raided her village. Two years ago my Rangers rounded up this band of Osage renegades and she was among them But the Pawnee may be our real prize. She claims to be the granddaughter of the chief of the Toyash, largest band of the Pawnee Picts.'

Satterlee seemed mildly impressed. 'Well, boy howdy. That'd be ol' Wa ter ra shah-ro. I know him.'

'I was hoping you might. What do you think of this girl's claim?'

'Could be bonyfide. 'Bout twenty grasses back, ol' Water ra shah ro's daughter got took as wife by a fur trader. Froggy feller. Wed her Injun style. Give the chief many gifts, cloth and mirrors, junk like that. Took her to St. Looey with him. Pawnee never seen hide nor hair of 'em again.'

'That would fit the girl's story. Claims her father was a Frenchman who abandoned her mother in St. Louis shortly after she was born. The mother tried to make her way back across Arkansas, but never got farther than the Lovely Purchase, the big Cherokee reserve south of here. There she sickened and died. The Cherokees raised her daughter, who's now seventeen. She wants to return to her mother's people. When she heard of our expedition to the Wichitas, she came to me and offered her assistance in exchange for a safe escort back to her people.'

Dake rubbed his chin, nodding. 'Yeh. Taking them squaws home might stir up some Injun gratefuls.'

'Merely a carrot to balance the stick. In a sense the girls will be levers for bargaining, but we'll attach no outward strings. We'll restore the Kiowa to her people, the Pawnee to hers. Let magnanimity take its course. We hope for one

25

thing that the Toyash will be disposed to give up young Matthew Martin.'

'Ain't that Jedge Martin's boy? Pappy had his hair lifted by Pawnee last summer?'

'The same. Toyash raiders according to all accounts, and the son's body wasn't found. The Martins are important in the East and President Jackson promised the boy's relatives that the Army will do everything possible to recover him. We can only hope he's alive and well. However – our main purpose will be to summon as many bands of the plains tribes as possible to a great council. We hope to pacify the warring Kiowas and Osages. In addition, we want to make treaty with all the plains peoples and, to that end, persuade representative chiefs or headmen to return with us.'

'Waste o' time,' Dake observed succinctly. 'Plain goddam foolishness. Lemme tell you . . .'

'That will do, Satterlee,' Dodge said testily. 'I daresay the plains, the people, the parleys will all present ordeals of one sort or another But we're paying you to give advice and guidance *toward* the trip, not offer blatant pessimism against it.' He tapped the map with his crop. 'We have little definite knowledge about the Wichitas . . . the Pawnee country. Suppose you tell us what you can.'

'Sure, Cunnel.' Dake sauntered over to the map table. 'Reckon you could produce a pinch o' tonsil tonic? Got me a turrible dry.' He cleared his throat. 'Tongue's all squoze up.'

'Little wonder.' Dodge glared at him. 'Apparently you haven't heard that General Winfield Scott has abolished the Army's whiskey dole. All posts are quite dry.'

'Aw, sho. Must be just a drop o' talk grease around –?'

'*No!*'

Satterlee's knowledge of the mountainous country where the Pawnee Picts had their stronghold appeared to be extensive and thorough. He pointed out locations of trails and passes and waterholes; he gave ready answers for Dodge's and Poore's questions. Stennis glanced at MacPherson and Davis by the door, then sidled over to them and murmured.

'What's Dodge in such dudgeon about? He seems even more temperamental than usual.'

'Wurra, wurra,' MacPherson grinned. 'After you left to fetch Satterlee, General Leavenworth made a surprise announcement. He has decided to lead the expedition himself. Promptly the four humors did battle in Dodge's spleen – you could tell how incensed he was – but he held himself in. Then we heard a steamer bell at the landing and the general excused himself – wanted to see if the civilians who'll be joining us are aboard. They're supposed to arrive on the *Arkansas Belle*.'

Stennis nodded. Word had come from departmental head quarters that a German naturalist named Beyrich would accompany the expedition, courtesy of the U. S. Government; also the government would send a special representative for the purpose of setting up trade agreements with the plains tribes.

'After the general left,' MacPherson said, 'the good colonel exploded A warlock o' the glens couldn't pronounce such anathemas. But there's precious little he can do about Leavenworth's decision, seeing's the general now commands the whole Western Department of the Army. Kearny's not too happy either, as Leavenworth hinted he'll leave him in command here at Gibson.'

'If there's one thing the Dragoons don't need more of,' Davis observed, 'it's rancor at the top ranks.'

They had conversed in whispers, but Kearny swung from the map table with his iron stare 'Gentlemen, you have my *permission* to move nearer and give a sharp ear to what's being said *here*. You may find it enlightening, even useful'

Sheepishly, the three subalterns came over to the table.

Dodge bent over the map, marking in new information as Satterlee enlarged on the problems they'd face. The mountain man continued to take a cheerfully negative view of the whole business and Dodge, never noted for patience, was restraining himself with difficulty.

Lately just about everything had conspired to turn the colonel irate. He was still smarting from heavy criticism he'd drawn for marching that first contingent of Dragoons five hundred miles to Fort Gibson in howling, freezing weather. Numerous cases of frostbite had been reported; many weakened soldiers had fallen ill Then the delays, one after another, in getting the expedition underway.

They'd be setting out three months later than originally planned. Even a greenhorn could see sense in not tackling the Great Plains at midsummer, but the War Department which had insisted on this mission was back East. Finally the blow to Dodge's pride and ambition: Leavenworth, not he, would lead the most spectacular journey in U. S. Army history.

'Commanch'll be the big rock in the trail,' Satterlee was saying, 'but you won't get nowhere with no grand parley less'n you get the Pawnee on your side.'

'That's why we're counting on you,' Dodge said. 'You have had closer relations with the Toyash than any other American.'

'I dunno, Cunnel. Been three year sincet I . . .'

The door opened, General Henry Leavenworth strode in. He was fifty one, a long-faced man with a hawk nose. Like Kearny, he was all spit 'n' polish. Seven years ago he'd built Fort Leavenworth to defend the eastern end of the Santa Fe Trail and he had more than a passing interest in seeing the service develop a strong mounted arm. He'd taken over command of Fort Gibson a few months ago, following the resignation of General Matthew Arbuckle.

'Well, Colonel, our civilians were on the boat. Our trade man, our Prussian botanist, even an artist. And one wife, b'God. I've installed them in tents on the campus. Would this be Satterlee?'

'Yes, General.' Dodge glared. 'Did you say *wife*, sir?'

Leavenworth nodded. 'The government fellow brought his lady along. I assumed he'd planned to leave her at Gibson during his absence, but it seems she's set on accompanying him and he doesn't object . . .'

'Out of the question!' Dodge snapped. 'A woman on this trek? Absolutely not. I trust you told her as much.'

Leavenworth touched the looping black horns of his mustache and smiled. 'Tried. A determined female, I'm afraid ' He glanced at Kearny, whose face also showed stern disapproval. 'Perhaps you gentlemen would care to try your powers of dissuasion?'

'I most damned certainly intend to try.' Dodge said. He whacked his crop against his leg and looked at the others. 'Gentlemen, you'll attend me, please. We'll welcome our guests. Ben, I'd like you and Satterlee to come too.'

'Sure, Cunnel. Dake?'

Satterlee shrugged. 'I'll mosey 'long.'

The men left the headquarters building and swung across the parade to the gate.

The fort, a palisaded square of barracks buildings and corner blockhouses, sprawled on an inclined elbow of land in a bend of the Grand River. Gibson was still the westernmost Army post on the American frontier, southernmost of seven cantonments that, stretching down from Fort Snelling on the upper Mississippi, guarded the Western border. Empty wilderness billowed away to north and west, a tangle of chaparral swamps engulfing the bottomlands to the south. The Grand River slashed the desolation like a sparkling snake, running clear as crystal for another two miles before losing itself in the mud heavy Arkansas. A broad shelf of rock created a natural landing for supply steamers which docked here when the water was high enough to let them negotiate the Grand's submerged sandbars The *Arkansas Belle* was drawn up, her twin stacks making traceries of smoke on a blue washed sky. Two of the Callicutt sons, Verl and Asa, were lounging by the stone dock, watching roustabouts unload provisions and equipment for the garrison.

Verl Callicutt glanced toward the officers and two scouts as they passed along the road He nudged his kinsman and said something; Verl looked. Dake grinned and tipped his hat to them. Stennis ran a finger around the tall stiff collar of his coatee which mercilessly gouged his sore throat. Damn all Army collars and damn all Callicutts.

MacPherson elbowed him, murmuring, 'Quite a battle it must have been.'

'Battle?'

'Don't ply me with innocence, laddie The nasty edge of a bruise shows round your neck Ho ho, the Callicutts, was it?'

Skirting north of the stockade's river side, the road became a straight lane flanked by officers' quarters, homes of married soldiers, mess halls and a hospital Around the stockade's other sides were scattered forage barns, stables, storehouses, carpenters' and farriers' shops, the sutler's

29

store and warehouse. Coats of whitewash protected some buildings, but fierce weathering was steadily hammering the best of them into decay. A skimpy row of elms, oaks and pecans relieved the grim cheerlessness of the dirt street. Patched and worn tents as well as crude log houses lined the officers' row. Leavenworth halted his companions by one of them. A young man in civilian clothes, his back to them, was bent over a wash basin scrubbing his face.

'Herr Beyrich,' said Leavenworth.

The young man straightened up and around, toweling himself. 'Ah, General! I did not see you.'

Carl Beyrich was slightly built, with a fresh apple-cheeked face capped by smooth blond hair. His corduroy suit was stained and rumpled, and the limp tops of some chicory plants dangled from one pocket. His eager brown eyes wanted to take in everything at once.

Another man came ducking out of the tent. A strong-looking fellow in his mid-thirties, he was in his shirt-sleeves and the shirt was blotched with dried paints. His cravat was a loose knotted kerchief around his brown throat; his rugged big nosed face was somehow familiar. Then Stennis remembered him. George Catlin, the artist. Catlin had visited West Point several years ago, sketching everything in sight, otherwise wetting a fishline in the Hudson River or joining the cadets at Benny Havens's off limits taproom.

Leavenworth performed the introductions. Stennis was surprised that Catlin remembered him from among many cadets; he also knew Colonel Dodge and Jeff Davis, having met them in Michigan Territory prior to the Black Hawk War. Catlin explained that he'd obtained special permission from Secretary of War Lewis Cass to accompany the trek. As the men stood chatting, a couple stepped from a tent pitched a few yards away.

'Ah, Mr. Sherrod ... Mrs Sherrod,' said Leavenworth. 'I should like you both to meet my staff officers and my two best scouts.'

Randall Sherrod was a tall imposing man with a large cleft chinned face that was handsome in a fleshy, imperial way. He wore a salmon waistcoat over his frilled shirt and a double breasted plum colored coat with long tails that nearly reached to the bottoms of the yellow nankeen trousers strapped beneath his shoes. He had a ruddy, hearty, fortyish look of success; his accent was vaguely Virginian. His facile manner and easy smile were characteristics that Stennis had learned to look for in special governmental appointees.

His wife was something else.

She looked about half her husband's age, twenty three or so. Tall as most men, her Junoesque figure was set off by a green riding habit trimmed with gold braid. She looked as healthy and robust as the devil, an impression of raw boned vigor that combined with the bubbling humor in her strong boned face to make you discount the beauty in it. Then gradually you realized that she was beautiful, vividly so. Her eyes were very green, her skin very tan; her hair glowed like coils of copper wire.

'Madam–' Dodge came crisply to the point. 'I under stand that you've expressed a wish to accompany our mission.'

'I wouldn't miss it for the world.'

'Preposterous!' Dodge snapped 'No place for a woman, trek like that. Out of the question.'

'Oh? Perhaps I misunderstood–' Sweeping her green eyes to Leavenworth. 'You said, did you not, General, that two Indian ladies will accompany the caravan?'

Leavenworth nodded.

Dodge said glacially · 'I can hardly believe, ma'am, that you are serious. You, a delicate, gently bred white woman, cannot possibly –'

She laughed. 'But I can, Colonel. I'm young and quite strong. I am an excellent horsewoman and a good pistol shot. I'm accustomed to long hours in a saddle or on a wagon seat and I am no stranger to hardship. Heat, cold, hunger, thirst – I'm on intimate terms with them.'

Dodge turned furiously to Randall Sherrod. 'Sir, the lady is your wife Surely you'll not consent to her being exposed to the dangers and privations of this journey'

'Afraid I've little to say in the matter, Colonel.' Sherrod's grin was bland as butter. 'Alexandra generally has her way. Besides, what she told you is quite true. She's accompanied me to many a rough and out-of-the-way place Tough as nails, sir -- never sick an hour that I can recall. Never a complaint. I'd hazard, too, that she can ride and shoot as well as most of your Dragoons.'

31

Dodge motioned to Ben Poore. 'Ben, step over here. Perhaps you can drum sense into these people. Tell 'em what we'll be facing on this trip. Why it's like nothing that's ever been undertaken.'

The tall scout walked up to Mrs. Sherrod, lifting the turban from his close-cropped hair. 'What the cunnel says is gospel, ma'am.'

'You have crossed the Great Plains, Mr. Poore?'

'Yes'm, many times. Only once at high summer by my lonesome, which foolishment I will not attempt again.'

'Yet, sir, you've agreed to guide this mission.'

'Yes'm. It is no fault of Cunnel Dodge's or Genril Leavenworth's that them brassheads in Washington City have wrangled over proceedings till summer and then have give orders it is got to be now.' Poore seemed ill at ease; he glanced at Satterlee 'Dake, you seen more'n me o' the far country. Tell Miz Sherrod what you think o' her going out there, a white woman.'

Satterlee gave a hitch to his belt and ambled closer to the group. His eyes were level on Mrs. Sherrod, Stennis noted disapprovingly, eyes alive with interest. Thank God he had the decency to stay downwind of her.

'Fact is,' he drawled, 'I don't reckon it is all that turrible a notion, Ben. You see –'

'What!' said Dodge.

'Just take a strong underholt on your humors there, Cunnel. I'm telling you straight it has been my noticing that most Injun women can gen'rally shade a man, Injun or white, when it comes to lasting out heat or cold. Pretty much that way with most ever'thing.' Dake grinned brashly. 'Had no truck with white ladies sincet I was a tad in Kentucky, but I 'member my sisters allus took sick from the pox and such *after* us boys did. Yessir, be blamed if I'd mind being tough as most women.'

Stennis listened in amazement. He wasn't sure whether Satterlee was serious or not. Mrs. Sherrod, however, was showing a bright-eyed interest in what the mountain man had to say. Stennis cynically suspected that this was the effect Dake hoped for.

'There, Colonel,' she said triumphantly. 'A knowledgeable man in your service has rendered the judgment which you invited!'

'Madam,' Dodge said icily, 'you will remain behind for the duration of this mission. That is my final word on the matter. I suggest that you occupy the period of your husband's absence with Scriptural readings and chaste thoughts, as befit your sex.'

Neither of the Sherrods took offense at his tone and words. Randall Sherrod appeared distantly amused. His wife smiled, a smile that was neither demure nor modest. Dodge gave a curt order that dismissed his staff, then headed back toward the headquarters building with Leavenworth and Kearny. Stennis, wanting to clean up, excused himself and started away toward the barracks where unmarried officers were billeted.

Somebody was stepping along beside him. Dake Satterlee.

'Where you ankling to, Loot?'

'The bathhouse.'

'Whooee, ain't that a grand idea! After you, you don't mind.'

'As you like,' Stennis said coldly. A bath could only improve Satterlee's pungent presence, but that didn't mean he had to start fraternizing with the fellow.

'Yessir,' Dake added with what Stennis took for an evil leer, 'she surely is a sweet-smelling thing, that lady.'

'See here, Satterlee –' Stennis swung around to face him. 'The lady is married, and if she weren't, she'd hardly be for the likes of you. I hope that's clear.'

'Clear as rain.' Dake gave him a crushing slap on the shoulder. ''Y God, Loot, that do be what I admire most about you. You are so goddam pluperfect gold-plated *honest*!'

CHAPTER THREE

The bugler's trumpet made a polished glitter as he swept it to his lips and blew assembly. The troops of the 1st Dragoons formed columns of fours in front of their barracks. Reins in hand, they stood at attention beside their horses. The air was warm and unstirring. Restive mounts stomped and jangled their bit chains; gear rattled and creaked Officers rapped out commands

Colonel Dodge stepped from the slab walled shack that served as his office. Yanking on his gloves, he walked to the orderly holding his roan. The orderly saluted, handed the colonel his reins, saluted again and wheeled away Dodge in his shabby buckskins stood where he was a moment, iron colored gaze moving across the resplendent ranks in front of him.

The Dragoons crackled with dash and color in their new full dress uniforms: double breasted coats of dark blue with spotless white gloves, gray blue trousers with three-quarter inch yellow stripes down the outseams. Caps were ornamented with gold cords, silver eagles and stars; their orange pompons were like bright badges. Ankle boots and spurs were rubbed to gleaming; sabers were belted over braided sashes of yellow silk.

At the order, the men climbed into their saddles and sat waiting.

Lieutenant Stennis Fry had enough poetry in his soul to appreciate an irony in the occasion. Looking to either side, a man saw the most bracing display of martial splen dor that the American sun had shone on. Looking behind him, he'd see as squalid a set of tumbledown shanties as had ever housed any hardluck soldiers These were the permanent quarters of the 1st Regiment of U S Dragoons. Arriving at Fort Gibson last December, Dodge had coldly rejected the poor lodgings offered his regiment; the dis gruntled Dragoons had pitched their tents on a site a mile west and named it Camp Jackson. Later they'd thrown up some oak shingled barracks of the crudest sort.

Today, June 15, 1834, they were turning their backs

on these miserable shelters in grand style. They were riding out to adventure

Dodge stepped into his saddle, settled his feet in the long Dragoon stirrups, then raised his hand and dropped it The bugler trumpeted advance. The troops moved out westward by companies, pennons snapping. Behind them rolled baggage wagons laden with tents, bedrolls, cases of rations and boxes of lead and powder. Ambulances stocked with medical supplies followed; seven head of beef cattle brought up the rear. Ahead of the long column were Ben Poore's four bands of picked scouts, men drawn from the Seneca, Osage, Cherokee and Delaware tribes.

The Dragoons rode belly in and chin high, glorying in their restored identity.

The mood that seized them after all these months was a mixed one of gala pleasure, schoolboy release and strutting dignity. It had taken a long time for the seed to bear fruit. Most of the men who had signed enlistment papers and flocked to Jefferson Barracks last summer and fall had been youngsters thirsting for adventure. Either itchy-footed farm lads or children of the coastal slums clawing for a chance, they'd needed training from the ground up. At first there'd been damned little to do the job with – no guns or uniforms were available. There were no horses and no stables to put them in. The men had drilled on foot with firearms long ago condemned; they had toiled at building barracks and stables and corrals. Their common pride had been mangled considerably, for they'd enlisted to be cavaliers, not carpenters. By October horses purchased from farms and sales barns all over the country had begun to arrive. The disgruntled recruits had found themselves not only spending hours at fatigue labor, but working constantly at mounted as well as dismounted drill. To fill their 'copious free time,' as the hard driving Kearny put it, there was the task of grooming each horse two hours a day – an hour above the knees, an hour below.

After the forced march to Gibson, Dodge's contingent had weathered out the winter at Camp Jackson under savage conditions. Wind, snow and rain had knifed in raw gusts through scores of cracks and crevices in the tents and make-shift barracks; the only true shelter they could find was by covering their gear and sleeping areas with buffalo robes.

The men had spent this spring grading and corduroying a supply road to the site of a new cantonment to the south, Fort Towson, and freighting stone for its construction

They had earned a right to pride. From a harum scarum rabble, they had developed into American Dragoons Still unseasoned perhaps, but toughened in the crucible of Steve Kearney's fierce discipline till they were as prepared as otherwise inexperienced troops could expect to be.

The pleasant morning was heralded by larks and towhees singing from deep summer grass silvered by dew. The buff colored hills of lush prairie rolled to the horizons like the swells of a frozen sea Stennis Fry was in Company A toward the column's head When he looked back, the mile-long procession made him think of a many colored serpent. The Dragoon uniforms added bright touches to the white-topped wagons; Dragoon horses made solid wedges of color The mounts were Thoroughbreds, Standardbreds, even a few Morgans; Dodge, to give him credit, had turned the crazy-quilt disparity of their colors neatly to use The mixed color animals were teamed to draw the wagons and ambulances. The solid color horses were divided into creams, blacks, grays, sorrels and bays; each Dragoon company was mounted on a different color.

Stennis twitched his shoulder with discomfort as the increasing blaze of sun against his back began soaking through his heavy wool coatee. These uniforms were im practically heavy and fancy for the plains – just two weeks out here had convinced him of that. . . .

Someone on a paint horse was riding up from the front of the column It was Dake Satterlee 'How, Loot!' he called cheerily as he rode past Stennis without slacking his pace.

Stennis turned in his saddle, gazing after the scout. Satterlee was heading for the rear of the train Stennis frowned Could that scruffy mountain man be entertaining more notions about Mrs Sherrod, after he'd been sensibly warned?

Dake was whistling brightly as he rode back the length of the column. The day was fresh; dew did a sparkling dance on the wind-pressed grass. It was pluperfect grand, by God, to be up of a morning without his head and in nards being cauterized from a night of raising the Old Nick. Course civil ee-zation was nice to get back to betimes, but he was set for another flier at the big spaces and a man wanted a clear head and eye to meet this country on its own terms.

Dake chuckled. He liked that long drink of water Fry, but the bluejay had best not rub Dake Satterlee too hard with his prissy Easternfield notions or he would find he'd taken underholts on a bearcat. Dake had no disrespectful hankerings after Miz Sherrod (at least he didn't reckon so); any man with lights in his head could see she was more'n just any hank o' hair and bone. But he'd speak to anybody it so suited him to, and wasn't no ornery shavetail going to gainsay him.

Dake passed along the blue columns of Dragoons, his lip curling in disgust as he eyed the solid wedges of color made by each company of proud prancing thoroughbreds. Jee'zus. Silly ass bastards, kiting off across the plains at high summer on these fat grain fed brutes. Wait till the grain ran out and they'd been on nothing but tough buffalo grass a day or so. Be like trying to wean spoiled babies. And that one bunch of creamy white horses Hadn't anybody figured out what bright targets they'd make in open country?

Up ahead, George Catlin and Carl Beyrich were pacing their mounts casually alongside the column. Catlin halted, pointing at a hackberry tree. Beyrich piled eagerly and awkwardly off his horse and hurried over to it He tried to break off a branch and gave a yelp, jerking his hand back. Dake cantered over to him, grinning.

'How, Dutchy. Don't you know better'n to grab aholt a full growed hackberry? For a feller's s'posed to know his weeds . . .'

'Many plants I have studied about I have not yet seen, Mr. Satterlee.' The round cheeked botanist looked oddly like a querulous infant as he sucked his bleeding thumb. 'I was quite aware, but in my exuberance forgot, that the *celtis pallida* bears a wealth of thorns.'

'Bet you don't forget no more.' Dake winked at him and then reined over by Catlin. 'How's things going with you, paintslinger?'

'Never saw such a sight!' Catlin waved an enthusiastic

37

hand at the caravan. 'It's an American panorama. Think I'll go up on one of those hills for a better view.' He patted the easel, palette, paints and brushes lashed to his saddle, eyeing Dake in the curious way he had of sizing up a subject. 'Sometime, Satterlee, I'd like to paint you if you're willing. . . .'

'Dunno 'bout that,' Dake said cheerfully. 'Be hell scraping all that there paint off after'ards '

Guffawing, he heeled his mustang and rode on.

Just behind the last company rolled the baggage wagons Oshel Callicut was lead teamster, heading up a dozen other drivers, among them his sons Dake grinned, tipping his hat to Oshel who, three days after their tussle at LeBarge's, still wore a fat blue black mouse under one eye. Oshel snarled at his team, cracking his brand-new whip above their heads. As he passed them, Dake gave each Callicut son the same jaunty salute Verl and Asa gave him dirty looks in return Their brother Tute was unable to handle a wagon He sat up beside Verl, his right arm muffled to the elbow in a dirty bandage from which splints protruded His eyes were red rimmed from pain and sleepless nights, and they were yellow with hatred as they followed Dake

Yessir, Dake thought, give him a half chance and ol' Tute will try to even up for that busted wing The thought did not greatly disturb him.

Two armed soldiers rode beside the next wagon, one to either side. A third man handled the reins The pucker holes at front and back of the canvas cover were tightly drawn so that Dake couldn't glance inside But he guessed that this wagon contained two girls, one Kiowa and one Pawnee, and that the guards were under strict orders concerning them.

The last wagon in the procession was driven by Alexandra Sherrod She was strong and straight on the high seat, wearing gloves on her hands but handling the reins as well as any man Dake reined alongside, then wheeled his mount and paced her wagon. He whipped off his hat, grinning.

'Morning to you, ma'am! Don't see your man nowheres about '

'Good morning, Mr. Satterlee. I'm afraid my husband

38

has been taken ill by the motion of the wagon. He's always affected thus when we commence a journey' She turned her head, looking through the canvas pucker into the wagon bed. 'How are you faring, Randall?'

A groan answered her.

Dake grunted 'Know an ol' *hivernant* remedy mought help. You scrunch up some buffler berries and mix 'em with a pint o' bear taller. . . .'

Alexandra smiled at him. 'Don't concern yourself, Mr. Satterlee. He'll shortly gain his "sea legs"; that will do him nicely.'

She didn't seem to be undertaking a lot of distress on her husband's account. In fact her no nonsense tone hinted that she was out of sympathy with him. Dake judged that was because most, if not all, of Randall Sherrod's difficulty was the amount of whiskey he'd taken on last night Ben Poore had told him that Sherrod had been drunk and talky at a private party, Poore had the man sized as a blowhard and a lightweight. Dake wondered what had attracted a woman like this to a man like him She was strong and competent, but sure enough all female Even in a worn calico dress, a prim high necked dress that made no secret of those big breasts, she sat that wagon seat regal as a queen, coppery hair curling richly out from the frame of her poke bonnet.

'I must thank you, Mr Satterlee,' she said 'I'm sure your intervention helped me persuade Colonel Dodge against his better judgment that even "a delicate gently bred white woman" can endure the rigors of this journey.'

Dake grinned. He's had a feeling the colonel would wind up on the short end of any debate with Miz Sherrod. She was as womanly as she was strong, a hard combination to argue with 'Glad I could be of service, ma'am. But got to admit to being curious.'

'About why I should wish to accompany this mission?'

'Yes'm.'

'A woman can yearn after adventure, excitement, as a man does, Mr. Satterlee. Does that seem possible to you?'

'Yes'm.'

She gave him a speculative look. 'You are an unusual man to think so. How I envy you the life you must have lived . . . to know all this country.'

'Not all, ma'am.' Her glance put a little curl of heat in him. He wondered what she thought about his coming back to ride beside her wagon. Suddenly Dake wasn't quite comfortable. 'Too big for any one man to know all. But have been across a goodly piece of it '

Her eyes turned forward again. 'How hard will the going get, Mr Satterlee?'

Dake shrugged. 'Depends how tough a body is. Ain't no country for whites to be crossing at high summer. July's the worst. Come then, we'll be right in the middle o' the plains '

'Yet like Mr Poore, you've consented to help guide the expedition. For his reason?'

'Kind of. Only I'm working for Ben, not the cunnel Ben's a friend o' Dodge's, I'm a friend o' Ben's ' He chuckled. 'Anyways I'm part Injun myself. My maw's maw was a Creek '

'And you know the Pawnee well, I understand '

'Yes'm ' His red kinships didn't seem to concern her· her glance at him was straightforward, not down the nose 'I wonder can I ask, ma'am, where did you learn to ride and shoot?'

She laughed. 'No great trick, considering the circumstan ces For one, I was raised on a farm Pa was a gentleman farmer in Massachusetts, but he preferred riding to hounds. He liked horses and guns and he liked dressing out his own game and he liked a warming dram. He was a big man, big and driving and loud, and his three sons were the images of him. My mother died when I was very young. So you may consider what I grew up surrounded by.'

Dodge wondered how with kin like that she'd come to marry such a ninny as this Sherrod But he decided against wondering aloud.

Colonel Dodge came riding up from the front of the column at a brisk trot He was speaking to the men he passed exactly as suited his fancy, treating officers and troopers alike Dake kind of liked him for that. He was a hard old coot, but wasn't locked into a lot of damnfool rules like these regular Army men. Dodge spoke briefly to Oshel Callicut, also to the troopers guarding the wagon ahead, and then he rode up to the Sherrod wagon and fell in alongside. He gave Dake a coldly curious look.

40

'Good morning, Colonel.'

'Madam!'

Dodge saluted her with his riding crop, kind of jauntily. He seemed in better humor than he'd been three days ago. With some reason, Dake figured. Not only had Stephen Kearny been left behind to command Fort Gibson, Henry Leavenworth was temporarily out of Dodge's hair. Paper business would keep the general at Gibson a few days longer; he'd catch up with the Dragoons before they reached the Canadian. So the honor of launching the expedition had fallen entirely to Dodge. . . .

'Where is your husband, Madam?'

She explained that Sherrod was wagon sick.

'Regrettable. But this is no work for you; I'll assign a trooper to drive your wagon.'

'Really, Colonel, I'm managing splendidly.'

'Ain't no string o' taffy, Cunnel,' Dake grinned. 'Never seen the beat o' her.'

Again Dodge's cold look 'I believe your place is out on scout. Will you kindly get back there?'

'Sure, Cunnel. Morning to you, ma'am.'

West of Fort Gibson were belts of hill country fairly well forested with post oak, blackjack and other hard scrubs. The Dragoons passed through mottes of forest all day. That night they made bivouac in a big clearing at a well timbered site. Sunset was a molten pool on the horizon as they halted in the woody crook of a stream that was already shrinking with the advance of summer. The bivouac was pitched in uniform lines that formed a square. The horses were picketed out to graze on the available grass, but not before they underwent the daily brushing.

As acting Assistant Quartermaster, Stennis Fry was kept jumping. He'd been doing so ever since he had been assigned the lofty title two days ago. He had been assured that his brightness and his bustling efficiency had recommended him to this position of eminence and power. If that were true, he wished that he'd been less the eager beaver Any sort of breakdown in procedures of commissary and transportation, any problems at all pertaining to feed or forage, were promptly brought to his notice He was expected to provide solutions for problems that he was convinced were

41

largely insoluble. He bitterly wondered if the quartermasters of Caesar and Napoleon had been addled with the same hopeless task of making requisitions and keeping estimates up to date. And whether they too had gotten their shavetail asses blistered by superiors whenever they'd lapsed.

It was a nasty job.

Stennis was not in particularly shining humor as he angled his mount across the camp square to check on the troopers assigned to groom the horses. Tevis was grousing bitterly to Murphy and Brander as the three of them worked side by side on their mounts.

'... Ain't enough a man's got to spend an hour er so cleaning up his own nag, he has got to handle hosses for ever'one on sick call 'n' what-not Then he has got to swamp down the ambulance horses. Then there's the beasts belonging to the goddam officers. Then there's a whole passel of non coms who've got too goddam lazy. . . .'

The grinning Murphy turned his head and saw Stennis; the grin froze. He gave Tevis a savage nudge. Tevis turned, a wiry feist of a man in his mid twenties. His coal-black hair bristled like his temper and his olive-skinned face was sullen.

'You,' Stennis said coldly, 'are required to put in no more time grooming these animals than is necessary to keep them healthy.'

'Yeh,' Tevis said surlily.

'*What?*'

'Yes, sir.'

'I'll overlook it this time. But any more talk if it reaches me will land you in trouble. Deep trouble.'

'Yes, sir.'

'Jeez,' Brander muttered, 'will you lookit that?'

The Kiowa girl and the Pawnee girl had left their wagon, which was somewhat isolated in a blackjack grove outside the square. They were heading for the thick woods that ranged around the stream. Men down the line left off whatever chores they were doing to watch them. By now everyone in the regiment had heard about the two girls, but hardly anyone had caught a glimpse of them. Stennis found himself staring too, as they passed not a hundred feet from the soldiers and himself.

42

'Back to work,' he said 'Snap into it!'

Something seemed awry in the scheme of things. Stennis couldn't quite put his finger on what it was. Then he realized that the sound of axes had ceased He'd assigned a detail to fetch wood and they had been chopping in the forest pretty close to where the Indian girls had gone into the woods to reach the stream.

Lightly kneeling his horse, Stennis trotted him into the woods. But the chopping picked up again and Stennis pulled the bay to a halt, grinning a little. Bohannon, in charge of the detail, must have let the men have their look as the girls passed, then he urged them back to work. Stennis took off his cap and sleeved his forehead, wishing he could open his blouse against the heat as some of the men had done. Damn the maintenance of dignity. Anyway it was pleasant here in the trees. It was a moment of solitude, dappled whisperings of oak leaves, a cooling toward twilight. The branches were ridged by golden sunlines and shadows printed the forest aisles; the noises of the camp seemed remote.

A movement caught his eye.

A blended flicker of shadow against shadow, then a man's form cutting between the trees Flecks of light paled his hemp-coloured hair. Asa Callicutt. Moving with intent stealth through the woods, so intent that he didn't see Stennis and his horse in the trees some yards to his left. And then he was gone from sight.

Stennis gazed after him, puzzled. Maybe he'd better determine what Asa was up to.

He gently drummed the sorrel's flanks, moving him slowly through the trees. Once he glimpsed Asa's back ahead of him, then the trees swallowed him again. Stennis heard a woman's angry voice. He touched spurs and twisted through the trees and came into a wide glade bordering the stream.

The two girls were standing on the bank, backs to the water. Asa was close to them, but not facing them, as Stennis burst into the glade. He'd already swung around, hot-eyed and tense, to confront the officer.

'You skulking dog,' Stennis said coldly. 'Do your skulking somewhere else.'

Asa's gaunt cheeks sallowed with temper. 'Don't read

43

no psalms to me, bluejay. I ain't one o' them sojers o' yourn. I will go a-walking where it so pleases me.'

'You will leave these women alone. I will not say it again. If I find you molesting them, I will shoot you like the dog you are.'

Asa's hands were clenched around his rifle, and now his knuckles paled as open rage flickered in his face. He started to bring the weapon up. It might have been only a threatening gesture, but a man could get shot waiting to find out. Stennis didn't wait. His saber was slung from his saddlebow and he brought the long curved blade whining from its scabbard.

Asa jumped back as Stennis kneed his mount forward. Gripping his weapon's barrel two handed then, he swung at the man and horse. Stennis parried the blow with his saber and jabbed at Asa's shoulder. Asa howled and tried to aim his cumbersome weapon at close quarters. Stennis arced a second slash under his guard, giving him a wicked cut on the arm.

Asa dropped the rifle. He started to back away, at the same time fumbling the tomahawk from his belt. A thrown tomahawk could split a man's head like a melon, and Stennis didn't hesitate. He lunged the sorrel forward. Asa tried to leap to one side and swing his hatchet, but the big horse's shoulder smashed him in the chest and bowled him over.

Stennis went on past him, reined around and came back as Asa scrambled to his feet. His tomahawk had gone flying from his hand. Seeing where is was, he started over to it. Stennis whipped up behind him as he bent, again knocking him butt over teakettle. This time Asa got up slowly. Stennis came cantering back, put a boot against his chest and shoved. Asa sprawled on his back and lay there glaring up.

'Get up,' Stennis told him.

He was fed up with the callow arrogance of these Callicutts. He wasn't finished and Asa understood that he wasn't. Stumbling to his feet, Asa tried to break for the woods. Stennis promptly wheeled his mount across his path, then deliberately crowded him back toward the creek, goading him relentlessly with the saber. When he tried to veer to the side or run, a twitch of reins was enough to cut him off. Finally he made a dive for his rifle. Stennis straddled him with the horse and put a deep saber nick in his unin-jured arm.

Again Asa got warily up. Stennis backed him hard against the bank, again pricking him with the saber. He plunged down the bank and lit on his back in the shallows. He lay with his arms bleeding pinkishly into the water, a greenish scum lapping at his chin.

'Now get out of here,' Stennis said. 'Leave your weapons.'

Asa scrambed out of the water and ran, crashing into the woods. Stennis wiped the saber dry. The girls had pulled to one side; they stood together and watched him. One of them came forward. She touched her saucy right breast.

'I, Ona,' she said.

The other girl commenced to giggle.

Stennis hadn't seen them up close before and he was surprised how pretty the one called Ona was. She was slim, quite small, with a skin the color of dark honey. Her face was a study in exotic tilts and slants that were rather orien-tal. Her eyes were brown, but they were a white girl's eyes; she must be the half-breed, the Pawnee. She wore a blouse of red calico and heavy skirt of blue wool, Indian colors worn in an Indian way, and her heavy black hair was bunned severely at the back of her head. A beaded belt clasped her narrow waist, a many-stranded necklace of white and purple wampum circled her neck She was seventeen or so.

She indicated her tittering companion. 'Her, Buffalo Calf Girl.'

The Kiowa was brown skinned and had a flat chubby face like LeBarge's daughter and whatever else she looked like was lost in her pullover buckskin blouse and wraparound buckskin shirt. Her giggling rasped his spine like a stone scraping on glass.

Stennis, far from suave with the opposite sex, had no idea what the hell protocol one was supposed to follow with these dusky creatures of the plains. Several bawdy sugges-tions he'd heard from fellow officers who had jested about the possibilities didn't seem suitable to the occasion.

He swept off his shako. 'Ladies –'

Buffalo Calf Girl clapped her hands over her mouth. The gesture appeared to register astonishment; in any case it shut off her idiotic giggling. Ona blinked in apparent surprise, though otherwise her face remained as still as a

45

carved Toltec mask. Stennis was a little unsettled himself. Even if the courtesy were unfamiliar to them, he hadn't expected such a reaction.

What the devil were they staring at?

The girls bent and picked up the water vessels they had been filling. Both of them kept fascinated eyes on him. Stennis said, 'Uh – well Goodbye,' and clapped on his shako and rode through the trees back to camp.

CHAPTER FOUR

'I am tremendously excited!' exclaimed Carl Beyrich. 'Such botanical specimens. The like of them no naturalist in Europe has seen Many are not even described in our books. But they will be; this my notes and sketches will ensure. A new country this truly is, my friends.'

'The Indians might argue that,' George Catlin grinned. 'But it's certainly full of sights no artist − no American artist − has captured. I have a full pad of drawings already and some notes of my own'

'Ah, then posterity can smile,' MacPherson said dryly, 'since it'll lack no record of a long, hot, dull journey No less than five of our officers are keeping detailed journals. Details of one tedium after another.'

'The expedition is hardly underway, Mac,' Stennis objected. 'And you know the reasons for it and what's at stake.'

'Och You sound like Dodge.'

The four of them were riding on the right flank of the column, making idle talk By now, three days out from Camp Jackson, the routine of the march had loosened, its various elements jogging out of formal arrangement and into more congenial patterns. Dodge's own free wheeling ways tended to encourage the slackening, and it was a way to cope with increasing monotony. Even the flow of fresh June landscape palled on the mind The land was less timbered now, and the vivid blooming slopes of wild plum, dogwood, black locust, red bud and serviceberry were thinning away Colorful mats of honeysuckle, violets and jack-in the pulpit persisted along the way, but no longer relieved the eye.

'Come on, Mac,' said Stennis 'I've no brief for Dodge or his methods, but there's more to this mission than any private ax the colonel may be grinding'

MacPherson chuckled 'That's no lie, laddie. The rest is pure politics and not just Henry Dodge's He has an eye on a territorial governorship, if you didn't know. Some say Andy Jackson has promised him one if this expedition bears likely fruit. Old Hickory's own intrigues are clear as glass. He wants Texas for the Union; why else has he sent his friend Sam Houston there? Merely to stir up American settlers that the Mexican Government invited onto their land in good faith. Lead 'em to a break with Mexico.'

'Washerwoman's talk, Mac. I'm surprised you take it seriously.'

MacPherson sighed. 'Very well, you bright-eyed idealist, why are we being sent to treat with tribes whose main stamping grounds are on Mexican territory? Like all Indians, they've become partly dependent on white man's goods – eh? Several times Dodge has mentioned trade agreements. Why the great sweat to wean these tribes away from dependence on the Spanish at Santa Fe? To gain the paltry trade of savages? No, it's their friendship we're cozening for, and I'll give you one guess why.'

Mac paused, a wry frown twisting his face. He rubbed a hand across his belly.

'What's wrong?' Stennis asked.

'Ah, a touch of stomach cramps. Naught that total abstention from Army fare wouldn't cure. It'll pass.'

They were close to the rear of the caravan, jogging past the Indian girls' wagon Both girls were walking alongside it, chatting. The Kiowa's high giggle rasped Stennis's nerves.

She was a born troublemaker, he thought dourly. Two nights ago there'd been a ruckus near their wagon, when Private Tevis had been caught tussling in the grass with Buffalo Calf Girl Her cries had attracted a sentry. Tearfully she had insisted that she'd been out strolling and Tevis had attacked her. Dodge had ordered Tevis flogged, afterward issuing a general order that was a warning: any man caught molesting either girl again would be summarily executed. Tevis had heatedly insisted that the Kiowa had deliberately teased him on, and Stennis believed it. He had no fondness for Tevis, his sullen ways, his grousing and malingering, but that girl's whole manner testified that Tevis hadn't been more than half to blame. . . .

Stennis lifted his shako and sleeved sweat from his face. The Kiowa gave a loud titter. Both girls were staring at him, half-amused, half awed, exactly as they had the other day. He reined quickly on, his face burning.

'Dammit, I don't see what's so funny!'

48

'Why,' Catlin grinned, 'it's all that nice hair of yours. Looks quite white in the sun.'

'What kind of nonsense is that?'

'No more nonsense than a black cat is to most white folks. The plain tribes regard a white buffalo as sacred. Your hair color is as rare on a young man as on a buffalo. I'd imagine that's what gets 'em. You're sort of a white buffalo, Lieutenant.'

MacPherson gave a hoot of laughter, then bent forward across his pommel, grabbing at his belly His face was twisted and shining with sweat. 'Goddam!'

Stennis reined in, then reached over and caught his friend's rein. 'Come on, Mac. You'd better see Surgeon Haile.'

'Very well, laddie. Lead on.'

MacPherson clutched his pommel, head bowed against his chest, as Stennis swung his horse around and, leading Mac's animal, cut away toward the column and the regimental surgeon's wagon. Catlin and Beyrich, unasked, flanked MacPherson on either side, ready tó catch him if he began to slip Mac's face was colorless; he looked as if he might topple from his saddle any moment.

What was it, Stennis wondered – something he had eaten, a touch of grippe or dysentery? Strange how swiftly it had grabbed him.

As they neared Dr. Haile's place toward the rear of the column, the surgeon was already moving his wagon out of line and pulling his team to a halt. Too, a half a dozen soldiers were piling off their horses. All were clutching their stomachs, sweating heavily, or otherwise showing signs of pain and discomfort. Stennis dismounted, helped Mac off his horse and then walked over to the surgeon.

'What's going on, Doc? Are all these men sick?'

'Looks that way.' The surgeon was a small man, round and rosy, whose face quivered with comfortable jowls, he chewed a cigar stub as he talked. 'I'll need time to examine them properly. MacPherson down too?'

Stennis nodded.

'Fry, listen, do me a favor. Ride up front and tell Dodge to halt the caravan for an hour or so.' As he spoke, Haile was already shucking off his coat and rolling up his sleeves. 'I want to know if any more are coming down with these

49

men's symptoms – stomach pains, headaches, heavy sweats. And I want them to report here on the double. . . .'

Since it was already late in the afternoon. Dodge called a halt for the day. As it turned out, men up and down the column were complaining of sore bellies and headaches. By nightfall, more than fifty of them had taken to their blankets They were burning up with fever, unquenchable thirst, intermittent attacks of teeth-chattering chills. Dodge strode through the camp inspecting the situation, talking to a man here and there, his face grim and worried.

No doubt about it, Haile told him Bilious fevers. Au tumnal fevers His treatment was to boil up Peruvian barks for quinine, which he administered with generous doses of whiskey.

Next morning, few of the men felt any better The ones unable to hold their saddles were loaded into ambulances; the less ill were somewhat isolated by being ordered to ride behind the wagons.

So it continued as the days and miles rolled by. Daily, men fell ill and dropped out in batches When the ambulances were overcrowded, they were loaded into baggage wagons. The ones still able to ride were relegated to the rear of the train, and every day their numbers increased. Henry Dodge fretted and fumed, his temper tapered off to an extremely short fuse He saw the whole mission, and with it his own plans, collapsing in an inglorious fizzle of weak bellies and diarrhea. . . .

Precautions seemed useless. The troops began to show traces of solemn dread tinged by panic Dodge imposed an iron order on the men by adherence, day and night, to a strict, dreary and unvarying routine Each morning, at the first pink break of day, the company buglers blasted away the shreds of sleep You unlimbered a legion of sore muscles, then stumbled through the usual preamble of as sembly, muster roll and sick call You breakfasted and were on the march by eight

The weather of late June was turning hot and sticky. By nine o'clock you could count on your Army blouse of heavy wool becoming a hotbox. By afternoon you were roasting in your own air tight corner of hell, drenched in sweat and tormented by a prickling heat rash. Your only

50

consolation was that the buttsores and chapped thighs of the first few days were hardening out.

Four o'clock brought night halt. You bivouacked in one of the four squared-off lines, flung down saddle and gear and picketed your horse out to graze. If there were grass and bushes, you systematically beat them for snakes. These Christawful plains were infested with more snakes than you'd ever seen, especially rattlesnakes. An average of four or five were turned up and killed at each campsite. Where wood was scarce, you scoured up the abundant buffalo chips. . . .

Covering about fifteen grueling miles a day, the regiment reached the Canadian River on June 25. It was a pleasant place to halt, the banks shaded by lush old cedars and mantled with thick green grass. The river itself was clear as glass, running down to its muddy terminus in the Arkansas. They laid over by the Canadian for a day to give the slightly afflicted a chance to recover and to weed out those unfit to continue the journey.

Here General Henry Leavenworth, accompanied by a small detachment of mounted infantry from the 7th, caught up with the Dragoons. The general had set out days after the regiment had departed, but his little group had moved faster and more swiftly than the mile-long Dragoon cavalcade, and none of the general's men had come down sick. His arrival and his assumption of full command did nothing to sweeten Dodge's mood.

However the general and colonel were of a single mind in one respect: the mission must not be abandoned because a relative minority of men were ailing. Most of the regiment was holding up well and only wanted toughening to the rigors of plains travel; the men would soon become acclimated. For twenty-seven soldiers deemed too sick to go on, half-shelters were built and floored with springy cedar cuttings. Six volunteers were left to tend their needs.

The 1st Dragoons crossed the Canadian and pushed on.

Bobbing black humps of buffalo had been sighted almost daily, but never at close range. Henry Leavenworth, usually reserved, became enormously excited at each appearance of a herd. He had an ungovernable itch to dust off a bull bison. Of which Ben Poore dryly commented:

' 'Tis an itch a man best get scratched and have done with it.'

On late afternoon of June 27, a sizable herd of buffalo was spotted. Leavenworth recklessly spurred away after them. Dodge and George Catlin, also bitten by the bison dusting bug, followed his lead. Dodge succeeded in killing a fat cow. Meantime Catlin was charged by a bull. He fired his rifle at the beast and missed, then wounded him with his pistol and drove him off.

Ben Poore angrily cussed out the trio· 'Three goddam fools got no better sense'n to charge a whole herd of buffler by themselves don't deserve to be alive. Genril, Cunnel suppose'n you both got your asses busted chasing buff? Then we got no leaders, we ain't got a soul knows enough 'bout our orders to manage the outfit, make the decisions. You want to bag some bufflers, you leave me pick the time and the place.'

Leavenworth and Dodge soberly agreed.

At midmorning of the following day, a rest halt was called close to the base of a hill that resembled a great squashed cone. It was a typical stop. Men settled wearily on their hunkers. They passed a few laconic words. They fired up pipes and cigars in a futile effort to cut the fierce stench of their animals' leisurely voidings.

A number of men assembled around Dr. Haile's wagon for dosing with quinine and whiskey. It was doubtful, Stennis thought, whether more than half of them were afflicted by any malaise worse than a mighty thirst. However, it wasn't in his province to shake up malingerers. All he had to do was collect the latest sick list from Haile and take it to the colonel.

He rode back to the front of the column. Dodge and Leavenworth were squatting on the ground, talking. 'Poore is right, Colonel,' Leavenworth was saying. 'This running for buffaloes is bad business for us We are getting old and should leave such amusements to younger men. I am determined not to hazard my limbs or weary my horse any more with it.'

Stennis swung to the ground, saluting as he handed Dodge the sick report. The colonel scanned it, frowning 'At this rate, we'll never ...' He glanced up as a rider came swiftly around the long curve of the squashed hill. 'Hullo. Satterlee . . . and he seems in a hurry.'

Dake dropped off his gaunt mustang and come over to them, grinning. 'Genril, Ben 'n' me spotted a small bunch of buffs, five of 'em, grazing t'other side o' this hill Right size stand for you boys to scratch that mean itch o' yourn on. Ben says get up a party o' five six and we'll give 'em a whirl.'

Leavenworth sprang to his feet. 'Damnation!' His words of a moment before were forgotten. 'Mr. Catlin!'

Catlin, in company with Carl Beyrich and Randall Sherrod, had come riding down from the rear of the column. The three civilians were idly chatting, and now they stopped and looked at the general.

'Buffalo!' Leavenworth shouted 'We're getting another crack at them, man! Come with us. You too, Beyrich '

'Nein.' Beyrich shook his head. 'I have no stomach to kill those wonderful great beasts. You will pardon me, sir.'

'Sherrod?' demanded the general.

Randall Sherrod smiled quickly. The smile seemed slightly forced. 'Er, why . . . buffalo, eh? Splendid. Glad to, General.'

Leavenworth's eye pounced on Stennis. 'Lieutenant, you'll round out the party. Come, gentlemen! Let's not dally.'

The six men rode up the long swell of hillflank. Where it began to curve off toward the other side, Ben Poore was waiting. He said nothing, just pointed. Off right at the base of the hill was a deep-grassed vale and a scatter of blackjack oaks. Five of the shaggy beasts were grazing there.

'Bull and four cows,' Poore murmured.

The bull was an old giant. His shaggy coat had diminished to tufts of matted, mud clotted hair and patches of bare bleached hide. The shedding, well-advanced in the June heat, was aided by his constant rubbing now against the blackjack, scraping away cushions of dead itching verminous hair.

'My Lord,' Leavenworth whispered excitedly. 'He must run over half a ton.'

53

'Over a full,' Poore said. 'Best see how our stick floats 'fore you take him, Genril –'

But Leavenworth set his spurs with a whoop and charged down the hillside. The others poured after him. Catlin yelled at Stennis to join him in bringing down the cow farthest to the left, Stennis shouted back agreement.

The bull raised his head. His pendulous beard swung. He snorted and hooked his horn into the earth, then lumbered away with Leavenworth and most of his party in full pursuit.

Stennis and Catlin charged through tall mottled grass under the blackjack. The cows scattered. They rode after the one that Catlin had singled out. A thick ironwood rearing across their path caused the two men to split apart, riding to either side. Catlin saw the low hanging limb, camouflaged by texture of shadows and leaves, too late. It caught him across the chest; his riderless mount galloped away. Stennis pulled up ten yards from the ironwood and trotted back. Catlin was sitting on the ground, holding his head in both hands

'Are you alive, George?'

' 'Solutely not. Neck broken.'

A musket shot Then another. And a man's voice shouting as if in pain.

Catlin said : 'That sounded like the general.'

Stennis spun his mount and put him at a hard run through the grove toward its south edge. He heard Ben Poore call out. On the heels of the shout, a heavy body came crashing through the trees. The bull heaved into sight, apparently turned his way by the two shots. He had been hit, his right flank streaming blood. Spotting Stennis, he veered in his wobbling run, horns raking the air.

Stennis touched spurs and sent his sorrel away at right angles, clearing the bull's path. He brought up his musket, cocked and took hasty aim, and pulled trigger. A misfire He dropped the musket and clawed the pistol from his belt.

But the bull had slowed to a massive lurching halt; his knees were folding. Dake Satterlee came through the trees at a gallop. He stopped, seeing the buffalo almost dead on his feet, and raised his rifle. He and Stennis shot simulta

54

neously, even as the bull crumpled to his knees. He plunged down, legs kicking, shaking the earth with his fall.

'Satterlee, was that the general?'

'T'were Hoss hooked a hoof in a pothole and throwed him. Leastways he hit the bull. Where's Catlin?'

'Lost his horse, but is all right The general?'

'Dunno. Go have a look, Loot. I'll catch up the paint-slinger's hoss.'

Stennis rode quickly to the end of the grove. He saw Leavenworth being helped to his feet by Ben Poore. Close by, Randall Sherrod sat his horse and stared at the ground. His face was pinched and white, drained of all expression. The general's horse was struggling in the grass with a broken leg. Dodge dismounted, placed his pistol to the animal's head and fired.

'Damn you, stand away!' The general sounded outraged as he shook off Poore's hands. He stood erect, straightening his coatee. 'Nothing at all the matter . . . perfectly well.'

A twitching qualm seized his face. He fought the pain threatening to double him. Then, almost before his knees could start buckling, he simply passed out on his feet. Dodge and Poore caught him as he fell. . . .

CHAPTER FIVE

The general had paid a price for his buffalo; two of his ribs were fractured. All that could be done was to apply the doubtful treatment of a tight wrapping. Rest and quiet were also in order, but Leavenworth refused to remain in a provisioned camp with a couple of guards, as Dodge suggested. Not only was the general as obdurate as Dodge, he outranked him. Leavenworth was placed in a wagon; the caravan moved on. . . .

Two days later the column limped into Camp Washita, Captain Dean's camp on the Washita River thirty miles above its confluence with the Red River. The Washita was a wide muddy stream with high, thickly wooded cutbanks The troopers made camp under the trees, welcoming shade which softened the sun's glare if not the punishing heat

With Leavenworth out of his head in fever, any decisions as to the next move lay with Henry Dodge. Dean's two companies of infantry, garrisoned here in tents nearly two hundred miles from Fort Gibson, formed the last American post on the edge of the Great Plains The toughest part of the journey by far still lay ahead. Half a hundred men were too sick to go on, nearly as many were on the verge of collapse At least eighty horses and mules were too disabled to take up the march. The general state of things and the brutal distance remaining to be covered plus the return journey meant that no one, not even a War Depart ment which rarely commended prudence, would blame Dodge for turning back

The colonel assembled his officers. He ran a crisp and impersonal eye over the dusty drooping lot He whacked the omnipresent riding crop against his palm as he told them that they would follow the same course as they had by the Canadian. They'd lay over by the Washita a few days and give the men a respite Men unfit to continue would be weeded out, shelters erected for them. Afterward the command would be reformed, the companies equalized as to numbers. Disabled animals would be put out of the way. And the regiment would push on. . . .

That was all. No appeal to their advice or their good judgment. Merely a declaration that raised no question of abandoning the mission. Nor was anyone particularly surprised. But on every side, as he moved among the tired troopers of his company, Stennis was aware of angry muttering and grousing. There was no ominous or mutinous sound to it. Not yet. The men might be well along to hating Dodge's guts, but they respected him now. First out of fear. Second for the iron discipline he'd begun to enforce lately Stennis smiled thinly at the thought. Back at Camp Jack son they'd complained that Kearny was too hard, Dodge was too soft By now most were ready to drastically revise the judgment.

After handing Dodge the report, Stennis made his way back to his company, feeling weariness tug at his heels There was a sort of tiring that finally ate into a man's marrow and wasn't abolished by sleep. A weariness compounded of heat exhaustion and a constant press of duty that involved niggling, tiresome, repetitious details, never a jot of excitement.

Glory, he thought wryly. So far the 1st Dragoons had offered anything but. If a man couldn't occupy himself with something splendidly worthwhile, better he idle his time away pleasantly Stennis thought longingly of the cool lawns of Jefferson Barracks where you could let a horse out at a brisk gallop among the ancient oaks Of nearby St. Louis with its genteel yet pleasure loving flavor of Old France Of the *chic* mademoiselles.

'Quit it, goddam you! Stand still, you wall eyed son of a bitch, or –'

Tevis was grooming his horse, the job he hated most; the animal was restively jerking its head away from him Bohannon was seated cross legged at a fire, a small leather-covered book pressed open on his knee He was laboriously writing in it From time to time wetting his pencil stub on his tongue He glanced up now, scowling.

'Tevis, be watching your treatment of the beast. You been warned –'

Tevis ignored him, giving the horse a savage kick in the flank It squealed and lashed out with both hind feet Tevis, red faced with anger, clung tight to its headstall and pulled his foot back for another kick

57

Stennis, still some distance away, moved swiftly forward. 'Stop it!' he ordered.

Tevis booted the horse again. The panicked animal wheeled in a half circle, dragging the slight trooper with it. Tevis lost his grip and fell. Scrambling up, he reached for a knife at his hip.

'Tevis!' Bohannon roared, coming to his feet. 'Did you hear? *He said stop.*'

Tevis turned, head hunched between his narrow should ers The firelight flashed wickedly on his eyes and he kept his hand on his knife hilt. His mouth was twisted crazily.

Stennis pulled up beside Bohannon. 'That's enough, Private. Come to attention.'

Tevis didn't move.

Stennis felt a personal sense of despair. What could you do about the noxious bitterness growing daily in a man? How could you handle it?

Captain Whit Mulady, company commander, had also witnessed the scene. Now he came stamping up, his boiled-looking face tight with anger 'You heard the lieutenant. Take your hand off that knife. Come to attention.'

This time Tevis obeyed

'Private, I've warned you what any more such outbursts would earn you. Do you see that tree?' Mulady pointed at a young oak.

'Yes, sir.'

'You will cut it down and trim off the limbs. Then you will carry it around the perimeter of this bivouac for a full hour or until tattoo. Get to it.'

Tevis silently got a handax Stennis walked over to the captain 'Whit,' he said in a low voice, 'that tree is too heavy. He'll hardly be able to lift it. And his back is –'

'Pity I've had enough of that fellow's foul temper. Maybe this will break some of it out of him.'

'It won't. It's not the answer.'

'Fry, you're too damned soft with these men. You won't win their respect that way.'

'Captain, you can make a man snap too, but respect is something else. I just think the punishment should help induce a man to fit the mold. If it won't, if it only makes him more recalcitrant, why inflict it?'

Mulady stared at him. 'You think too much, Fry, do

you know that? Carrying the log is regulation punishment. He'll carry it. That's all.'

It's degrading and stupid, Stennis thought, but he said nothing as Mulady turned on his heel and strode away. Stennis glanced at several men who had left off grooming their animals to look on. 'What are you men "soldiering" around for? Get back to your duties.' He moved over to the fire where Bohannon was standing with the nicely neutral look of an old non-com.

'What is that book, Sergeant? I've noticed you writing in it every night.'

'Oh, this.' Bohannon's face flushed; he slapped the leather notebook against his leg. 'It's, um, a sort o' record I'm keeping, sir. Of our journey.'

'A journal? I didn't suspect you of a literary bent.'

'Oh, nothing like that, sir. It's just a record o' sorts. Quite a few are keeping the like. Why, there's Lieutenant Wheelock – he's keeping the official journal – and Sergeant Hugh Evans is keeping one and Mr. Catlin –'

Bohannon was almost squirming with embarrassment, embarrassing Stennis too. 'Quite true, Sergeant. More the better, eh? Carry on.'

Supper fires were being laid around the squared encampment as dusk sifted down. Stennis prepared and ate his usual monotonous fare of beef and beans, then crossed the camp to the field hospital that Dr. Haile had set up under the trees. He and his assistants were treating a dozen more ailing soldiers. The surgeon had a harried, nerve-ragged look! he'd been puffing one cigar after another down to stubs.

'Never saw anything like it,' he said. 'Fever, ague, dysentery, sunstroke! Jesus. How can men be expected to improve under these conditions? Rolling and tossing all day in these damned wagons and this heat.' He took a wet shred of cigar from his mouth and eyed it distastefully. 'And I'm damned near out of cigars. You wouldn't have ..?'

'No.' Stennis said. 'Sorry.'

Haile grunted. 'I suppose you want to see MacPherson.'

'How is he, Doc?'

'Holding his own. As much as you can say for anyone.'

MacPherson was sitting with his back to a tree, a blanket covering his legs. He raised a hand and grinned weakly as Stennis came up. 'Sit ye doon, Sten. It's a fine evening.'

Stennis settled on his haunches, gazing worriedly at his friend. Mac had lost weight; his fair skin was sprinkled with sweat. 'How are you making it, fellow?'

'As the old song has it, taking the low road, laddie But I'll make it, never you worry. Still, I wish all that lovely hair o' yours did bear a bloody charm with it. Might help me damp this damned boiling in me guts.'

'You should have stayed at the Canadian.'

Mac's eyes flicked blue sparks. 'Not I. Nor will I stay at this place, mannie. I'll see the mission through.'

Or die trying. Stennis did not know what to tell him, and after a few more minutes of talk, he left Mac and returned to the company bivouac.

A man came staggering along the line of fires, his slight frame bent almost double under the weight of an oak trunk carried on his shoulders. Tevis was barely able to lift one foot after the other. From time to time he stopped, head down, to shift the log for comfort When he came near Stennis, he stopped again. Raised his head His opaque glare focused on Stennis and he spat. Then staggered on.

We will kill him, Stennis thought, or he will kill himself fighting us. And what will be served by it?

Tute Callicutt's colorless eyes followed Dake Satterlee as the mountain man crossed the west side of the camp, heading for the river. A pure hatred consumed Tute He'd never felt anything so intense in his life. Unless it was the rat of constant pain that gnawed at his arm.

Satterlee disappeared in the thick shadows and trees beyond the throw of firelight. Tute's gaze dropped to his splinted wrist. It was wrapped many times in a strip of calico that was filthy and stained. *Jesus!* Just moving it brought knifing agony. The hatred vanished in a twinge of fear.

Suppose the goddam thing had to be cut off? What would he do then? One handed man couldn't handle a team for shucks. He felt a thin comfort as he looked at the hard-bitten faces of his kin. Daddy and the boys would take care of him. No worry on that score. Just that a one-handed man wasn't worth shucks on his own account, and that was bad.

Oshel took out his pipe and a greasy buckskin pouch from which he took tobacco, packing the pipe. He pawed among the coals with horn calloused fingers and produced a live coal that he dropped into his pipebowl, puffing it alight. Then he broke the silence.

'How be that arm o' yourn doing, boy?'

'Well enough, Daddy. Better'n she was.'

Verl glanced up from the stick he was whittling on. 'That's a lie for certain sure,' he said slyly. 'He favors it all the time. Iffen you ast me –'

'Nobody did!' Tute snarled. 'You shut your goddam face!'

Oshel puffed his pipe a few times, then took it from his mouth. 'When you look at that arm last, boy?'

'She's all right.'

'Unwrap her. I be taking a squint.'

Tute held his father's stare for a long moment He wet his lips and silently undid the caked knot and unwound the cloth. It stuck on the last few turns and he had to set his teeth hard together before ripping off the last layer. Verl and Asa craned their heads avidly.

'Nearer the fire,' Oshel said 'Hold it out.'

Tute swallowed. It was awful. Worse than it felt, if that was possible.

'Gawd,' Asa whispered. 'Lookit that now.'

Oshel's frosty glance tipped up. 'Them red streaks up your arm, boy, that's blood poisoning. Iffen you didn't find the guts to peek at it, you still knowed it was swole again its size. I oughta larrup your hide for not saying some'at.'

Tute felt an ooze of sweat under his clothes. 'Nobody gonna take this hand offen me You hear?'

'First it is gonna get cleaned up,' Oshel said. 'Then we'll say what's to be done. Asa, fetch some water.'

Asa picked up his hat, got to his feet and headed for the trees.

'Not from the river, you sorry cottonmouth,' Oshel rumbled 'From the water wagon, damn you! And take this pot along. That hat o' yourn don't even hold brains.'

61

Asa brought the water. Tute kept fighting back throaty squeaks of pain while his father carefully washed the dis colored arm, clearing away blood and matter. It was still a sickening sight. Tute could hardly bear to look at it, a thick dread clogged his throat.

'It's throwing bits o' bone,' Oshel announced. 'That ain't good. Ain't no smell anyways. That's somep'n. All right. We gonna wash this thing ever' morning, ever' night, ever' rest stop. But first whiff of corruption I get, Tute, this hand is gonna come offen you above the break.'

Tute worked his jaws, swallowing. 'You cain't do that, Daddy.'

'I can. Can and will should need arise.' Oshel's eyes were gray flint. 'You hear me, boy, and hear me plain. This here wrist is bad infected. It will kill you like a pizen baited wolf without the pizen gets worked out. I will keep it washed clean. Ever' chance you get, keep it in water hot as you can stand. In a few days we will see Verl, get a clean hunk o' cloth and that jug I got hid under my wagon seat. Nothing like good sipping corn for cleaning out a body's evil humors'

'Don't you worry, Tute old son,' Verl said, all grimacing reassurance now. 'We will take keer o' that Satterlee done it to you. Won't we, Daddy?'

Oshel tugged gently at his beard. 'We will bide our time. Iffen Tute gets a hand took off, we will take off both that buckskin man's. You have got my word on't.'

Dake splashed and spluttered in the Washita's warm muddy current awhile, then stepped straight out into a wild plum thicket growing low on the bank. He'd left his clothes here. The condition of his buckskins gave him pause. Seemed a sight of bother for nothing, sluicing off your dirt just to climb back into a set of duds this gamey He had bought himself a new suit of nicely tanned hides off a Cherokee woman before they'd left Gibson, but they were alread stained and sweaty, ingrained with dirt.

Hell, he didn't mind dirt. Never had before. Now he felt self conscious half the time That Sherrod lady was under his skin; he knew it and couldn't find any good reason for it. Hell, he hadn't even spoken to her since that morning they'd set out except for 'How-de-do, ma'am.'

She was a sightly creature for certain sure, but so were some squaws and a few crib slatterns. Come down to it, he couldn't think of a good reason any woman, least of all a married one he hardly knew, should grab him in this wise.

Dake shook most of the water off and pulled on his buckskins. What the hell, at this point he didn't smell aught higher than any sojer boy. They all rode under the same hot sun, sweated alike and got the same dust blown in their teeth. Maybe an easeful dude like that Sherrod could keep clean somewhat, but nobody else could. Anyway, Dake thought pridefully, *he* had taken a bath, by God. And had taken one every day they'd been camped by the Canadian.

He walked back toward the fires, passing the Callicutts again, their mean eyed looks amused him.

The wagons were pulled up around the square like white-shrouded buffers between the cherry fireglow and an ocean of outer darkness The Sherrod wagon was drawn up under some trees apart from the others; behind it, the two Sherrods were talking. A sharp rise in their voices yanked Dake's attention. Jesus, sounded like a real set to between them. Sherrod was apparently drunk as a lord, but that was nothing new.

Dake heard a smacking sound It made his skin goose-flesh Three more slaps followed it, hard and flat and savage, more like blows than cuffs On each of the two last ones, Mrs Sherrod gave a sharp little cry.

Dake pulled up from his slouched position. His muscles turned hard

Sherrod came around the corner of the wagon. Yep. Rolling all right Stinking, rotten drunk Booze worked different ways on different men. It turned Sherrod meaner than a bobcat in heat. He went lurching away into the trees, not looking back

Dake got slowly to his feet, glancing around. Nobody in the vicinity outside of him had noticed the set to He ambled over to the wagon and stepped around its tailgate. Alexandra Sherrod was leaning against the wagon box, her head down, one hand pressed to her face. Her back was to him, her shoulders shaking.

'Miz Sherrod.'

She jerked around. Firelight raced redgold on her hair;

wetness penciled her cheeks. She wiped a quick hand across her face. 'Mr. Satterlee . . . what brings you by?'

'Are you all right ma'am?'

'Right? Of course. Everything's right. How could it be otherwise?' Bitterness stung her voice; she was fighting for control. She swung her head away and the light shone angry red on her face where she'd been struck; her lower lip was split at the corner and she dabbed at it with her thumb. Half-turned away, she whispered: 'Will you go? Please?'

Dake walked away, feeling anger bubble hotly in him. Keep out of it, he thought; it is none of your mix. Caution making a bid to flag down rage and not succeeding. Dake wasn't the temperate sort. Swinging partly around on his heel, he headed for the trees. A glow from the fires made a ruddy fog of light deep among their trunks. Sherrod was easy to locate. He was quietly cackling to himself. Like a loonie.

Guided by the sound, Dake came to a break in the trees where firelight and starshine blended in, a reddish uneasy pallor. Sherrod stood there, unsteady on his legs. He was draining a flask. He flung it away, swearing, and owlishly let his eyes follow its bouncing twinkle across the loam. It came to stop by Dake's foot and Sherrod's glance moved upward.

'By God! It's you.'

Dake didn't speak. He moved in on Sherrod slowly, feeling the flesh of his arms ripple with tension. Easy now, he warned himself.

Sherrod's hair was mussed, his clothes rumpled; he had a seedy unshaven look. 'By God!' he said again. 'It's the calf-eyed lout who camps so near to us every night. You have your gall, fellow, do you know that?'

Dake still said nothing.

'You ludicrous idiot!' Sherrod laughed, swaying on his feet. 'Don't you think we're on to your little game? We've had many a laugh about it, my wife and I. We . . .'

'I just seen your lady wife, and she wa'n't laughing.'

'You filthy border trash! Don't presume to tell me what you've seen. And don't ever interfere in what's of concern to my wife and me, us alone. Or by God, I'll –'

'You'll what? Like you done with Leavenworth? Stand

64

with a loaded gun in your hand and watch a buffler trample me?'

Sherrod hiccoughed. 'Wh . . . what?'

'Reckon I'm the only 'un really noticed. When the genril got throwed in that hunt and the buff bull rushed to gore him. Hadn't been for me and Ben turning the bull with them shots, he'd a finished Leavenworth right there. You was a sight closer than us and in a sight better position. You could a raised your musket and pinked that bull square Only you was froze to the spot tighter'n a cow chip in January.'

Sherrod's face sagged and went putty colored. 'You bastard,' he whispered.

'What's really souring your craw, Sherrod, you found out what you're made of. And it's a dose you can't keep down and can't spit out neither. So you suck your fancy flasks dry and knock your lady wife around. Makes you a man some'at.'

'You bastard,' Sherrod spat. 'Keep away from my wife, do you hear? Stay away from our wagon!'

Dake nodded slowly. 'That's a bargain, Mister. But you got a part to keep to. Which is you don't never lay a hand on that lady wife o' yourn without she asks.' His voice hardened. 'Never again.'

'Who the hell do you think you're talking to, fellow? I'll do as I damned – *arrrgh!*'

Dake's fist had travelled no more than six inches. It was enough to double Sherrod over, wheezing and clutching his midriff.

'It sure ain't none o' my business,' Dake observed, 'but I vow, you think a man with edication and all –' his fist thumped Sherrod's right kidney, staggering him '–'ud have more sense'n to ignore a purely sensible suggestion. Now I got another –' the fist slammed into Sherrod's opposite kidney '– which is not to let himself get caught taking a heavy hand to his wife again. Otherwise he could just get sliced up into bitsy strips –' the fourth blow sank again into Sherrod's soft belly '– and hung up to dry for jerky.'

Sherrod crumpled to the ground holding his belly, making noises like a sick hen. Dake toed him lightly in the ribs. 'You think about it. Meantime, best get offen that damp ground soon's you're able. Man could catch his death.'

Dake swung around and walked back to camp.

CHAPTER SIX

The Dragoons celebrated Independence Day with the wet, dirty, grueling business of getting teams and wagons across the muck bottomed Washita. The river ran considerably deeper than its muddy and sluggish appearance would indicate. It was midnight when the last canvas hooped wagon had been floated to the opposite bank. Afterward Dodge let the wet, weary men throw their blankets where they wished and drop into dead-spent sleep.

They roused out, grumbling and cursing, at the usual reveille hour, to assume the march again. The disabled animals had been shot; the troops had been reorganized into six companies of forty-two men each. Those too sick to go on would remain in Captain Dean's camp with a couple of company surgeons to tend them. General Leavenworth had contracted typhus; his condition had taken a serious turn for the worse. He would remain here. Others seemed to have somewhat improved, among them Sandy MacPherson. These were given the option of staying with Dean or continuing with the column, and MacPherson elected to go on.

Dodge's biggest professed worry was food. Neither food nor water had been a problem so far. The troops had dined on an abundance of antelope, wild turkey, catfish, caught at every river crossing. But Dodge respected Ben Poore's opinion, and Poore's assessment of what lay ahead was gloomy· you couldn't predict how things might be any given year, but what to generally expect this time of summer was damned near no game or water. And the column had enough rations for just ten more days. . . .

Sixty miles and three days beyond the Washita, they struck the first sparse woods of the Cross Timbers. Sten nis had heard travelers talk of this thick sunless belt of blackjack timber where whole acres of trees lay blown down in jackstraw tangles that had become overgrown by rioting bramble and thorn. As usual, though, no fireside anecdote had done justice to the facts. Stennis had never seen such a terrible stretch of country. . . .

Then men got out firewood axes and set to breaking trail through the cross fallen timbers. The saber, that standard fixture of Dragoon gear which had proven so useless to the Indian-fighting horsemen, turned out to be dandy for hacking one's way through near impenetrable thickets of timber saplings that had sprung up between tangles of fallen trees. Briarlike undergrowth flourished everywhere too, its thick thorn armed branches shredding clothing and flesh at a touch, lacerating men and animals alike. 'Anyways,' said a grizzled soldier, 'we finally found a use for the goddam cheese knives.'

For three days they labored through a fanged jungle of deadfalls and scrub, days that seemed to drag on forever. It wasn't merely the ordeal of opening up by slow feet a road for the wagons. The journey was an unending plunge through gloom; a dark depression seeped quietly into the guts of everyone. The Indians whispered fearfully through out the passage. Their race had made this cruel wilderness the source of a hundred superstitions.

On the afternoon of July 9, they emerged from the Cross Timbers Dodge called a halt for the day close to a sallow trickle of creek. The men moved sluggishly; they were exhausted, crabby, temper-bitten. Many climbed down the bank and squatted by the water, officers and men congregating in groups apart.

Stennis soaked a handkerchief and wet his hot face; he scrubbed at the dusty beard caking his jaws. His ears hummed with what appeared to be a touch of fever; most everyone was touched by it. He rolled his itching shoulders against his dirty sweat-stiff shirt and dipped the handkerchief again. He thought worriedly of MacPherson, who was in bad shape again and worsening. All yesterday Mac had ridden slumped almost insensibly across his horse's withers. Before nightfall he'd joined others in a wagon that was filling with a new batch of the sick. Damn such stubbornness! If only he'd stayed by the Washita. . . .

There was a commotion up the line. Stennis got to his feet and moved that way. Some men were pointing and motioning, and now he saw what the fuss was about. A band of perhaps thirty Indians were coming up on a slight rise beyond the trees. They sat their shaggy, wild-looking ponies at a careful distance and remained there, just watching. The Dragoons fingered their weapons and muttered among themselves.

Dodge hurried up now, halting his mount. He studied the Indians, then turned his head as Ben Poore and Dake Satterlee reined up beside him. 'What do you make of them, Ben?'

'Renegade bunch, from the look. Osage I'd say. No women or kids, no tipis, just what they can lug on their hosses Wearing trade cloth and what nots. Plenty o' guns too. They know the white man, all right. But it's dead sure they never seen no sojers like you this far west'

'Not enough to dare attack a column this size. Should we ignore 'em, do you think?'

'Dunno, Cunnel. That is a grubby looking crew. Could be troublesome if they got it in their heads to go after our hosses by night, some'at like that.'

Dodge slapped his riding crop against his thigh. 'Very well We'll ride out a short way and you can try palavering with the beggars.'

As soon as Dodge and Poore started their horses across the shallow stream, two Indians broke away from the group on the rise and came torward them at the trot. The two parties met on the streambank Dodge spoke firmly and clearly, his voice carrying. 'Tell them the warriors of the Grandfather come in peace We bring gifts from the Grandfather for all people of the plains.'

Poore spoke a few words, reinforcing his speech with sign talk. The bigger of the two Indians replied, flexing his fist around the feathered lance he carried. His arrogant manner was a clear match for Dodge's own. A big thick trunked man in his thirties, he had a feral hard lined face. His scarred coppery torso was naked to the waist; he looked powerfully muscled, yet lithe as a cat He wore his hair long, free of adornment, under a filthy turban; it hung lank and greasy down his back

'Says he wants sugar and tobaccer,' Poore translated.

'He'll have them.'

'Says he seen some cows. He wants a cow.'

'Very well.' Dodge's tone grated a little.

The leader promptly made a third demand: a bar of lead and a keg of powder. Dodge, plainly nettled by now, said with a snap of finality. 'Tell him these things will be brought to him.'

Randal and Alexandra Sherrod came walking along the line to see what was going on. Mrs. Sherrod looked particularly handsome in a maroon riding habit that enhanced her tall figure. Only the fading bruise on her cheekbone marred her fresh beauty. (Everyone had speculated about that bruise.) A marvel how she'd kept herself up, seeming to thrive on heat and hardship.

'Tell him the Grandfather wishes him peace and a long life,' Dodge said and then, his patience used up, began to turn his horse.

The Indian spoke sharply. He was not looking toward the colonel.

Dodge reined up. 'What did he say?'

'Says he wants the Fire Hair. Says —'

'What!'

'Says he will give many presents for her. Means Mrs. Sherrod.'

'By God!' Dodge quarter turned his horse toward the Osage. 'You tell this damned insolent savage —!' He paused, lowering his voice to a curt flatness. 'Tell him it is impossible. She is wife to a man.'

Poore spoke again. The Indian drew himself up. He spat deliberately and laughed. His answer was harsh and contemptuous.

'Says for the white dogs to keep their gifts. Their white sluts too. Says he will take what he wants when it so pleases him.'

'*You tell him,*' Dodge shouted, but the Osage had already wheeled his mount away.

Dodge didn't hesitate. He clapped in his spurs and rammed his horse up beside the Indian's. His big arm shot out. He grabbed a fistful of the Osage's long hair and yanked him sideways. It was done too fast for the startled Indian to react; he was simply spilled from his horse and dragged away as Dodge spurred into a run. He hauled the wildly stumbling Indian along beside his mount for a good ten yards, then let go. The Osage plunged on his face, flipping head over heels in the dust.

Dodge pulled his animal to a halt and swung around,

jerking a pistol from his belt. The Osage lunged to his feet, his face snarling and dust-caked He found himself looking at Dodge's leveled pistol. The hair had fallen back from the right side of the Osage's face and he had no ear on that side, only a knurled scar.

, 'Ben!' Dodge's voice was thick with anger. 'Tell that lot on the hill if they make a move, I'll kill him. Tell them!'

Poore already had his rifle trained on the Osage's companion. He was a trimly knit youth in his teens He had the sly bony look of a gaunt wolf; his hawk irised eyes shone with fury. A deep scar grooved his lower lip, warping it to a nasty grimace His resemblance to the big Osage was unmistakable. Son or younger brother. He carried a double barreled English rifle; he'd started to swing it in Dodge's direction, but Poore's weapon had stopped the move.

The Osage's men had been taken completely off guard by the suddenness of it. Now an uncertain ripple of movement ran through them, but it was cut short by Poore's shouted warning. Stennis's heart was pounding in his chest; he'd been certain that Dodge's rash move would rip the situation wide open

'Tell them to get out of here,' Dodge said. 'If they come near us again, we will fire on them '

Poore spoke The big Osage walked to his horse and swung onto its back. He yanked his lance out of the earth where it had fallen impaled, then looked at Dodge. The pistol was steady. Both Osages heeled their ponies back to the rise, and moments later all the Indians were gone. Like smoke.

Dodge and Poore came back across the stream.

Mrs. Sherrod moved forward, her face a little pale. 'Thank you, Colonel. You are a gallant man.'

Dodge smiled grimly 'It was not done entirely on your account, ma'am. That savage had to be faced down and his insolence chastised This band was small. But on the far plains yonder, the Indians will outnumber us many times over. They have a mysterious talent for spreading occurrences such as this like wildfire. I shouldn't be surprised if by the time we reach the Wichitas, our coming will have been long known ... also that the Indians there will be aware that we are not palefaces to trifle with.'

70

Poore said dryly: 'Cunnel, you have things reasoned out all that close when you went after the big 'un?'

'No, I simply lost my temper. The fellow's insolence galled me beyond restraint.'

'Nevertheless, it was handily done, Colonel,' said Sherrod. 'I congratulate you.' He took his wife's arm. 'Come, my dear. We'd best return to our wagon.'

As they walked away, Poore grunted: 'Coulda been our scalps out there, Cunnel. Them Injuns had cut loose, we'd a been sitting ducks, you and me'

'It worked for the best, Ben. I drove a lesson home.'

'Ain't so sure. Rec'nized them two after a bit Big bastard you dumped on his ass is Skinned Ear. Used to be large noise in Osage councils. Kid was his brother. Cut Face. Bad Injuns both. Whole crew of theirn likewise. Too much brushing agin white man's ways turned 'em rotten Got run outen their tribes and took to raiding for their wants. Skinned Ear heads 'em 'cause he's tougher and meaner'n the lot Lost his face with you. Got to make it up some ways or he'll lose 'em. Likeliest way is to revenge hisself on you'

Dodge laughed. 'Nonsense. How would he manage that?...'

Three days of struggling through the Cross Timbers had deepened the sullen depression that hung over the column Dodge decided to extend the halt, laying over at this spot till tomorrow. He sent the scouts out to hunt for buffalo, but they returned empty handed. The food situation would be grave before long. Meantime sickness continued to eat into the Dragoon ranks.

The first death was reported at six o'clock that evening. Private B F Chaney of E Company died quietly in his blankets Combination of bilious and heat exhaustion, said Dr Haile. His tone indicated that he expected others to follow Chaney before long.

Sandy MacPherson was too weak to sit up any longer. He was consumed by fever that came and went between attacks of teeth chattering chills His rational moments were few. Sitting beside him in the dimming light and listening to his feeble efforts at talk, Stennis felt a thickening despair. Mac's skin was gray and dry, his voice a husky rattle.

71

'Wurra, wurra. Don't look so unhappy, lad A man's name and appointed hour are writ in an angel's book ... eh, who's that angel?'

'I don't know, Mac.'

'No matter. It's how a MacPherson meets his fate. Claymore belted on and tartan snapping No slippers and fireside memories for us.' He grimaced. 'Although this damned way is neither. A wee sip o' that water, please.'

Stennis held up his head and tipped a water jug to his lips Mac drank and lay back. A sardonic grin curled his lips. 'It seems a petty thing to die for,' he whispered. 'Just because the lumpwits who run the military system must commit nine out of every ten possible blunders whenever fresh ground is being broken It's the Black Hawk War all over, lad If some manner of strategy or logistics enjoys success once, apply it with a rocklike nuance to every circumstance So scores, hundreds, thousands must always die for the myopic stupidity of the brass balled muddleheads on top. Aye, I'd have left the damned system erelong. But rather it had not been this way.'

His eyes closed, he slept

Stennis gazed glumly across the sick camp At one fire, Alexandra Sherrod was helping the Pawnee, Ona, brew medicinal tea A whiff of it made his nostrils quiver – nasty-smelling stuff At first Dodge had objected to the women exposing themselves unnecessarily to sickness, but Mrs. Sherrod had been her usual insistent self If nothing else, their presence would cheer the men, and Ona knew medicine secrets that she averred would help The white woman and Pawnee seemed to be getting along remarkably well; Mrs Sherrod was trying to communicate with Ona in her own tongue and Ona would shake her head and laugh, her white teeth shining

Stennis sat brooding at Mac's ashen face Soft footsteps made him look up Ona was standing there Her large eyes were luminous, she spoke soberly. He wearily shook his head to indicate that he didn't understand. She tried a few English words, slowly and haltingly.

'Your friend ... very sick.'

'Yes'

'Mebbeso Pawnee med'cine help. I make. My mother show.'

Stennis's eyes stung with the quick anger of despair. 'Squaw medicine?' he burst out. 'Chants? What in God's name good is all that heathen mumbo-jumbo? A man is dying!' His voice cracked. 'Dying, don't you understand?'

She might have understood half the words. But she grasped the tone perfectly. Without speaking, she turned and walked back to the fire. Mrs. Sherrod had caught the byplay between them, and now she wiped her hands on her apron and came over to Stennis. Her expression was taut and cold.

'How dare you?' she said quietly. 'That girl was trying to help in the best way she knows. Also, for your information, some Indian cures, some of their herbs and drugs, are far more efficacious on particular ailments than anything that civilized physic can devise. And if she should believe that chanting will help, what of it? I suppose you've never worn asafoetida or had blister plasters on your ankles.'

Stennis's cheeks warmed. 'You're right, ma'am. I am sorry.'

'You might tell her so.'

He did his best. Going over to Ona, he said. 'I am upset about my friend. I hope you will forgive me for speaking as I did.'

But she wouldn't look at him or reply. Would not or could not. He realized that his words had cut so deeply, it would take more than a mere civilized apology to redeem him. Ashamed of himself, quite depressed, he started away from the sick camp.

He encountered Dr Haile returning from the main bivouac, carrying his case of surgical instruments. Haile had chewed his cigar to shreds and he looked furious. Stennis remembered that awhile ago somebody, somewhere down the line, had begun yelling in obvious pain. A few minutes later a soldier had dashed up saying that a teamster had gotten hurt, was bleeding something fierce, and could Doc come on the double?

'Know what all that howling was about?' Haile demanded. 'Know what it was?'

'No,' Stennis said

'It was that stupid son of a bitch Tute Callicutt! That busted wrist of his. The goddam thing was bloated and suppurating. Then it turned gangrenous. So Old Man Calli-

73

cutt sawed it off with a butcher knife. Just like that!' Haile made a slicing motion with his hand. 'You think those stupid swill sippers had the sense to come to me when the corruption first showed?'

'I suppose not.'

'Goddam right not! I might have saved the hand. At the least I could have amputated cleanly. The old man did a butcher's job. No bleeders secured, no sutures, no stump flaps! He was pumping blood like a stuck pig, so the old man thrust the stump into a fire and Jesus, you never saw such a mess. Ahhh!' Haile flung the cigar away, his tone savage with disgust. 'Did what I could. Made a second cut farther up and took off two inches of bone, then secured the flaps Who knows? He may live.'

Stennis left Haile muttering to himself and headed toward his company line.

He was passing the cluster of baggage wagons when pandemonium hit. Shots and shouts carried from beyond the wagons. Men were scrambling to their feet, yelling questions, trying to wrest sense from the confusion. Indians after the horses, Stennis quickly guessed. The animals had been picketed out on grass west of the camp; today's encounter with the renegades had caused Dodge to post a heavy horse guard. But hitting by surprise in the early dusk, Indians could create havoc.

Stennis veered toward the wagons on the run He passed a thick motte of trees and, coming around them, blundered into the path of a phalanx of riderless horses charging right angled past the grove. He leaped awkwardly backward, tripped and rolled on the ground. The horses thundered by, bannering dust Several riders, hugging their ponies' backs like burrs, raced in their wake

Stennis scrambled to his feet, pulling the pistol from his belt. He fired point-blank at the nearest brave. Missed. But the fellow's pony broke stride, caving in its run and then cartwheeled in a fall. The rider hit the ground plowing up a shroud of dust, somersaulted and surged to his feet in an agile bound.

Cursing, Stennis fumbled for his powder flask The Indian was running after his fellows; in a moment he'd be lost to sight. Just then three soldiers came boiling around the trees, muskets in hand. Stennis whipped out an order

74

and the three men drew bead and fired. The Indian spilled to the ground.

Stennis and the soldiers reached him quickly He was struggling to get his wounded leg under him; now he whipped out his knife.

'Take him alive,' Stennis said.

After a considerable tussle they disarmed the man and dragged him to his feet. 'Damned if it ain't that bastard with no ear,' said a soldier. It was. Skinned Ear himself. They had a prize He stood quivering in the soldiers' grasp, his cable muscled body tensed for any advantage that might be seized.

Stennis said curtly: 'Bring him along. . . .'

The raid had cost the raiders more dearly than it had the Dragoons. Two of Skinned Ear's men had also been captured. He and a dozen others had stolen up on the picket lines, dusk covering their approach, but had been discovered almost at once The sentinels had opened fire, killing one renegade and wounding two more The rest had been driven off, melting away into the near dark Skinned Ear and a pair of companions had succeeded in cutting one of the picket lines and stampeding the animals off, but the bravado act had cost Skinned Ear his freedom and a bad leg wound.

Dodge ordered the captives brought over to a fire. He kicked up the embers, spraying a burst of ruddy light over the three wounded men, he grinned 'Nice work, Mr. Fry. You've counted big coup.'

'Border'll be a heap quieter with this 'un's fire damped,' said Ben Poore. ' 'Pending what you got in mind for him, Cunnel '

Skinned Ear stood with his arms folded, ignoring the blood pumping from his leg. Firelight painted highlights on his muscled torso; his face was contemptuous in its sinewy disregard of his captors

'Got in mind?' Dodge echoed 'Why, nothing, Ben Just insurance against more trouble with their crew Three good hostages are worth a bit of trouble and a few horses. . . .'

CHAPTER SEVEN

Dr. Haile was summoned to patch up the injuries of Skinned Ear and his two companions. Though satisfied that their wounds would discourage any attempts at escape for some time, Dodge ordered them securely ironed inside one of the depleted supply wagons. A blacksmith hammered shackles into place round their ankles; attached were yard long chains which were bolted to the thick bed of the wagon box.

Next morning, after the Dragoons had taken up the march, a band of horsemen who were assumed to be Skinned Ear's renegades was reported trailing them at a distance. But they never ventured nearer than a half mile to the rear of the column. Finally they pulled off altogether and there was no further sign of them in the days that followed. Apparently unsure whether their leader was dead or a prisoner, they'd given him up as lost. . . .

Beyond the Cross Timbers, the Great Plains had their real beginning. The Dragoons found that everything they had ever heard about them fell appallingly short of the reality. A horizon-reaching vastness, like the billows of a molten sea which had cooled ages ago, unleashed itself on their senses. The country was a treeless immensity of muddy rivers and glaring skies and hot eternal winds that shrank all of man's august pretensions and crushed him mentally to his knees.

The days and miles ground by. Despite the regimen and routine that Dodge still doggedly enforced, what little posture and strut the proud Dragoons had retained now wilted away on the summer blasted plains. Where the days of June had been sweltering and sticky, the days of July were dry and sizzling. Before, you'd felt you were stewing in a closed boiler; now you were roasting on an open spit and the heat was savage and punishing and implacable. Your heavy wool uniform, standard issue, had been a sweaty hotbox; now it was a filth-stiffened torment on your boiled, rash bitten flesh. Where you'd let your coatee hang unbuttoned, you now discarded it altogether. Goddam the regulations, said the men, and the officers kept their silence and then followed suit, declining to mention the breach in their reports. Shirtwear, since the Army didn't issue any, was a colorful variegation of linseys, flannels, cottons, even a few silks and cambrics. But all of it soon took on the mock uniformity of any grimy, sun-bleached, sweat-blotched rags.

Still forced to cover fifteen miles a day, the men became bred to the bone with exhaustion. It was part of the furnace-like chimera that each day brought. So was the routine. Even the cycle of rest stops had a dispiriting monotony. Flies hummed in clouds; men made vacant underpitched attempts at talk. The horses stood head-down, emitting dry blubbering noises; they voided bladder and bowel with juicy splattings whose rich green stink quickly made each halt unbearable. Then the buglers would trumpet brassy signals; again the soreness of movement would begin. . . .

The water situation was exactly as Poore and Satterlee had predicted. The few streams that hadn't dried up were reduced to saffron straggles. Where water had pooled deeper, it stood stagnant and greenish. Tepid, foul to the taste, muddying at a touch. The same was true of such miserable seeps as the scouts guided them to. By now, however, with travel between waterholes stretching to days, the men were not finicky.

The problem of food was becoming urgent. The men were put on half rations, then on quarter rations. Parties of Indians went out daily to reconnoiter for buffalo. The fruits of their foraging were a few isolated bull bison who were old and defeated and whose meat tasted like it. Divided among the few hundred men who could still keep food down, several tough and stringy buffalo split up fine and didn't last long. But they did stretch the diminishing supplies.

The scouts' bleak predictions were borne out again when the high-strung throughbreds began to fail. They had no bottom for the poor forage, bad water and killing heat to which the plains-bred mustangs of the scouts stood up easily. The purebreds became rib-gaunt and began to limp; lather and dust caked their fine coats with a muddy crust and they were sorry things to behold.

Against all Dodge's expectations, the health of the whole command continued to deteriorate. Men's bowels were on fire; fits of flux and vomiting attacked nearly everyone. All countermeasures taken proved useless. The sick list swelled every day. A few men improved; most did not. The severely ill were consigned to the supply wagons. That these didn't become overcrowded was due partly to the rations being nearly used up, partly to the fact that almost daily the stricken were slipping into coma and death. The trail became dotted with fresh graves All that could be done was what had been done before. When a place with fairly good water was reached, a sick camp was set up; provisions and two well volunteers were left with the ailing.

Stennis Fry recovered from a mild onslaught of fever; the blistering heat didn't sap his vitality as it did that of most. But like most, he found the empty vastness of these parched wastelands a terrifying depressant. His worry for MacPherson worsened it; he didn't know what, outside of pure Scot grit, was keeping Mac alive, for he sank a little more every day.

Dodge listened to the medical reports, his face grim and haggard. He'd ceased his dogged insistence that the men would become conditioned. Instead he assembled those who could still stand and gave them a snap-to speech in his hot intense style. They had a job to do – *at all costs* – and they were going to do it by God if he had to drag the last living man of them through by his ears.

The lecture produced an outbreak of mutinous grumblings. The old bastard was pushing too far. But conditions weren't really favorable to either mutiny or desertion and the only remaining choice was to stick fast and hold on. Also, perversely, a fresh shot of hatred for Old Ironguts was the bracer needed at this point Men hugged their hate to them and nurtured it. And let Dodge's fierce will flail them on. . . .

Another night camp. The usual squared beacons of flame. Dake Satterlee and Ben Poore squatted by a solitary fire, cradling their scalding cups of coffee between calloused hands and reminiscing on better days. Private Tevis came slogging by on his circuit of the camp, carrying two saddles on his back. Passing them, he had a wild cock-eyed look.

Poore grunted. 'That bluejay gets his tail in one crack after t'other. Glutton for punishment detail.'

'Leastways they can't find no trees for him to tote around way out here,' Dake grinned. 'Puts me in mind o' Eph Bassett when we was trapping the Blackfoot country few year back. Bunch o' us was holed up for the winter. After a month ole Eph started to get ornery and awful-eyed like this Tevis. One night he cut loose and went after all of us with an ax. Had to heave him in a crick to cool off.'

'Yeh. There's gents get that way.' Poore gazed glumly at the fire. 'This here's a jinxed outfit, Dake. Good 'un to shake free of whilst the getting is good.'

'You thinking on't?'

'This child'll see the job through. Don't let that hinder your hankerings, though.'

Dake swigged his coffee, tossed the cup aside, yawned and stood up. 'Feel like stretching my legs a spell, ole hoss. See you later.'

Poore shot him a quizzical look, but said nothing. Dake ambled away down the campline. Old Ben was too wise to stir up the pot, but his concern rankled a mite. Hell, he'd kept his word to that Sherrod ninny not to approach his woman, hadn't he? He wondered if he looked moony to Ben, who knew him pretty well. Fact was, the belly-deep confusion he felt about Sherrod's lady hadn't dried up yet. Otherwise he'd likely shake free of this fool outfit, all right. Taking green troops onto the high-summer plains. Going on with near to a third of 'em down sick. Jee-zus!

He saw Catlin, Beyrich and Sherrod talking by a fire and said a howdy as he passed them. Only Catlin and Beyrich replied; Sherrod's blotchy face merely took on a pizen-mean look. Hell with that sour-bellied bastard. Must be that all the lizard pee he swilled down secured him against mortal affliction. But you had to hand it to the paintslinger and that Dutch pilgrim. Liverish with fever, they wouldn't slack up for anything, Beyrich still hot as all hell after strange weeds, Catlin still toiling away with paints and sketchbook. Regular as sunrise, the both of 'em.

Dake swung over toward a man who sat alone, staring into his fire. MacPherson had given up the ghost last night and Stennis Fry was taking it pretty hard. Dake felt obliged to say a word; he cleared his throat.

'Sorry about your friend, Loot. He was a right fine sort.'

'Thank you.'

Dake walked right on, not wanting to intrude further. Took a spell for a man to lay his ghosts, but Fry would be all right. Had a curious stuffy way about him, but you had to like him for all that.

Later Dake might wonder if he'd deliberately ambled in the direction of the Sherrod wagon. At the time he didn't particularly think about it one way or the other; still he couldn't deny who was on his mind. And presently his way took him close by the wagons, drawn up in a line just east of the camp square. There she was, cleaning up some supper odds and ends, and he was going to ankle straight on past. But she glanced his way with a pleasant smile.

'Good evening, Mr. Satterlee. Would you like some coffee?'

Man couldn't refuse coffee. Besides his guts were cauterized by the fearsome brew that Ben Poore had concocted of seep water and chicory.

'Yes'm. I thank you.'

He came to the rear of the wagon and accepted the graceful cup she handed him. Real china, by God. Real coffee too. 'Ain't that fine! Ain't had the like sincet I was in St. Looey last.'

'Oh?' Kneeling, she went on scouring dishes in a shallow pan of water. 'When was that, sir?'

'Unh, last year it was.' No point mentioning it had been in the fancy salon of Madam St Pierre's, the town's plushest bordello, and he'd taken coffee because Madam didn't permit liquor on the premises.

She straightened up, wiping a film of sweat from her forehead. Not a strand of that redgold hair was out of place, Dake noticed admiringly, and her plain calico dress was neat as a pin. She was the kind who'd fit in wherever she was. Kind of woman who mothered strong men – with a fine sturdy body surely built for it.

'I must look a sight.'

'Yes'm Just the prettiest.'

'Oh Thank you.'

She smiled straight at him and he took the opportunity to look for bruises. Nary the tinge of one. Not that he was surprised. Even a mean dog could be learned new habits and he'd served Sherrod a pretty tight lesson. But the shadow of misery around her eyes and mouth was plain as speckles on a pup. A nerve quivered in her cheek. Sure enough. That bastard's drinking and his worsening ways had her worn fine as froghair.

'You needn't look so closely, Mr. Satterlee,' she said quietly. 'I can tell you that he hasn't struck me again. He kept me awake half that night, groaning about his stomach. But I shouldn't guess you'd intended to injure him very severely.'

Dake's face burned. He didn't know what to say. Finally he muttered: 'No'm. Just tickled his belly and sweetbreads a mite.'

'You are kind, but I fear it's kindness misplaced. Oh, I shan't deny it feels wonderful to have a champion. I'd nearly forgotten the feeling But I can hardly encourage such gallantry, can I? It's really quite a hopeless business.'

'Might help to talk about it some'at.'

'No. Please –' She bit her underlip. 'There is no help for what is. People cast their lots and then live their lives as they must. I am not a whiner nor a weakling. I have that pride, I hope.'

Dake, never a halfway man, figured he might as well shoot his whole bolt. 'Sure you do, ma'am. Just it helps to talk betimes. A body reaches the end of being strong.'

Well, he'd hit the mark there. Her eyes dilated and she looked away.

'It is all of one piece, Mr. Satterlee. What can I say? My father died and my brothers were all married ... had families of their own to look after. Suddenly there was nobody. And then Randall was there. He was the brother of Father's best and oldest friend He said the right things and I believed them. I was to learn that he had a talent for saying the right things and saying them very well.' She made a small, impatient gesture. 'I was only seventeen, which is not very important. Not any more. We've chased down every will-o'-the-wisp, it seems, to the east of the Mississippi. And now west of it. One time it might be cotton in New Orleans. Another time, a scheme for selling off a wilderness tract in the middle of nowhere. No venture was successful, and finally Father's money – what he left

81

me – was gone. A friend of Father's in the nation's capital obtained this appointment for Randall. It is steady work at least.'

And it hadn't changed a goddam thing, Dake thought. She stood half turned from him, twisting her hands together, so that – sensing the true depth of her agitation – he wondered how much she'd left unsaid. The drinking, sure. Cards? Other women? How much bad mouthing, how many blows or beatings? Thinking on it gave a wrench to his innards.

'Reckon that man o' yourn needs someone to look after him,' he said gently.

'Yes' Her head tucked down 'I have to, that's why I'm here, why I go where he goes, everywhere. . . .'

Somehow, Dake was never sure just how or why, she was up close to him. Crying against his shoulder. Seeking the comfort she needed. There was no more to it, he was sure. But his arms were tight around her and the moment turning into a whole world more for him, silken womanhood and soft firm pressings that a man'd be stone cold dead not to heed, and his heart near stopping in his chest.

It was half dark by the wagon end, the wagon itself half-concealing. Nobody to see And in a few moments they pulled apart. In the same instant, Sherrod came around the wagon.

He halted, swaying. Primed full for sure. His face was puffy and discolored, yet it went livid in a second.

'You,' he said in a strangled voice. 'You dirty chaw-bacon scum!'

He bulled straight at Dake, who wheeled away from his awkward lunge, murmuring, 'Go easy there. Go easy –'

But Sherrod was beyond listening. He waded after Dake in a fury, plunging a hand under his coat. It came out with a little Allan's patent pistol that needed only a jerk on the trigger to send an ounce of lead into a man's guts.

Alexandra Sherrod screamed. And Dake stopped retreating.

He took one long step, caught Sherrod's wrist as the pistol whipped up, and twisted The gun barked like a feisty mutt; he felt the ball fan his scalp. Dake twisted again and the gun fell to the earth. He kept twisting, forcing Sherrod to his knees.

'You better listen,' he said coldly.

Sherrod howled like a gutshot coyote. He clawed at Dake's wrist with his free hand. 'I know what I saw! God! I'll kill you! I'll kill you both!'

Dake held him like that, helpless on his knees, not knowing what else to do. Jee zus. Dandy kettle of fish this was. What in hell . . .?

About a dozen men were coming on the trot. Some enlisted men and several officers, Fry among them. Ben Poore, Catlin and Beyrich right behind. They came to a stop and then Dodge was shouldering through them at his stock, driving stride. His eyes snapped up the scene with a glance.

'What was that shot? What in hell is this?'

Dake let go of Sherrod, who almost fell over. He staggered to his feet and turned a yellow-eyed look on his wife. 'You strumpet! Whore! You –'

Dodge stepped forward, his hand cracked across Sherrod's mouth 'Curb your tongue, sir! I want an explanation and that damned fast!'

'Ask her! Ask him!' Sherrod was shaking like a palsied man. 'This swine was holding my wife, fondling her –'

'Quiet!' Dodge's stare ran cold blades through Dake. 'Well, Satterlee?'

'Reckon he thinks he seen what he thinks he seen, Cunnel. Wa'n't what it seemed, that's all.'

Dodge waited a moment, then snapped: 'That's all?'

'That's all. Rest ain't nobody's mix-in. Yours neither.'

Sherrod made a sudden lurch at Dake, who promptly stepped backward. He could smack this pipsqueak just once and he wouldn't rise in a year of Sundays. He wondered why he didn't; he felt curiously detached Guilty? Well, a mite, maybe. He could sure-hell see how it looked to these men.

'That's enough!' Dodge roared. He caught Sherrod by the shoulder and flung him reeling against the wagon box. He hung there, fingering his broken lip.

'I demand satisfaction,' he said hoarsely.

'That is suitable,' Dodge said grimly. 'The pair of you can square off right here.'

'In one of your border-style dog falls? I wouldn't soil my hands on this swine! He ought to be shot –'

'Ah, you want a gentleman's satisfaction. Is that it?'

Sherrod hesitated. He swallowed. His gaze flicked to Dake and he snarled, 'Yes!'

'Very well.' Dodge smiled wolfishly. Dake remembered that the colonel himself had a hellfire deadly reputation as a duelist – guns, knives, fists. 'Satterlee, you're the challenged party and have choice of weapons. Sabers? Pistols?'

'I never even held one of them frogstickers.'

'Pistols, then; I have an excellent brace and will provide them for the occasion. Also my services as referee. Sherrod, you may name your seconds.'

'Colonel,' Alexandra said in a shocked voice. 'Please –'

'Be still, Madam,' Dodge said coldly. 'Your misgivings are belated. Sherrod?'

'Will you second me, George?'

Catlin nodded.

'And you, Beyrich?'

The naturalist shook his head. '*Nein – nein*. It is a barbarism I cannot countenance.'

Sherrod's glance moved to the officers, pausing on Lieutenant Jefferson Davis. 'Mr. Davis?'

'I am agreeable. However, I should remind the colonel that dueling is forbidden by regulations'

'Damn your twopenny Army rulebook,' Dodge said irritably. 'No mention of this affair will be made in any report or correspondence.' His frost fire stare swiveled across the officers. 'I trust that's understood?'

Davis shrugged 'As you say, sir'

'Very well, Satterlee Choose your seconds.'

It seemed like a sight of nonsense. 'Ben?'

'Proud to, hoss.'

'How 'bout you, Loot?'

Fry's hesitation came as no surprise; he sensed the young officer's distaste for the situation, he was groping for words of refusal With no real hope of convincing him, but sure that he'd like Fry in his corner, Dake said· 'I ain't liking this dueling fooferaw. Just playing out what I been dealt. I ain't gainsaying what this man seen. Just he's thinking wrong. Can only give my word.'

Fry fetched him a real surprise.

'That's good enough for me. I'll second you, Satterlee.'

'I think we may settle the affair with dispatch,' Dodge said. 'So it doesn't interfere with ordinary business, we'll hold it before reveille tomorrow.'

Sunup was faintly flaring on the horizon's edge as the party of men tramped out on the plains toward a slow-swelling rise. It was some distance from the bivouac square. Conducting the proceedings in the shadow of its other side wouldn't only keep them private, it would also, at this very early hour, ensure against flat sunrays hitting either duelist's eyes.

Stennis still felt reluctance at his own involvement. He hadn't till now been aware of feeling friendship for Saterlee, but his readiness to take the scout's word about compromising circumstances indicated liking. Very well. Still dueling struck him as infantile and – what had Beyrich said? – barbarous. Yet the regulation against it had been ubiquitously blunted by so many Army hotbloods who had a penchant for picking quarrels and secretly consummating them by the code that it was merely stale print on paper. Leave it to the free-wheeling Dodge to ignore it openly.

They reached the spot.

Dodge said dryly: 'Would either gentleman care to extend an apology?'

Dake shrugged. 'Am willing to call off fireworks any time. But ain't making apology for some'at that ain't so.'

Sherrod merely shook his head tightly. He was bareheaded, wearing fawn-colored pantaloons and a ruffled white shirt. The complete duelist-at-dawn. His face was pale except for being drink-mottled; he wasn't altogether steady. He must have spent six sleepless hours dwelling on this one. A weak, petulant fellow whose spirit was in his mouth, Stennis thought. Aside from the spiritous courage in his belly.

Dodge opened the lid of the engraved mahogany case and passed the matched pistols around for inspection. Then, in full view of everyone, he swabbed the grease out of each pistol barrel and flashed a cap on each nipple for clearing. He tested both weapons, ramming the wrapped balls down against their charges and setting caps where the heavy curving hammers would strike true. He fired each gun at an outcrop some yards off. Rock dust puffed from an identical shot with each clear, whiplike report. The weapons were incredibly accurate. He loaded and primed again, then handed a gun to each man.

'They're hair-triggered. Careful, once you've loaded.' He scuffed off a patch of ground with his heel, walked twenty paces off and marked a second position. 'Very well, I count to three. Each man fires. If neither is hit, you either go through the business again or consider honor satisfied. Make ready.'

The two men walked to their positions and stood sideways to each other. They used both hands to cock their pieces, then pointed them skyward A light wind combed the curling prairie grass. It touched up the morning cool, but Stennis felt sweat already damping the cambric shirt against his back. He felt tension in his companions; only Dake appeared peculiarly relaxed.

Dodge counted

Sherrod fired on the instant. The ball whipped the sleeve of Dake's upraised arm. Wet darkness dyed the tanned leather.

Dake never stirred a muscle. His face was stonelike as he lowered his pistol to eye level. Sherrod stood paralyzed, his eyes wide and staring Dake dropped his barrel and shot into the ground The weapon's discharge at a touch kicked up dust nearer Sherrod's feet than he'd probably intended.

'Hell,' Dake said mildly. 'Missed.'

From a sophisticated man, his gesture would have been *opéra bouffe* From Satterlee, it was a simple declaration, plain as words But how would Sherrod take it? A glance at his outraged face gave the answer He'd had a bad scare, but in his eyes Dake had deliberately made him look the fool.

'Blood has been drawn,' Dodge said, 'and, I take it, honor satisfied.'

Dr. Haile was already moving toward Dake, but Sherrod shouted · 'No! Let's see how strong his guts are!'

'Man,' Dodge said coldly, 'what does it take to pound a point home to you? I declare this affair ended If –'

'Unh unh,' Dake drawled 'Stand off, Doc, ain't but a scratch Cunnel, we will play the waltz out again '

Silently Dodge reloaded and primed the weapons. They

took places. Sherrod's face was shining wet. He was starting to shake.

'One-two-three –'

Pink dawnlight slashed along the barrel of Sherrod's
weapon; he fired. This time Stennis saw Dake's big body
jerk to the ball's impact. He just stood there. Sherrod's
jaw dropped. Dake lowered his gun and shot into the ground.

A murmur ran through the watching men.

'There's an end of it,' Dodge said peremptorily.

Sherrod stood motionless, his eyes oddly glazed. Then
he jerked like a man startling from a trance. '*No!*'

'Satterlee, I hope you'll not be such a fool,' Dodge said
crisply.

'Sorry, Cunnel. Sherrod named the tune and I am just
playing out the waltz. No, you stand back, Doc. I ain't a-
bleeding to death.' The whole right side of his buckskin
shirt was wet red.

The pistols were charged once more.

This time Sherrod had the self-control to take a careful
aim. But the decision was too late. By now he was shaking
so, he made a clean miss.

Dake's raised pistol sank to a level on Sherrod's chest.
This time he didn't lower it. The seconds stretched out
long and aching. Stennis felt his skin gooseflesh; his mouth
was dry. God, he thought.

Sherrod's face was pasty. He stood crumpled and swaying, the empty gun sagging from his hand, hitting the
ground.

'Shoot!' he screamed. 'Shoot, for God's sake!'

Dake shrugged, tipped up his pistol and fired into the
sky. Then he turned, walked over to Dodge and handed
him the weapon. 'Dandy balance, Cunnel, but a mite touchy.
Want to wash and clean these nice shiny play-things straightway so's the barrels won't foul. Not now, Doc, I just got
nipped in the armpit. Skeeter bite. You best look to Mr.
Sherrod. Seems in mean shape.'

Sherrod had fallen to his hands and knees. He threw up
in the grass.

Alexandra waited by the wagon, watching her husband
weave unsteadily across the camp, which was in a bustle
of activity as the Dragoons prepared to resume the march.

Randall came too close to the rear of a skittish horse that was being saddled by an ill-tempered soldier. The horse's hind hooves lashed out, missing Sherrod by inches. He stumbled aside, then stood blinking.

'You damn fool!' yelled the soldier. 'Stay out o' the way!'

Randall didn't answer. He came on toward the wagon. An hour ago he'd returned from the duel so badly rattled that his teeth were chattering. Without a word to her, ignoring her questions, he'd dug out one of his few remaining flasks and disappeared. A few moments later, seeing Dake Satterlee crossing the camp, she'd felt an overwhelming gust of relief. Neither man, apparently, had been hurt.

Then and there, Alexandra had made her decision.

Randall came plodding up. He was seedy and beard-stubbled; his clothes awry, and even in the revulsion she felt, she had to steel herself against pity.

'Why isn't the team hitched?' he said surlily. 'You're so damned handy at those things. Or finding someone to do 'em.'

'Hitch your own,' she said quietly. 'You'll be hitching your own from now on.'

'What? What's 'at mean?'

'It means I've moved every stich I own out of this wagon. It's all yours now, Randall. I only waited to tell you that.'

'Moved? Moved?' He looked wildly around, squinting his reddened eyes. 'Moved where?'

'Everything I own is in that wagon yonder.'

He followed her pointing finger. 'My God – with those squaws? You're joking!'

'They helped me move. I've made friends with them – as you should know, since you've objected loudly enough – and they were fully agreeable to the idea.'

'You, you can't do that! I'll tell Dodge. . . .'

'The colonel has given his approval. Don't you understand, Randall? It ends here. I've had enough.'

All the color washed out of Sherrod's face. He grabbed at the wagon box for support. 'You can't do this, Alex,' he said hoarsely.

'It's done.'

'The humiliation – the scandal . . .'

'Since when did those aspects concern you? I've lived

88

with them for seven years. Your wine and your women, your –'

'A man does these things!' he cried. 'Haven't you any compassion?'

'No, no more. I have a little pride left, I think. I mean to keep it.'

He caught her by the wrist, leaning close. 'Ah. I see. It's the mountain man. You'll be free to proceed with that affair. But you can't really want that smelly illiterate. This is merely your little revenge!'

'You are beneath contempt,' she said quietly. 'Let me go.'

She twisted against his hold and broke it. He fell off balance against the wagon box. He began to cry, tears running down through his beard stubble. Alexandra felt sick. Not again, she thought. Not this time. Tears. Regrets. Promises. No more.

She walked quickly away. The Pawnee, Ona, was waiting for her by the wagon, her face somber.

'You cry,' she said. 'He cry. Maybe is no good, what you do?'

'No. No good, Ona. But worse not to do it. I think we should get the wagon into line. . . .'

CHAPTER EIGHT

'Evening, Sarge.'

'Top of it to you, Mr. Satterlee.'

Dake paused in his leg stretching, sank down on his hunkers beside Bohannon's fire and dug out his pipe and tobacco pouch He filled the pipe, curiously eying Bohannon as he slowly scribbled in the little book spread open on his knee. He'd pause, shake his head, mutter to himself and then scribble some more.

'Would you be spelling the word uncertain u n s-e r-t a i n?'

Dake meditated as he got out his Mexican tinder cord, flint and steel *eslabón* 'Think she's spelled without no *a*.'

'Na, that ain't right. There's an *a*, I'm sure.'

Satisfied, Bohannon wrote on. Dake deftly struck a spark into the tinder cord and blew it to a ripe coal He grinned. Worked like a charm every time He puffed his pipe alight, squinting at the little book. 'What's new in turkey tracks, Sarge?'

'I'll thank you not to mock me literary efforts. That's what Lieutenant Fry calls 'em.'

'Ole Loot oughta know. Never had more'n two year o' schooling my own self. Be pleasured to hear what you writ.'

'Well, then.' Bohannon cleared his throat. ' "July 14 Today as usual. Corporal Menlo died, also Privates Tibbetts and Moran We buried them. Soon we will come to a big village of the Comanche says Ben Poore Maybe four days Our supplies is about run out Will be in unsertain straits if the Comanche is not kindly disposed to us. He will have food but we will need plenty and if he is not disposed to surrender it I wonder what we will do. Maybe fight—" '

Dake chuckled around his pipestem. ' "Scuse it, Sarge. But even Dodge ain't *that* big a fool.'

'Agh,' Bohannon grunted 'I know you scouts think poorly of the man. But he has sand in his gizzard, that you must admit.'

'Yeh Enough he's on a fair float to getting his hair lifted. Ours too.'

90

'D'you truly think there'll be trouble with the redskins?'

'Never learned t' head off any Injun's thinking One thing sure. They decide t' take us on, they will wipe us up like backfat on a hot griddle.'

They chatted awhile longer. Bohannon defended his commander, though his heart wasn't much in it. He was a direct man, simple and stubborn and loyal to his service, and Dake liked him for it. Afterward Dake continued his stroll along the north line of the camp, replying to hellos here and there. Officers hailed him familiarly, which it struck him they hadn't as recently as yesterday. Must be the duel this morning had made a difference. Lieutenant Jefferson Davis had been impressed enough to observe that he'd never seen more gentlemanly behaviour on a field of honor.

Honor counted as a big coup to the likes of Davis, a southern 'cotton aristocrat.' Dake still considered it a goddam foolishment, particularly in that he'd just stood and let that Sherrod ninny take potshots at him. He'd been damn lucky that he was still alive to think about it. One shallow groove along his right arm and a nick in the far chest muscle on that side where his only marks for it. Yeh. Goddam lucky. 'Is this how you expiate your sins?' Dr. Haile had acidly inquired while bandaging Dake's scratches. Untangling Doc's meaning, he supposed that was it. He'd contributed to busting up a man and his wife; how was he supposed to feel?

Fact was, he felt a spark of pleasure that she'd quit Sherrod and guilt nudged him on that account too. He also felt a mite sorry for Randall Sherrod. This country had a way of trying a man's mettle as no civilized temptations ever did; it sharpened the best and worst of his nature. He'd seen other ninnies like Sherrod; they never stood a show out there. Hell! Did she still have a feeling for him or had stern duty alone kept her by him this long? And what difference could it make for Dake Satterlee? His thoughts kept tracking back to the moment when she'd stood close against him, filling his arms with a satiny warmth and lush maturity whose memory still thickened his blood.

Best he not go near her again. Best all around He'd troubled her house enough. Dake kicked savagely at a clod of earth, grunting as a twinge grabbed his stiff armpit.

He was nearing the wagons and decided he had better skirt wide of them. No sense taking a chance on his resolution being weakened again He circled towards the outer darkness, away from the fires. He could make out a sentry, his muskets shouldered, pacing a slow watch in a brief area where two wagons were drawn up. One held Skinned Ear and his pair; the other was occupied by the two squaws and Alexandra Sherrod. The guard also commanded a view of the food wagons and could watch for soldiers attempting to raid them.

The plains had soaked up part of the day's heat and a light wind was up, stroking the short curling buffalo grass. Dake felt his way on silent moccasins, the darkness sliding past him like silk. He was occupied with his thoughts, yet alert

He picked up a few sounds that weren't quite covered by a drift of minor noise from the camp. Faint sounds, but close by and seeming out of place. He halted and listened.

His lips stretched. Sure enough. A man's whisper. A girl's soft, bold, cajoling giggle.

That damn Kiowa. She had sneaked out in the dark to meet some man. No surprise, that. Buffalo Calf Girl had a lusty reputation back on the Lovely Purchase. A hot-eyed sixteen and full of the Old Nick. White man's ways had bashed the old Injun rules all to hell. Passing strange some man hadn't filled her belly with a kicker before now. One trooper or teamster with more hots than good sense hadn't been enough impressed with Old Ironguts's warning or the example he'd set with Private Tevis. Hell, maybe it was Tevis again. Whipping hadn't dimmed that bastard's crazy ways a whit.

Dake couldn't make out a thing in the thick dark, but judging they were somewhat to his right, he veered left to avoid them.

Then he pulled up short again The voices were getting louder and turning pretty wild. Man sounded demanding and angry. The Kiowa, scared and shrill. That damn girl. Tease a man without mercy, then play coy. Dake sympathized with the man. Woman like that, be she red or white, was the worst sort of tramp. Hell with her.

He started to move on, but the girl gave a sharp frightened cry. He heard tussling sounds in the grass; the man was cussing wildly. Dake knew the voice then. Asa Callicutt's. Damn little fool, trifling with a wild man like Asa. Dake gave an oath and headed in that direction.

He saw two dark twisting shapes on the ground. Moved in, bent and grabbed a handful of long hair. The howl of pain told him it was Asa's. Dake dragged the struggling man to his feet. Asa, startled crazy, began yelling like all fury; he grappled Dake. Son of a bitch was wiry strong. For a moment it was all Dake could do to counter his groin-hitting eye gouging tactics. Then Asa landed several hard jabs in his short ribs and Dake furiously seized his neck, thumbs tensing instinctively to jam deep in the soft throat hollow, a thrust that would kill instantly.

Dake barely caught himself in time. He switched holds, bear hugging Asa and toeing behind his heel, then leaning hard and tripping him and going down with him. In mid fall, as Asa's arms flailed loose. Dake clamped an armlock on him. Asa was half helpless as they hit the ground. Then completely helpless as Dake changed to a full headlock.

'Quit it!' Dake snarled in his ear. 'Quit yelling, you goddam fool, I ain't no Injun, I'm trying to save your silly ass –'

Asa stopped shouting and struggling. But too late. The guard by the wagon had caught the commotion out in the dark. Silhouetted against firelight, he was coming this way at a cautious trot. Dake let go of Asa and got to his feet. The girl, damn her eyes, had begun a wild screeching.

There'd be no stopping it now. Old Ironguts had made his threat. And a promise. Whatever else you might say of him he was a man who kept his word. . . .

Tute Callicutt lay in his blankets, staring up at the velvet night. One folded arm cradled his head; the other lay across his chest. He did not look at its bandaged stump. Didn't have to. The pulse of dull pain kept him in constant awareness of it. And all he had to do was move it to waken a tearing anguish.

Goddam the old man. Taking it off like he was butchering out a buck.

Wouldn't hear of the surgeon touching it. Had no faith

in leeches. Maw had died because a sot of a sawbones had messed up the breech birth of her fourth son. Maw and the baby were buried next day. So was the sawbones; Oshel had seen to that. Hill justice, raw and sudden. A shot from ambush and a sheriff who was Callicutt kin and winked it away: killing by a party unknown.

Doc Haile was a different sort, but try telling Daddy, Nossir, son. Will take off that rotten limb of yourn my own self. Now you get to swigging this corn lightning. Tut had been drunk and loose and giggling when Daddy started in, Verl holding him. Till the blade hit a fat nerve. Be he doused in hellfire one day, it couldn't be any worse. If Doc Haile hadn't come and acted quickly on the fire-blackened blood-spurting mess, he'd be fueling Old Scratch's bonfires right now. Days of fever and delirium had followed; he had become a near skeleton except for his ballooned arm. Then a clean healing had taken. But he was still weak as a kitten.

Tute twisted restlessly, quieting at the burst of pain. Couldn't blame Daddy; he'd acted for the best as he saw it. But Jesus . . .

The camp square was pretty still now, after all the bedlam earlier. Fires crumbling to cherry coals sent out faint glimmers here and there. A dim red shine played on the blanketed shapes of his father and brother close by. He knew they weren't catching any shut-eye either.

'Daddy,' Verl said softly.

A long silence. Then Oshel's weary rumble: 'Yeh, boy.'

'What we gonna do about Asa?'

'We done all we can for Asa. A fitten burial. Some words said. Hush your mouth, son. Let your Daddy think on't.'

Oshel sounded much calmer than he'd been, but his tone still bore an ominous edge. Verl took the hint.

Tute squeezed his eyes tight shut, wetness tingling at the corners. Only a few hours gone. Asa had been alive and full of cussedness. Now he was cold clay in a prairie grave.

Why in hell'd he have to get dog fever for that no-good Injun bitch? She'd known Asa had a fierce itch for her and had played on it like an angler baiting a hook. Sashaying past him betimes, switching her pert ass like a feather duster Black eyes twitching aside looks full of sin and promise. Had poor Asa near busting out of his drawers.

Same as with that Tevis bluejay. Same thing all over.

And Dodge hadn't been about to listen to Asa's side any more'n he had to Tevis's. Kiowa had carried on with tears and wailing over how 'Asa had offered her a pretty present if she'd meet him. Poor dumb Indian gal, what did she know about such things?

Not that she had Dodge fooled. She didn't by a damn sight, Tute was sure. But Ironguts had vowed the next man to molest one of those girls would be shot like a polecat. Summarily executed was how he'd put it to Oshel who had roared his protests for naught, arguing that he and his boys were civilians. No exceptions would be allowed, said Ironguts; all had heard his warning. Nor was the punishment any more nor less than would be inflicted on any man of his regiment, enlisted man or officer, who'd ignored his ruling. It had to be.

So it was. What could Asa's daddy or brothers do? Stand by and watch while soldier guards marched Asa to the center of the firelit square and a dozen more soldiers formed a tight row, muskets gleaming. One crashing volley. Powdersmoke like a pale shroud on the scene. And it was over.

At last Oshel broke the silence, his words coming slow and labored. 'Hark to me, sons. We Callicutts got three people to settle with. That Kiowa. Satterlee . . .'

'Daddy,' Verl broke in, 'Satterlee, he tried t'do right by Asa. Spoke up for him right pert. Tol' Dodge that Injun bitch was most t' blame.'

'You forgetting the turn that buckskin man done your brother Tute?' Oshel's voice had a whip-edge cut that made Tute's innards curl. 'I made a promise I ain't forgot. His two hands for Tute's one.'

Verl held his tongue, which was smart. Oshel's tone made plain that another such remark would get him whopped silly. Tute didn't say anything either. He couldn't raise his sights above the mad hatred that flared in him at the mention of Satterlee's name.

'Satterlee, I said,' Oshel rumbled. 'And Dodge. Three to settle with. But in God's good time, boys. I will say when it's to be. . . .'

CHAPTER NINE

Colonel Henry Dodge tramped heavily up and down, kneading the frayed riding crop in his fists. His jaw was grim, his thoughts split between anger and impatience. Damn! Why the first desertion now? Now, when they were so close to their contact with a plains tribe? Three to four days to a main Comanche village if they maintained a steady march. Yet, because he was certain that the success or failure of the whole mission rested on this initial contact, Dodge had the nagging, frantic feel of a man fighting time: even an hour's delay could set him on edge.

The men were breaking camp. Non coms shouted orders; equipment clanked and creaked. Dodge ran his gaze over the sunburned soldiers moving about their familiar tasks. Little resemblance here to the regiment that had ridden out from Camp Jackson in highstepping splendor a month ago. Bearded and dirty, uniforms bleaching to scrubby rags on their scarecrow frames, many of them hollow eyed from the ravages of sickness, they looked no better than any ragtag gang of border militia. There was little talk, most of it muted and sullen. The rocky morale was worsening. Still, though they might crab and gripe and move sluggishly, they were toeing the mark, by God.

Let his officers, damnfool regulars all, mutter about his methods; the damned book wasn't worth a hoot or a whistle out here. They'd resented his leadership from the start because he was a political appointee, not one of their own. Regardless of what the mission accomplished, once it was finished and the official reports filed, his military and political enemies would be howling after his scalp, calling for his dismissal The execution of a civilian, Asa Callicutt, would raise a special stink. The fools! No command wanted to give such an order. The vow he'd made to place any woman-molester in front of a firing squad had seemed necessary at the time; he still deemed it so. No leader could afford to renege when his word was put to the test as it had been last night. Let 'em hate his guts; discipline had been maintained. Anyway the President would stand behind him as always.

Old Hickory knew how to crack a whip with both soldiers and politicians and make the bastards jump.

Dodge squinted briefly against the swollen sun, hardly topping the horizon yet, but holding the promise of another broiling day. Its heat was already soaking through his faded red-flannel shirt. He swore softly. Damn these blistered plains. Damn the stupid timing of this expedition. Damn the plague of miseries, one after another, that had bogged the mission down from the first. Above all, damn the swamp of red tape and the brassheaded ignorance of War Department officials whose decrees had forced inadequate preparations: heavy wool uniforms, poorly chosen equipment, insufficient food. Future military forays on the plains would benefit by their example. Unquestionably. Damn thin consolation.

His adjutant, Lieutenant Jefferson Davis, came up and saluted. 'Sir, I've accounted for the muster roll and sick list of each company. Apparently Private Tevis is our only deserter. However, one of our civilians is also gone. Mr. Sherrod.'

Dodge was only mildly surprised. That would explain the two missing horses. The loss hadn't been discovered till this morning, for the regimental animals, picketed under heavy guard, were all there. But the scouts' mustangs had been in a separate bunch and the ne'er-do-well half-breed scout who'd been delegated to guard them had been approached well after midnight by Private Jack Tevis, bearing a bottle of whiskey. The scout had wakened this morning with a splitting headache. Claimed Tevis had offered him a drink, then knocked him out. More likely he'd drunk himself to a stupor, for he was reeking of the stuff.

'Where the hell did Trevis get the whiskey, I wonder?' Dodge mused aloud.

'I ran into Dr. Haile, sir. He had a profane complaint. Says someone stole a bottle from his medical stores.'

'And there'll be other stores missing from a food wagon,' Dodge muttered. 'That pair of unbalanced fools! I'd prefer letting 'em meet the fate they richly deserve. But ...'

Lieutenant Stennis Fry came up at the trot, mounted on a tough, wiry mustang borrowed from the contingent of scouts. Behind him were Dake Satterlee and a half dozen troops likewise mounted with full gear. Outside of Davis,

Fry seemed to be the only officer who wasn't semi-prostrate with Army diseases; the soldiers chosen to accompany him were also in good fettle.

Fry snapped a salute. 'Ready to go, sir! I've drawn four days' rations for each man.'

'Glad you're feeling so bright-eyed and bushy tailed. Mr. Fry You may have a long trek ahead. They have at least three hours' start on you.'

'Davis has determined that Private Tevis is the only deserter from our ranks. However, he was accompanied by Mr Randall Sherrod' Dake Satterlee gave a little start, Dodge noticed 'Tevis must be brought back I'll take no chance on his example setting off a rash of desertions This outfit is riding a tight enough edge. We're moving on without delay; you'll catch up with us.'

'Yes, sir. And Mr. Sherrod?'

'Bring back his horse,' Dodge snapped 'He can return with you or continue his way, as he wishes It's my sincere hope that he'll choose to go on all by himself.'

Randall Sherrod took a swallow of whiskey from his last remaining flask, wiped his mouth on his grubby sleeve and gazed across the blasting monotony of summer plains that rolled ahead of them. The midday sun broiled down on the scorched grasslands and nothing moved in all that buff tan desolation God, what a terrible country. He held the small flask to his ear and shook it, made a wry face and thrust it back in his pocket

Sherrod hadn't spent this long in a saddle in some years; his backside and thighs were starting to chafe Thinking of the long, grueling journey ahead of him, he groaned softly. But physical discomfort, he'd already decided, was the least of his worries.

Tevis ricked slowly alongside, muttering to himself now and then. Something about him put an uneasy flutter in Sherrod's stomach The fellow's moods alternated between violent opposites. He would ride for many minutes in surly silence, refusing to respond to questions by so much as a grunt. Suddenly and for no reason, he would launch into a savage tirade against some object of his spleen Dodge The Dragoons. The goddam Army. An ascending spiral of hatred that was wild and irrational.

If he takes a dislike to me, Sherrod thought, what will happen? He dwelled unhappily on the days and nights that must be spent in this man's company More and more he was regretting his decision to leave the caravan. The raw vastness of the country seemed more appalling than ever; empty and endless in its undulant flow to the horizon. His eyes ached with the heat; flinty points of light danced in his vision.

God, why had he listened to this fool? Already, only a few hours away from the camp and the sun hardly at mid morning arc, a first sodden clutch of fear and loneliness was gripping him. At least the caravan had offered decent company and safety of a sort. . . .

If only Alex hadn't turned on him. He'd had a cold-bellied sense that no amount of remonstration or pleading would bring her back. She'd threatened to leave before, but he'd never truly believed that she would. He did love her; he needed her. God, how could she desert him, knowing it?

The naked shame of it burning in Sherrod's guts had forced him to one of the rare moments of honesty he dreaded He couldn't remember when he hadn't been a coward. As a youth, he'd been dogged by fear of failure till it became an obsession. Until he was afraid of being afraid His father, Virginia gentleman, hero of Lord Dunmore's War and proud Tory during the Revolution, would never brook failure in an only son. Very early, Sherrod had learned how to carry off small necessary subterfuges, a zeal of desperation urging him to masculine pursuits which he'd mastered to perfection because they did not come naturally to him. He'd lived the pretense successfully for years, till marriage to Alexandra had cracked its bold gloss. His fight for strength had ended, for Alex was strong enough to lean on. Unwittingly, she had destroyed him. Alex had destroyed him. With that thought, as always, his moment of honesty had been past, drowned in a fog of whiskey.

It had been the worst of all possible times to be approached by Tevis, who had dropped sly hints that he planned to desert and would be willing to take along some company. Tevis had guessed from talk he'd heard that the gov'ment gentleman might be his man. A shrewd guess.

Sherrod had snatched gratefully at an offer that would remove him from reminders of his disgrace.

All Tevis had wanted in exchange for bringing him out safely was a thousand dollars, payable on their arrival at St. Louis. He thought Sherrod was a rich man. Very well, Sherrod had thought; he'd scrape the money together somehow. And Tevis, obviously a tough, wiry product of the frontier, had made their prospects sound good. Trail back was a ling hard 'un, he'd allowed, but a lone man 'ud stand a sight better chance making it out than a whole goddam outfit that was dying on its feet. Two men alone could move a sight faster and smoother than a long crawling column. Good strong horses. Rucksack of food. Rifles. These were all they needed. There'd be a little game along the way to be snared or shot, enough to fill a lone traveler's belly, and he'd marked the different watering places in his mind. Hell, yes, he had it all worked out but the doing. Hardest part'd be stealing a bait of food and a couple horses and slipping away, but they should manage right smart by night. Camp would be asleep, darkness would cover, nobody'd allow for a man to desert way out here. . . .

Sherrod rubbed a shaky hand over his face. God, he needed another drink already. Panic bit at his vitals; he began to shake all over.

He reined in his horse.

'Tevis,' he said, and the soldier looked at him and slowly pulled up. 'I have changed my mind. I am going back.'

Tevis gave him an unblinking stare. 'We got a bargain. You going back on't?'

'I'm afraid so. I have changed my mind.'

Tevis raised his musket from his saddlebow. He did not point it, but the gesture was ominous. 'You had best change it back then.'

'God, man! This is a foolish thing we're doing. We'll never make it, even if –'

'You owe me,' Tevis said in a monotone. 'You gonna keep your part.'

'I –' Sherrod stopped himself. Saying he had no money, he suddenly knew, would be a fatal mistake.

'Get on.' Tevis motioned with the musket.

Sherrod moved ahead of him, a brassy-sick taste on his tongue. His whole body jerked to the crash of two quick

100

shots. But they hadn't come from close by. And he was untouched. He twisted his head. 'Tev –'

Tevis, he saw at once, would not answer. He was slipping sideways from his horse in a dead loose fall. He hit the ground like a sack of meal. Dust boiled up in a cloud and settled; blood patched the back of his shattered skull.

Sherrod sat frozen and staring. He saw a slow fray of powder-smoke hanging over the crown of a swelling hillock a hundred yards to his left. White smoke settling and that was all.

Sherrod leaned against his horse's neck, sick with horror. My God . . . who? Or what? He'd never felt such a rush of stark, unreasoning terror. Yet he couldn't move. He searched the silent roll of land with his eyes, coming always back to the hillock.

Nothing. No sign of a thing. A smash of death, sudden and senseless, and nothing more.

Like a man in a trance, Sherrod gathered his reins and turned his horse back in the direction they'd come. He rode very slowly, like a man picking out a trail on a mountain ledge. As if a single misstep would be his last. His eyes quested all around. Still nothing. No more shots. No enemy in sight. Only a wash of hot heavy silence that seemed to mock his helplessness.

Sherrod's nerve cracked. He screamed at his horse, kicking in his heels, lashing his hand up and down. The animal jumped and settled into a stretching run, Sherrod flattened against its mane.

A second shot. He was only dimly aware of it, for the bullet had already slammed into his horse's side and it was plunging to the earth, pitching Sherrod over its head.

'Well?' Stennis said.

Dake Satterlee had been walking about studying the ground; he straightened up. 'Some'un's cut onto their trail,' he said. 'One man, barefoot hoss.'

'He's following them?'

'Seems 'at way.'

Stennis peered at the trampled earth and crushed grass. It bore the hoof and wheel marks left by the Dragoon column yesterday. A trail so plain that he hadn't appreciated Dodge's sense in assigning Satterlee as guide, since he and his soldiers need only trace back a route that Tevis and Sherrod were bound to follow Now, only a few miles along, Satterlee had spotted tracks of a horseman who had come up from offtrail.

'What does it mean?' Stennis wondered aloud.

'Reckon a body'd have to ask him,' Dake grunted as he moved over to his horse and swung up. 'Sign says this fella's been follering our outfit Pulled back outen sight 'hind a rise when Sherrod and Tevis come along, then cut back on the trail Only now he's follering the two o' them.'

'How the devil do you tell all that?'

'Old sign, fresh sign, track covering track ' Dake shrugged. 'Still don't say who this gent is or what he's got in mind '

'Indian?'

'I'd hazard so.'

Stennis frowned. 'Perhaps one of that band – Skinned Ear's?'

'If t'is, he is by himself '

Stennis put his mount forward, raising and dropping his arm, and the soldiers fell in behind him. They set a brisk pace along the well marked trail, Stennis feeling a tension between his shoulder blades, a pleasant tingle of excitement. This was resolving into more than a mere chase after deserters

He glanced thoughtfully at Satterlee jogging beside him. He wondered what was going through the scout's mind. Mrs Sherrod and Satterlee. Somehow the thought seemed less ludicrous now. Satterlee might be unlettered, a wild man of the plains, but he had resources and intelligence that Stennis appreciated more and more Very little escaped him and his judgment aways proved out sound and sure. Most of all, Stennis remembered the duel and how the scout's courage had put a so-called gentleman to shame, revealing him for what he was.

But you had to weigh Mrs. Sherrod into the picture. An unfortunate situation. Though a man like Satterlee gave no clue to his deeper feeling, the duel had made it clear enough. Stennis silently sympathized with him.

Occasionally Dake signaled a stop so he could study the sign. He allowed they were gradually overhauling Tevis

102

and their mysterious follower. Ought to come up on 'em before noon. Everyone best watch sharp.

The quick pace had sweat pouring off the men; furnace heat pounded and punished them. Just moving your eyeballs in their sockets brought gritty pain. Stennis muddily wondered that anything, even the occasional bison or band of mustangs that the column had sighted, could survive this stupendous wasteland from one year to the next. How did the Indians manage? Living on stuff that your stomach couldn't sustain Knowing just where to dig for water in a dust dry streambed. Unaffected by conditions that slowly tore the white man down, body and spirit...

Satterlee pulled up, lifting a hand.

'What is it?' Stennis asked.

'Sounded like a couple guns. One shot, then t'other. Wait a bit.'

When another shot came, Stennis faintly picked it out. 'We'd better waste no time,' he said. 'Forward to the trot!'

He didn't want to push the horses too hard Nor did he want to run heedlessly into something unexpected. So that it was some minutes before they picked up the figure of a man stumbling across a rise ahead. He was half running, half staggering, toward them. Stennis held the trot. Another minute and he identified the man as Randall Sherrod.

He was half out of his wits with terror, babbling incoherently. What Stennis managed to extract from him was that two shots had killed Tevis, but Sherrod had not seen anyone When he'd tried to run for it, another shot had killed his horse. He had hugged the pitiful shelter of its carcass, waiting, but no more shots had come. So he'd started back down the trail.

He was a miserable sight, clothes covered with dust, face streaked with tears and sweat, eyes staring like a crazed man's. Stennis said as gently as he could, 'You look used up, Mr. Sherrod. Suppose that you climb up back of Private Kline there and we'll push along.'

With Sherrod mounted behind the soldier, Stennis waved the patrol into motion To Dake he said quietly: 'Only one man was trailing them, yet two quick shots killed Tevis – the two you heard first. He coudn't reload in a second flat. Would he have two rifles?'

'Wouldn't need two, Loot. Just one two barreled gun. Like that brother o' Skinned Ear's was toting. 'Member?'

Stennis remembered. The boy called Cut Face. And his nice shiny double-barreled English rifle.

They found Tevis's body where Sherrod had last seen it. His horse stood by, reins trailing As the men approached, a cloud of flies droned up from the sticky darkness of Tevis's broken head Dake warily circled the hillock from which Sherrod figured the shots had come. He studied the ground in its vicinity, then came back to the others.

'He cut off the trail a ways back, Loot, and come up behind that hill. Dropped Tevis but figured killing Sherrod's hoss 'ud do for him, so left him afoot. Then whupped his own hoss away and is long gone. No use tracking 'em. Never catch up.'

'Think we'll see him again?'

'Most like. Long as he figures Skinned Ear is alive and we got him. Been follering us Then follered Tevis and Sherrod for the plain hell. Wouldn't pass up catching a couple of us alone thataway.'

They buried Tevis where he had fallen Stennis said a few words while the men stood with heads bowed. Then they mounted and rode back the way they had come, Sherrod on Tevis's animal. In a couple of hours they overtook the slow moving column.

Dodge listened with coldly savage patience as Stennis told him the story. Afterward he took out his wrath on Sherrod, calling him a disgraceful poltroon and regretting that he couldn't claim him in his command for about five minutes. That would be sufficient time to have him shot for desertion. As it was, Sherrod had better goddamned well stay out of his sight.

About midafternoon, a lone horseman appeared a mile or so behind the column. He came no nearer, just followed steadily, matching its pace The solitary apparition began to spook the men; whisperings of 'Tevis's ghost' spread up and down the line. Dodge tried to puncture the ominous nonsense with the counterword that the man was a single Indian, Skinned Ear's brother, but the mood of many was already on hairtrigger and the rattled whisperings continued.

Finally Dodge sent out a patrol with orders to take the fellow prisoner. It returned empty handed Before they'd reached him, the rider had vanished like smoke into the prairie swells. They had searched for an hour, with no luck. At least, it seemed, they had driven him off. But he was soon back, holding the column's wake at the same distance. One minute he was nowhere, the next he was there.

Ben Poore talked with Skinned Ear awhile, riding be hind the wagon where he and his companions were shackled. He repeated the conversation to Dodge. 'Ear wanted to brag some. Says that's his little brother follering all right Says his men knowed Ear wa'n't dead when they never found his body. But figured they couldn't take him from so many sojers, so gave up. All but Cut Face. Says he won't never give up.'

'Then he'll be a long time trying,' Dodge said crisply. 'Unless he can find a way to steal deep into our camp and break his brother's chains.'

CHAPTER TEN

The distant presence of the Indian rider continued to have an unnerving effect on the men. Dodge dispatched another patrol, then another, to run him down. These fared no better than the first. The fear talk did not dissipate. But the real fear was of things more tangible than ghosts or trail dogging redskins. Thirst. Hunger. Fever. Each day following the one before it with a desolate monotony, except for getting hotter and harder. These were the true enemies. . . .

The midsummer heat poured like a blistering fluid over the trudging column. Dry grass powdered under wheels and shuffling hoofs; clouds of tan choking dust billowed. The tawny-tufted undulations of baking earth swelled to a weirdly hovering rim of distant mountains The air quivered incessantly; mirages shimmered from time to time.

Where was the Comanche village? They should have reached it by now. At least come upon some sign that it was near Food. They must have food soon. They must have fresh horses The faltering, overdriven thoroughbreds were starting to drop More men were relegated to the jouncing wagons where they rolled and tossed in delirium. Men continued to die Surgeon Haile himself came down with fever and was dangerously ill.

Poore was dismayed by their failure to find the summer lodges of the Kotsoteka Comanches He fanned scouts out to look for sign. They finally found it. But all of it pointed to a dismal indication that the Kotsotekas had deserted their town site weeks ago. Probably anticipating an unusually severe summer, they had packed their lodgeskins and household goods and moved to some likelier place. Wind had obliterated their tracks; only a few discarded objects, a broken cradleboard or a cracked cooking pot, half buried ashes of old fires, marked the site.

It was a bitter blow to Dragoon hopes As they pressed on, it began to seem a fatal one By now the ovenlike temperatures had clamped fiery fists of drought on the last streams. Nothing remained but stagnant puddles filling hollows where buffalo had wallowed. The men dug holes in streambeds where dampness survived. Horses almost trazed with thirst had to be fought on an iron rein. The parched and impatient soldiers had to be watched too. Erratic start-ups of hot, dry, hard-blowing wind increased their misery. The pace of the column began to limp. More and more of the emaciated thoroughbreds were dying on their feet. A stench of sickness simmered like a tangible miasma around the men and animals.

Once again Dodge flailed the assembled men with a savage, driving speech. But there was no tinder left to seize the sparks he threw out. Yet a few hours later, as if the heavens couldn't deny his fierce will, clouds began massing across the sun and turned dark-edged. The wind cooled and held steady. The men gazed at the sky and murmured. The pious prayed aloud.

Then a cry ran up and down the dusty column. 'Buffalo!' At first it brought little response. Many had reached a point where the mere thought of food turned the belly rancid. All they could think of or hope for was the rainstorm which showed every promise of breaking, yet did not break. But it was true: a sizeable herd had been sighted and soon hunters' guns were roaring. Within the hour, even soured palates had perked up to the crackle and savory odors of roasting meat. Dodge ordered quantities of the flesh to be jerked and stored against the days ahead.

But there'd be no sun-drying of meat today. For by mid-afternoon the sky opened and torrents of water drenched the parched column. . . .

Alexandra gazed out the back pucker of the wagon cover, watching the soldiers capering like children in the pelting rain. They whooped and laughed and sang; they held cupped hands to the cloudburst and drank. Some hardy souls had braved official wrath to strip down to their drawers and roll in the mud. That looked like fun, she thought almost enviously.

Grinning a little, she looked back at the two with whom she shared the wagon. It was a bit damp but quite cozy under the canvas and thrumming rain. The three girls sat in comfort on their blankets and enjoyed the cooling air as Alexandra continued the English lesson. Far off and faintly, thunder rumbled.

Both Ona and Buffalo Calf Girl had a stumbling command of the language, sufficient for most purposes. But it pleased Alexandra to help them improve; little enough return for their hospitality. She tapped a pencil against her teeth, gazing at the worn copy book open in her lap. It contained fragments of Chaucer, Spenser, Keats, Shelley, copied long ago in her own schoolgirlish hand.

'Ona, do you think you can say the verse I read to you yesterday?'

Ona recited it without hesitation.

> ' "I am the daughter of Earth and Water,
> And the nursling of the Sky;
> I pass through the pores of the ocean and shores;
> I change, but I cannot die." '

Alexandra smiled. Ona had heard the verse read aloud only twice, but that was enough. She was quick and interested; her vocabulary and diction had improved in an amazingly short time. But Buffalo Calf Girl's power of concentration was limited. Unable to take the lessons seriously, she spent more time giggling over her mistakes than trying to correct them. Just now she was most absorbed in peering out at the young men cavorting in the mud. No doubt wishing she could join them. She really was a good-hearted soul, Alexandra thought, but a shallow mischief-maker too. The Callicutt boy had paid for his life for a flirtation in which Alexandra was convinced that the weight of the blame lay with the girl.

'Very good,' she nodded. 'Now, Buffy; can you repeat it? Try the first line.'

' "I am –" ' Buffalo Calf Girl tittered.

' "I am the daughter –" '

' "I am – daughter – of –" Uh . . .'

Alexandra sighed. 'Let's try another stanza.'

> ' "I bring fresh showers for the thirsting flowers,
> From the seas and the streams;
> I bear light shade for the leaves when laid
> In their noonday dreams." '

'That should be an easy one. I will read it again. . . .'

She realized that both girls were looking past her at the rear pucker. Turning her head, she saw her husband standing there looking in. Sight of him gave her a cold little start. She hadn't spoken to him since the day she left their wagon. She hadn't been near him since, and seeing him now, she felt a distinct shock.

'Hello, Alex.'

'Hello, Randall.'

She felt a faint half angry embarrassment, but she couldn't just turn him away. Her sharp edged disgust with Randall Sherrod had softened, but not her resolution to leave him It had been a long time coming, but once fixed, the decision was immovable. Still she felt a stab of pity. He had lost weight; a blond beard stubbled his jaws, and his eyes were haunted and nervous. The rain had slacked down to a steady drizzle that matted his light hair to his head.

'You shouldn't be in the rain, Randall '

'I, ah . . ' He swallowed, clutching the wagon box. 'Could we speak alone, Alex?'

'I'm afraid not. If you have anything to say . . .'

'Give me another chance, Alex. I beg you. It would be different this time, it really would, so much is clear to me that wasn't. Won't you come back now?'

Alexandra looked away from him, shutting her eyes tightly. 'Promises, Randall. Promises, promises! I'm sick to death of them '

'I don't blame you If I could only make you believe.'

'Why do you want to lean on me now? Have you run out of whiskey?'

'I don't need it any more, Alex I hadn't been without it in years and I've found I don't need it, I need –'

'I don't care, Randall Go away '

She kept her face turned from him. After a moment she heard his footsteps moving off. Buffalo Calf Girl began an uncertain giggle; Ona silenced her with one sharp word.

The heavy drizzle continued as the column moved on. The men had nothing in the way of waterproofing; after the first exhilaration of fresh coolness had worn off, they began to complain and curse the weather. So it went through the remaining gray hours of daylight and into the early

109

darkness after they'd made a cold, wet, fireless halt and dined off cold bison. Soggy buffalo chips wouldn't ignite, so the men huddled in groups in the wet darkness, shivering wet, warming themselves with a comradely griping.

Around midnight the storm picked up again. The thunder that had boomed distantly began to cannonade like massed artillery, slamming back and forth between horizons. The pitch black was flashed apart by white flares of intermittent lightning. It picked out men's hunched forms and the pale-topped wagons where the sick were sheltered There was little else to be seen and the continual roar of thunder drowned every other sound so that men had to shout to be heard.

Drenched to the skin, Stennis Fry slogged back and forth on the round of his duties How long would the storm last at peak fury? Cold or hot, wet or dry, he seemed to bear twice the burden of any other subaltern in the regiment. Bitter observation had shown him ways of avoiding many onerous burdens, but he'd refused to take advantage of them. A stern upbringing made any form of shirking repugnant. Still he was learning that hard work pointed only one road to success and not the easiest one. . . .

Stennis went out to check on the horses. Lightning and thunder had some of the high bred animals skittish, but they were securely picketed and the guards had everything in hand He cut back toward the main camp, passing back of the wagons.

A sound faintly reached his ears, making him pull to a halt.

Though muffled by rolling thunder, the noise was flatly distinct. A quick solid chunking, like an ax biting into wood. Not a large ax; it couldn't be swung with that swift vicious rhythm.

A hatchet. Tomahawk?

Stennis stood listening, a cold dribble running down inside his collar. He was mystified. There wasn't a scrap of wood available, wet or otherwise, to stoke a fire. What else would anyone use an ax on? He tried to isolate the exact source of the chopping. Seemed to be coming from one of the two wagons isolated from the rest. One sheltered Mrs Sherrod and the Indian girls; the other, the three Indian prisoners.

Stennis hesitated a moment longer, waiting for the next glare of lightning to show him something definite. Then a quick suspicion hit him like a blow. He started toward the wagons at a run. In the same moment, during a lull in the thunder, the chopping ceased.

The guard! Where was the guard?

A burst of lightning gave him the answer. Two more steps and he'd have stumbled over the sentry's body. It was crumpled in the grass a few yards from the prison wagon. Stennis stopped and grabbed his shoulder, saying 'Royton?' And rolled him on his back.

Rain laved Private Royton's face and glassy eyes; it rolled into his open mouth. His throat had been cut.

Stennis came straightening up just as a dark form sprang from the darkness of the wagon box, bounding out through the back pucker. He saw steel flash and grabbed for the upraised arm. Then the hurtling body struck him full-on; he went down with his assailant on top, the enemy's full weight driving him against the ground with a crushing impact.

He clung numbly to the sinewy wrist, holding the tomahawk away. The fellow was straddling him; lightning lit up a snarling face and scarred mouth. Cut Face. Stennis heaved upward, at the same time yanking the arm he held sideways, rolling the Osage on his side. Cut Face was quick as a cat. He doubled his legs under him and threw his weight backward. In an instant he was firmly on his feet and then, straightening his body, dragged Stennis up to his knees. Stennis kept a dogged grip on the Osage's wrist; he tried to wrap his free arm around Cut Face's legs and throw him.

The Osage's knee whipped up and cracked against his chin. It jolted him loose and knocked him on his back. Stunned, he saw the tomahawk sweep back and down in a blurred arc. Too late to twist away, but he tried. Then his head exploded with pain.

He twisted on the wet earth, holding his head. Hazily aware that the chopping had resumed, furious shattering blows. His senses ebbed away. Not long, for a few seconds. Rain beating on his face pulled him back to sick awareness.

He stumbed to his feet, the blood boiling in his head. Lurching over to the wagon, he grabbed at the puckered

111

canvas and stared inside as lightning washed the interior in a furious glare. The boards that anchored the Indians' chains had been smashed to pieces, the chain bolts freed. The prisoners were gone. Cut Face had chopped them free....

Stennis heard a muffled cry.

He squinted against the storm. Thunder pealed in his ears, lightning pinwheeled against his eyes. He made out the other wagon and a man climbing out of it, in his grasp a struggling woman. Other figures moving shadowlike ... a washback of darkness wiped out the scene.

Stennis stumbled toward the wagon. His senses whirled; he tripped and fell. Again he got laboriously to his feet, dragged the pistol from his belt and blundered on blindly. Slammed against the wagon wheel. Hung across it trying to focus his eyes.

Lightning gave him another brief clear view. Of four men moving away and hauling the three women with them. One of them screamed, thunder all but drowning the sound. Stennis's legs moved without violation, the earth tilting and heaving under him God ... they were taking the women away. He had to stop them.

He tried to shout, but if a sound came out, he couldn't hear it himself. He was aware of falling again, the earth rushing up to meet him.

Thunder crashed and rolled His brain sawed in and out of a dazzling sentience He was up again and trying to run. Another jolting fall Up again Lightning seized the outlines of the people ahead. Flicker-patterned glimpses that receded steadily, growing more distant. And then were gone.

His head swirled with misty impressions. Even these blurred away as a rush of oblivion swallowed him.

CHAPTER ELEVEN

In the cool dawn Dake Satterlee squatted by a small fire, cleaning his rifle with hot water, linen and ramrod while his soggy buckskins blotted up the heat. Wet deerhide was a stretchy greasy mess, a misery next to the skin. But it would have to dry on his back as the sun rose; he'd dally by a fire no longer than necessary to swab his rifle clean as a picked bone and be sure it was in prime working order.

Occasionally his glance roved across the plains, a sea of fluid gold in the flat rays of sunrise. Low down east, the sky was pale and new, flushing to a smoky pink higher up and chasing the last ashen color of night toward the west. The storm had quit a couple of hours ago and the day would be a soft scorcher, but not too bad.

The regiment had perked up. Men moved more briskly than they had in days, the night's wet cold only a memory, as they fell into column by companies. They had already been up a couple of hours, fanning out in patrols for a futile search of a wide area, trying to pick up sign which the rain had wiped out. But Dodge, anxious to make use of their renewed spirits and the relative coolness that followed a storm, was delaying no longer.

Dake dried every particle of moisture from his Kentucky long piece, then loaded it just as painstakingly Ben Poore sauntered up, gave a sober greeting and dropped down on his haunches by the fire He snorted quietly. 'Why'n hell don't you have the donkey cannon changed over to caplock?'

'No need. Can knock a flint off any good rock. Man gets way out in the lonesomes and runs out o' percussion caps, he is in trouble.'

'Not half the trouble he got if his priming gets rained into or his pan cleared out by a hard wind. Then where's he?'

'With a tomahawk and a couple knives to throw, not too bad off.' Dake grinned. 'Your arm waxing stiff, Ben?'

'Your bones'll feel frosty of a morning too, you live

113

that long.' Poore shifted on his heels, squinting across the plains. 'Dodge says you aim to quit us here. Fact?'

'Happen he tell you why?'

'Didn't need to. You gotten sort o' close to that shave-tail Fry.'

'Yeh, got to 'fess I like the cuss, for all his fusty ways.'

Ben wouldn't mention Miz Sherrod, just as Dodge hadn't, but Dake knew that both were aware of his deeper reason for cutting loose on his own just now.

Poore sighed. 'Kind o' like to taken the trail with you, I wa'n't bounden to guide this outfit.'

'Well, you know this here stretch o' country well as me, so I ain't no loss right here. I be catching up 'fore you reach the Wichitas.'

'Sounds like you plan on being gone a good spell.'

'Long as need be,' Dake said flatly.

'Looka here, hoss.' Poore took out his pipe and frowned at it. 'I don't need to tell what the odds is agin finding Fry or them Injuns or the women. Say you keep circling out till you pick up track. . . .'

'Their track's out there, Ben. Where' the rain let up, they started making track.'

'Rain kept up till the wee hours. They'd a been miles from here by then. You got no way telling which way they went, so you'll just keep circling out till you cut their trail. Boy, that could take days.'

'You ain't saying a lot I don't know. I might get lucky.'

'Blamed long odds agin it. Suppose'n you do, they already got a good eight hours lead on you.'

'They're all afoot,' Dake reminded him, 'saving that Cut Face. Four men, three women. One hoss can't carry more'n two and not very fast or far at that.'

'Four of 'em, one o' you.'

'Well, they got but the two guns we know of. Cut Face's rifle. One musket they lifted offen that sojer boy they knifed. Cuts the odds some'at. I got all the range with this piece, Ben.'

'Suppose'n you have, you reckon you will catch 'em in time to do them girls any good?'

Dake's face went hard. 'I surely hope so. If I don't, won't change nothing for four sorry redskins.'

But he knew with a hollow gutted certainty that Poore

114

had named the odds coldly and accurately. The picture of what had happened last night was too clear even if the rain hadn't wiped out all tell tale sign. With full darkness and a hellbuster of a storm to cover him, Cut Face had simply sneaked up to the camp on its south flank where the wagons were set off and exposed. Taken the sentry by surprise and slashed his throat with one quick stroke. Thunder had covered the noise he'd made chopping his friends free. With the women's wagon right by, easy to slip into it and carry all three off, the storm smothering that commotion too. On foot the Indians might be overtaken if their escape were quickly discovered; with female hostages, they could still bargain their way free.

But was it that simple? Skinned Ear needed only one hostage to bargain with, not three The Pawnee and Kiowa? Ear knew their importance to Dodge's mission; spiriting them away would be a proper revenge on the white chief who had shamed him in front of his men and had chained him in a wagon for many days. As for Alexandra Sherrod, Skinned Ear had desired her to start with A matter of convenience to bear her off with the others. Getting safely away with all three would give him plenty to crow in his blanket about.

As it happened, the escape and kidnapping had gone undetected for hours afterward. The storm had let up somewhat and the camp was settling down for the night when it had been noticed that Lieutenant Fry was missing. He'd been seen last by the horse guards. Minutes later somebody had stumbled over Private Royton's body and what had occurred was quickly determined. The time must have been right after the horse guards had seen Fry. Only thing that wasn't clear was exactly what had happened to Fry. His long billed shako had been found near the girls' wagon. Seemed likely he'd discovered the escape in process and tried to stop it and failed. But what happened then was anyone's guess. Didn't make sense that Skinned Ear would take Fry along too. But if he hadn't been killed, where was he? And why hadn't he raised an alarm?

Dodge came tramping up at his crisp stride, Randall Sherrod behind him. Sherrod looked pretty purposeful for him, and he was carrying a musket.

'We'll be on the move in a few minutes,' Dodge said tersely. 'Suppose it's no use trying to dissuade you to abandon this wild goose chase.'

Dake swung to his feet. 'You give up too easy, Cunnel.'

'Plague take it, man, that's not the thing!' The suggestion had touched Dodge's temper. 'I have a whole regiment to look after, a mission to complete. If I thought there were a ghost of a chance of recovering the women, I'd send a company out straightaway. You'd stand a better chance of finding a very small needle in a very large haystack.' He waved a hand at the glistening plain. 'Christ, man! You don't know which way they went. They've many hours' lead and are getting farther away all the time. Our scouts have covered all the ground in a square mile and more, not a trace of sign. And they'd have gotten miles away before the storm let up ... doesn't that tell you how hopeless it is?'

Dake merely nodded. No gainsaying that his chances weren't exactly as thin as both Dodge and Ben reckoned. Anyway he doubted that enough soldier boys could be mustered from this sickened, weakened outfit to fill out even a small squad, one that could match the driving pace he meant to set. He'd move better and faster by himself.

'Ain't blaming you none, Cunnel. Likely be a risk o' lives for naught.'

'What about your own, Satterlee?'

'This he-coon can make out on these plains well as an Injun can, don't you fret. My hide's to do with like I want. It ain't contracted to your Army.'

'Neither is mine,' said Sherrod. He moved forward, his face pale and firm. 'I'm going with you, Satterlee.'

Dake gave him a speculative gaze. 'That so?' He bent and picked up a rucksack at his feet. 'Got enough jerked beef and cracked corn here to carry a couple men for a week, Sherrod. But twice of it won't fill your belly worth a damn.'

Sherrod flushed. 'The whiskey is long gone, Satterlee. I've been filling my belly with rancid water since.'

'Ain't that a comfort.'

'It seems to have sustained me well enough. If you will not take me along, I will follow you at a distance. To stop me, you will have to shoot me. Do *you* have the belly for that?'

Jesus, willy nilly, seemed he'd be saddled with this ninny. 'Mister,' he said disgustedly, 'I don't give a bat from hell what you do long as you don't get in my way. I plan going a far ways. Going it fast and hard. Ain't one damn thing gonna slow me. Particular a pee-ant like you ain't.'

'I understand. You may not believe it, Satterlee, but when not rattled I am a good shot. I am also a damned good horseman. I was raised to be. I can keep up with you. If not, all you need do is leave me.'

Dake nodded, hard eyed. 'I will, don't you fret.'

Stennis crouched on his haunches, feeding buffalo chips into a skimpy fire. It hadn't been possible till now, midafternoon, to rustle up chips that had dried out enough to take fire. Still damp from last night, they were yielding plenty of smoke, which was the idea. Not, he thought bleakly, that even a smoke column which could be spotted miles away was likely to do him very much good now.

Carefully touching the crusted scab on the side of his scalp, he winced. It burned like fire to the touch, but the hellish pounding ache that had made him fear his skull was fractured had ebbed away. His brain was working all right, thank God. There wasn't much else to be joyful about.

After the pounding rain had revived him last night, he had stumbled dazedly on, he didn't know how far When he'd tried to take his bearings, he'd found he had lost himself in the stormy murk and blurred anonymity of undulating land. Finally he had collapsed again. He hadn't awakened till the sun was high. Reckoning it was then close to noon, he'd felt a real and sinking fear. For his disappearance along with the prisoners and the women had certainly been discovered hours ago. By now a search had been conducted and abandoned, those who were missing given up for lost. The column, of course, would simply push on.

At first he'd been thankful that the sun was out: he could hold a rough direction by it. Head north and he was bound to stroke the clear trail left by the Dragoons But three hours of steady tramping hadn't turned up a sign of

117

the column's passage. Either he'd cut east of last night's camp and the heavy rain would have wiped out those hoof and wheel marks or he had mistaken the direction from which he'd headed off from the camp last night He'd believed he had gone generally south, but in the murky wet he might easily have blundered off on any strange tangent.

Stennis felt tired as hell, his muscles full of cramps, as if he'd gotten no sleep at all. Exactly as anyone deserved to feel after lying out in the rain for hours, on soaked ground for hours more. His stomach was churning; his ears sang with a touch of fever. So he'd paused to rest on this shallow hill. After spreading out a little tinder to dry in the sun, he had scraped up a few buffalo chips and started his fire. He wasn't chilly and he had nothing to cook. And if his smoke could been seen very far away on so bright and clear a day, there was good reason to doubt that anyone was inside seeing distance. Really he was killing time and offering himself false cheer.

He wished, by God, that he did have something to eat. Some of the light-headed weakness he felt was pure hunger. His belly ached, his saliva worked on nothing. He had spotted several jackrabbits, but though he'd cleaned his pistol, it had misfired twice. The powder in his flask had gotten damp. He needed dry powder and a good rifle. But mostly he needed a canteen. He had slaked his thirst at a revivified stream a little while ago, but he could carry no water with him. And water, not food, was always the first concern. . . .

He tossed a few more chips on the fire. Then the distant crack of a rifle reached his ears.

Stennis crouched electrified, wondering if he had imagined it. He shaded his eyes and circled the horizon. Finally the two horsemen showed as black specks; after a few minutes of intent watching, he was sure they were headed this way. They had seen his smoke and had fired a response.

Excitedly he reached for more fuel to build up the fire and signal back. Then he let the chips drop. With his luck, these riders might well be hostiles of one complexion or another. He broke open his powder flask and inspected its contents again. Damn. Should have spread it out to dry. All he could do now was wait bare-handed and pray....

It was a good while before the two were close enough to identify. He felt a surprise at this illogical pairing – Dake Satterlee and Randall Sherrod – and then it occurred to him that perhaps it wasn't so illogical after all. They were leading a couple of extra horses. He waved his arm.

'Halloo, Satterlee!'

Dake gigged his mustang up the slope, halted and surveyed Stennis and the fire, and then shook his head. 'Loot, you do shave your luck finer'n any man I seen.'

'Are there others out?' Stennis demanded. 'Is the column nearby?'

'Hell, no. Ain't nobody out for a little afternoon prom-ee-nade but a couple of damned idjits like us. Here, shinny onto one of these here nags. You will have to fork him no saddle, but you are damn lucky at that. These two and Sherrod's was all I could persuade the scouts to part with and that for the last silver in my poke. Good solid mustang flesh anyways.'

'But did you pick up a trail? Did –'

'Tell you whilst we ride. Want to hear your story too.'

Stennis heaved himself awkwardly onto one of the horses. Satterlee swung his mount and led the way as Stennis talked impatiently, telling what had happened last night and since.

'Sounds like you hit ever' bump in the road, Loot. But why'n pluperfect hell didn't you roust out the camp 'stead o'skinning out after them Injuns by yourself?'

'I was dazed from the blow. Didn't really know what I was doing. I suppose I was more or less unconscious all night and far into the morning when the search was being conducted. I couldn't have been too far from the camp then, but I couldn't have signaled anyway. Couldn't build a fire with wet tinder and wet chips, and my powder's still damp.'

Dake unthonged the powder horn from his belt and handed it across. 'Scrape out your flask and take some o' mine. You are damn lucky we spotted that smudge o' yourn. Course a body can see it long ways out here. But still lucky we come this close whilst tracking the other party.'

'You did find a trail, then?'

119

'Yeh, and a peck o' good fortune we did. Only it warn't by chance. Sherrod and me started out a-searching right at dawn. Covered I dunno how much ground circling out and around hunting for sign the rain had wiped out. Still be looking hadn't been that Pawnee had her wits about her.'

Dake dug in a pocket and pulled out a shred of fabric. Stennis recognized it as a piece of Ona's red blouse.

'Shrewd 'un, that. Dunno how she managed it, but reckon the darkness helped. Dropped bitsy hunks o' nice bright cloth along the way she was dragged. Even so, took us near till noon to find the first piece and a spell longer to turn up the next. Then we had a direction and have moved right along. We picked up quite a few more, so know we are going right.'

Stennis felt a hard tightness in his chest, staring at the bit of fabric. 'But they had a wide lead on you and have widened it since. Do you think . . .?'

'Pawnee has bettered our chances by considerable. Pret' soon we are bound to come to where they was when the rain stopped. Then I will have straight sign to foller. We got hosses, they ain't. That is the big thing now, Loot. . . .'

Stennis's fire had pulled Dake and Sherrod away from the trail that Dake had been ferreting out. Now, as they returned to it, Dake found another fragment of cloth. Skinned Ear was moving roughly southwest. His exact destination wasn't clear, but he was heading for territory claimed by Mexico. Whatever else he might have in mind was a mystery, but none of it concerned the three who followed, aside from what it might mean for his captives.

As Dake had predicted, they soon found where storm's end had ceased to obliterate the sign. Now Dake pushed along swiftly, his observations quick and sure. Tracks of four men and three women. And one horse, Cut Face's, picked up during the escape and flight. But one animal was precious little use. Skinned Ear's half-healed leg was giving him trouble, slowing the pace, and finally he had mounted Cut Face's horse. He and the other two were badly hampered by their dragging shackles. The women were holding up well thus far. No more bits of cloth were found; with daylight close, Ona had left off marking a trail that was now plain.

An hour later Dake found where the Indians had halted

by a granite outcrop. They had smashed their shackles between chunks of loose rock till the links were broken close to the bands. The long chains lay discarded by the outcrop. Afterward the fugitives' speed had picked up. Dake's face was bleak as iron as he steadily followed track, bending deep out of saddle as if he were sniffing it out.

Stennis's sore head began to pound; he was getting nauseated, his vision turning fuzzy. The plains on every side of him seemed to heave and tilt like sea swells. Rest. He had to have rest soon. Twilight came. His brain felt suspended in its thick glowing amber and he had a hazy conviction that unless they stopped soon, he would float away on it like a drop of grease on a current. Twice he was jerked awake by shots as Satterlee bagged a couple of jackrabbits. Then the gray wool of dusk was pressing down and Satterlee's voice, roughened by strain, was saying they would halt for the night Stennis felt his horse stop; he slid off and sank down on the ground

While he and Sherrod rested, heads sunk on their knees, Dake built a sheltered fire, skinned and gutted the rabbits and quick grilled them. The smell of meat cooking revived Stennis's appetite and he tore ravenously into his portion. Afterward he lay with his back to a warm hummock, feeling almost restored.

Stennis thought of the golden skinned Ona. He'd thought of her more often than he liked to admit. Maybe he was here for the reason his companions were; maybe that was part of what had driven him in a blind pursuit last night. He toyed with the idea and found it not unpleasant; nothing in the mere speculation could compromise a man.

But speculation kept blurring into worry, concern, fear. So far the Indians had pressed anxiously for distance, pausing only to break the shackles. Allowing no time to work any mischief on the women. But they too must be in night camp . . . somewhere

Nobody had anything to say There was no need for words A few minutes after they had rolled into their blankets, all three were relaxed in sleep.

CHAPTER TWELVE

Dawn was only a gray suggestion when Dake roused them out to take up the trail. Stennis didn't see how any tracker could find his way in this murky pallor, but Dake appeared to have no trouble. A fragment of smudged earth, a single grass blade bent awry, was all he needed. He pressed forward at a steady pace. Sunup came; another long day began. Stennis felt better than he had yesterday, but the grueling pressure was starting to tell heavily on Sherrod, as it must on any man in his forties who was sadly out of condition.

Satterlee was like a machine of rawhide and steel wire. Indefatigable himself, he allowed no pauses for rest; only darkness and not consideration for himself or his companions had forced his halt last night When hunger moved him, he produced a handful of jerky or parched corn and passed some to Stennis and Sherrod, they ate without leaving their saddles A fixed goal burned in the mountain man Stennis was positive that if either he or Sherrod fell behind, Dake would abandon him with hardly a second thought.

Before noon they came on the remains of a rabbit feast. The Indians had camped here; Dake studied the ground and said nothing His companions didn't ask They pushed on At midafternoon they came on Cut Face's horse The spotted pinto was standing by itself in a shallow coulee and Dake cautioned them to move carefully; it might be a trap. But the animal had gone lame, that was all It shied at their approach; Dake steadied it with some Indian horse-calming words. He examined its leg and said it was just a pulled tendon, but the animal would be useless for some time so the Indians had abandoned it.

As they resumed the trail, Sherrod called hoarsely, 'Satterlee! How far ahead are they?'

' 'Bout three hour.' Dake answered without glancing up from the trail. 'I allow we will overhaul 'em at a goodly clip from here on Pace is telling something fierce on the women and Skinned Ear's leg is dragging more 'n' more '

They rode deep into the afternoon. Implacable heat

122

sweated and punished them. As always, the infinite monotony of vast swelling plains hammered at a man's senses and blunted them. Stennis felt the usual mild weariness, while Randall Sherrod rode in a virtual stupor of exhaustion. Stennis didn't know what, outside of sheer grit, was keeping Sherrod in the saddle. Grit it must be, for he hadn't voiced a word of complaint

Dake reined up so suddenly that Stennis nearly rode his horse into him.

'What is it?'

Dake motioned at a sunken stretch of prairie ahead. It appeared to be a high grassed, almost marshy lowland, the first such that any of them had seen in many weeks. A dense ribbon of greenery snaking across it indicated that a stream of some sort transected the low belt of land, spreading out a damp aura. The ribbon marked a deep growth of scrub oak, plum brush and willow along the stream's course.

'Track's fresh,' Dake said tersely. 'We are close onto 'em. And that place ahead 'ud be a likely 'un for 'em to stop and rest. They won't be looking for no pur'suit.'

He reined behind a rise of ground, then swung down and threw his reins. Stennis and Sherrod did likewise

'Mind now,' Dake warned, 'we move in slow. We have got surprise on our side, which only applies we don't get seen or heard. Wrong move could get Miz Sherrod or them girls killed. Remember it. You two foller me and where I walk Don't neither of you bat a winker less'n I tell you to '

Thumbing up the frizzen of his rifle, Dake shook priming powder into the pan and closed the frizzen down again. Stennis drew the pistol from his belt. Dake went down between the tapering rises like a shadow, Stennis behind him. Sherrod brought up the rear, his exhaustion suddenly transmuted to jittery alertness Where the sink began, the grass grew tall and rank, rustling along their legs.

Dake came to a halt. He whispered, 'Smoke,' and pointed.

Without knowing what to look for, Stennis would have missed the wisping transparency curling up from the trees. The almost smokeless fire that only an Indian built. Listening, Stennis heard nothing but a murmur of water.

Dake began creeping forward again, his companions moving warily in his wake. Gaunt fingers of dead brush at

123

the edge of trees snagged at their clothes. Satterlee moved in absolute silence, making Stennis sweatingly aware of the soft inevitable noises he and Sherrod made Actually, following Dake's lead, they passed through heavy brush and trees in comparative stealth.

A soft cry reached them. A muffled slap broke it off. Dake froze, his hand raised. They heard a sound of running feet.

'Come on,' Dake grated.

They tore through the brush, abandoning all pretense at silence. Burst into a clearing where the fire smoldered, the Indians only seconds gone. Ona must have heard something; one of the women had tried to cry a warning to the pursuers. Dake loped across the clearing and rammed through the thick scrub. The churning hush of water increased and then the trees ended on the streambank. It was a small river or large creek, swollen by recent rains. Here and there it broke to turbulent roils formed by thrusts of water-polished granite. Apparently the watercourse had worn down through a long underlying rock basin. Wordlessly Dake dropped to his haunches behind the willow growth. Stennis and Sherrod did the same, edging up beside him. Here they had a long view of the lower stream.

Not over a hundred yards away the Indians and their captives were picking their way slowly along the stony bank. They must be looking for a place to cross The three women, stumbling with exhaustion, were being goaded along by the Indians. Sherrod threw his musket to his shoulder. Dake clamped a fist around the barrel and forced it down.

'I can get one from here,' Sherrod hissed. 'Goddam you –'

'You won't fetch a goddam thing from here,' Dake murmured. 'Musket ain't worth shuckins over eighty yards. My K'ntucky 'ud fetch one, but just one. Then they would likely kill the women outright. Got to wait till we can get closer in. Get two, maybe three of 'em, at once. Give the women that much more chance . . .'

Stennis wryly eyed the pistol in his hand. Ineffective beyond a few yards. And Sherrod was shaking so badly with rage and tension, he'd probably miss his shot. But Satterlee was right, thin as the chance seemed.

The Indians had halted at a point where wet click shards of granite projecting from the streambed formed a bridge of sorts. They crossed over single file, herding the women between them. Scrub trees on the other side quickly swallowed them. The three men left their concealment and started down the bank toward the crossing.

Suddenly bushes crackled. An instant later somebody came running out of the scrub. It was Ona, she had broken away. Skinned Ear was lunging after her with long hobbling strides. She ran onto a tip of rock that abutted above the water.

Before she could leap, Skinned Ear had seized her by the arm. Ona wheeled on him like a young tigress, her fingers curving, tearing down his face. His hand smashed her open-palmed, felling her to the rock. Face darkly contorted, he bent, seized a handful of her hair and started to drag her up. His other hand whipped high; a knife glittered in it.

Dake's rifle was already sweeping up. There was an imperceptible pause between the instant it hung level and the high, ringing report. Skinned Ear jerked and spun, toppling from the rock. He dropped like a stone into the water.

For a moment Ona was motionless on her knees Dake shouted at her to get out of sight fast. She climbed swiftly off the rock and into a dense thicket. A moment later Cut Face came charging back through the scrub, his gaze swiftly questing He had just time to glimpse his brother's body in the water before Sherrod fired. A miss, but it sent Cut Face scrambling into the scrub.

The three men hurried toward the crossing, Dake reloading and priming his weapon on the run. As they went across the slick rocks, Stennis saw Skinned Ear's dark loose shape turning and tumbling in the downstream rush. Ona crawled from the thicket as they came up She began to talk volubly in her own tongue. Dake cut her off with a flat order: she was to wait here and not budge from the spot. Too spent to argue, she sank down on the bank.

'You are not hurt?' Stennis asked.

'No,' said Ona and her eyes followed him as the three men struck off into the trees, hurrying.

The riverbank scrub thinned quickly away into tall grass

125

that marked the open flat again. Dake raised a hand, warning his companions to slow. A trail of parted and trampled grasses cut toward an isolated island of scrub oak that rambled across the flat. Plain enough. The Osages were laid up in the close-packed oak, waiting for the white man to come inside gun range.

'Get down,' Dake murmured. 'We will snake along on our bellies.'

There came the squeaking cry of a woman trying to scream past a hand covering her mouth. Then a musket shot, as if the Osages had guessed Dake's intention; Stennis thought he'd felt the wind of the ball. Dake dropped flat on his belly in the grass. Another shot roared from the oak thicket, powdersmoke floating from its depths, as Stennis and Sherrod plunged down beside him.

Stennis lay with his face in an odorous crush of grass and rotting muck, heart thundering against his ribs. They were slightly outside musket range, but a bullet from Cut Face's rifle might find them in the half-sheltering grass. They had nothing to draw a bead on but a green tangle of stunted oaks at which they dared not fire for fear of hitting the women. If a man tried to approach the island from any side, the Osages need only wait till he was close and bring him down.

'Big rock over there,' Dake murmured, pointing. 'Maybe fifty feet. Foller me.'

He slithered away on his belly whisper-quiet, his body stirring the deep grass with a slight graceful undulation that an inexperienced watcher would mistake for an air current. He used his elbows to pull himself along, cradling his rifle on his forearms. Stennis followed, trying vainly to emulate Dake's silent glide. Stalks rustled and broke against his chest and legs; his pistol hampered him. Sherrod, panting along in his wake, was even clumsier. One of the Osages gave a hooting laugh. A rifle cracked; the ball slashed through grass and tore up clods inches from Stennis's legs.

Dake came to a quick stop. His tomahawk flashed and fell in a silvery sweep. A dull thud, a thrashing in the grass. Dake crawled on and Stennis, moving after him, gave a generous berth to the headless, slowly writhing body of a large dust colored snake. They reached the thrust of weathered and splintered rock lifting like a shallow loaf

126

out of the flat. The Osages fired a few desultory shots which chipped the crumbling stone

Hugging against it, Sherrod hissed: 'What in God's name is the good of this? If –'

A cry came from the thicket. A soft climbing sound of pain that became a pure wail. It could have been either woman, but Sherrod yelled: 'Alex!' And started to struggle upright.

Dake gabbed him by the arm. '*Keep down* –'

But the screaming went on. In a mad fury, Sherrod broke Dake's hold, lunged up and scrambled across the rock. Dake and Stennis moved simultaneously, each grabbing one of Sherrod's legs to haul him back. He tried to kick free.

Cut Face's rifle crashed. Sherrod's struggling ended. He flopped backward, they caught at him. His body fell bonelessly against their hands, turning as it slid down the rock between them. The ball had made a neat hole in his temple where it went in. Almost no bleeding.

An Indian's voice rose in a taunting howl.

'Randall! Randall!!'

That was Mrs. Sherrod crying above the howl and the screams. She hadn't been the one screaming. Seeing that Buffalo Calf Girl's shrieks brought nobody else out to be shot, they cuffed her into silence with two flat sounding blows.

'Satterlee, we have to do *something!*' Stennis whispered.

'Yeh.' Dake rasped a palm over his beard 'Got to take a clear bead on 'em and got to get 'em away from them girls afore we do. Do that, we gotta draw 'em out. Got a notion how, but be damn risky.'

'Whatever has to be done, let's do it!'

Dake outlined his idea in a few spare phrases. The risk was clear: even if the Osages were lured out away from the girls and into the open, chances were excellent that both Stennis and Dake would leave their bones to bleach with Sherrod's. With the bones of an Osage or two, if they were lucky. For only a rash or foolish white man engaged a red man hand to hand· Indian youths were trained to rough-and-tumble combat from infancy. Their skill with knife and tomahawk made closing with them on those terms near suicidal. Dake judged he could hold his own

127

in an equal contest, but not if two rushed him. While he talked, he was carefully filling his deerhorn charger with powder, also fillıng his priming measure to the brim.

'What I am gamblıng, Loot, if they know our guns is empty, they will come a-hustling at us 'thout their guns.'

'Why the devil would they do that?'

'Somep'n the plains Injuns got they call counting coup. Big medicine to come up next a live enemy and smite him.'

'Will they do that?'

'Told you she's a gamble. Iffen she works and I can cut the odds by one afore they reach us, it will equalıze things and give us a chance. Best I can do. You game for't?'

Dake would stand a chance against an equally armed Indian. What chance would Stennis Fry have? Damned little, Stennis thought realistically. But if he could divert one foe long enough, even if it cost his life, Dake might emerge the victor. And the women would be saved.

'Yes,' Stennis said. 'Get on with it.'

'Right soon, I think. You're a good man Loot.'

An agonized moan drifted from the oak island. Mrs. Sherrod. She was of sterner stuff than the younger girl. They'd have to do a good deal to elicit a sound from her.

It was what Dake had waited for. A chance to let the Osages think that the two whites were maddened by the second woman's cries into emptying all their guns. It must seem that natural. Dake scooped a bullet from his shot pouch and slipped it into his mouth, then swung his rifle up and fired. The echo was beat down by a second roar as Stennis discharged his pistol, aiming above the thicket. Dake was already snatching up Sherrod's musket; he fired that off.

As Dake had calculated, it goaded the Osages to a bravado move they couldn't resist. Seeing an easy kill of two foolish whites, the three came bursting out of the oak thicket. They spread apart as they raced toward the boulder, Cut Face brandishing his tomahawk, the other two armed with heavy butcher's knives. They made a sudden, vivid, savage picture, sunlight streaking their dark faces and bodies.

128

Even as they'd leaped out to view, Dake was recharging Sherrod's musket: now the preferable weapon with its short smoothbore barrel. His motions blended without a wasted gesture; he spilled the charger powder into the muzzle in one lightening motion, not losing a grain. Disregarding patch and ramrod, he spat the ball into the barrel and drove it home with a smart rap of the gunstock on the earth. Then primed the weapon and slapped down the frizzen.

The whole thing took only fleeting seconds, but in that time the sprinting Indians had nearly covered the distance to them. The one in the lead swung back his heavy knife with a furious whoop, about to overhand it at the mountain man.

Dake was down on one knee as he finished loading. No time to aim. He brought the musket level at his hip and fired at the leader. The bullet took him in the throat; an artery fountained as he went over backward.

The second Osage came straight at Dake, knife flashing. Dake had only time to raise off his haunches and half-brace himself, the musket clubbed in his fists but no time or leverage to swing it as the Indian hurtled full into him. The two went down in a struggling tangle, rolling over and over.

Stennis has his hands full with Cut Face, who lunged at him with a fierce yell, tomahawk raised. Stennis hurled the empty pistol at his head, then whipped out his hunting knife. Grappling Cut Face, he managed to seize the arm with the tomahawk. But he couldn't hold the Indian's lean greased body; it flowed like oil through his hands.

Suddenly he lost his grip on the arm. The tomahawk fell, the flat of its blade glancing off his head close to where it had laid his scalp open before. Silver sparks flailed in Stennis's vision. Dimly he knew that he was falling. The earth jarred against his back.

Cut Face was above him. Again the war ax swung up.

Dake shouted something. He was a dozen yards away as he leaped to his feet, holding the bloody knife he had wrestled from his opponent, then used to dispatch him. His voice brought Cut Face around in a half-turn. Dake's arm whipped back and forward. The cleaver-like blade

129

made a turning flash of wet crimson as it overended once in its flight.

It met Cus Face's chest with a terrible impact. He staggered back, then forward, dropping the tomahawk. He toppled across Stennis's legs.

CHAPTER THIRTEEN

After burying Sherrod and appropriating the weapons of the dead braves, they lost no time getting away from the place. Both Ona and Buffalo Calf Girl were nervous about darkness overtaking them close to where men had died, for unshriven by rituals for the dead, their spirits would be restless. There was a more practical reason for not lingering, and that was Alexandra Sherrod's mental condition. Her husband's death had left her in a dull, unspeaking trance. Tired as the girls were, they made no complaint as the party returned to where the men had left the four horses. With the women and Stennis mounted and Dake tramping ahead, they struck out toward the northeast.

Twilight was closing into dusk when Dake halted the party. They needed rest and food and he would fix up the moccasins he'd taken off the dead Indians. Alexandra's stockings were shreds, her shoes in ruin. The tough moccasins of the Indian girls had stood up well enough, but they might need spares before the trip was done. They ate some of Dake's cracked corn and jerky while, working by firelight, Dake used knife and thongs to tailor a pair of moccasins into service for smaller feet.

Ona matter-of-factly tended Stennis's wounds, and the hurts and bruises of her two companions. From an open hillside she had gathered plantain leaves which she'd macerated to a mash and spread on their cuts and scratches to hasten the healing. Now she was patching their tattered clothing and her own with ravelings.

All three were bruised, scratched, dirty, and of course tired to exhaustion; otherwise they seemed physically no worse for wear. His discreet questions put to Ona through Dake, had elicited the information that the Indians hadn't harmed the women except for a few cuffs to quicken their progress. Skinned Ear had not permitted his braves to touch them otherwise; apparently he'd had plans of his own for them.

Stennis found himself admiring Ona's quick, graceful

hands. She was quite as tired as her two friends, but she had a tough and resilient spirit too. He had never, Stennis thought bemusedly, met a girl who could touch her in that regard.

'Man can do worse'n a good Pawnee woman for a help-meet,' Dake commented without glancing up from his work.

Stennis flushed. 'You ought to know.'

Dake looked up, his stare hard and unamused. Stennis had the feeling he'd struck a private nerve. 'I'm sorry,' he said. 'I didn't mean ...'

'Forget it Loot.'

No telling much about Satterlee's thoughts from his weathered, bearded face. But his glances at Mrs. Sherrod told his concern just as plainly. He must be wondering too how deeply and in what way Sherrod's death had wrought on her.

Stennis threw some more chips on the blaze, peering at Mrs Sherrod in its fitful light The lovely face was as blank as smooth china plate, no feeling or expression in it. She would not speak nor would she move, even to eat or drink or help herself, except at a direct command. Ona had said that she'd held up well through the ordeal of captivity, so it wasn't that. Her stunned trance must have its source in Sherrod's death, which Stennis thought rather puzzling. She wasn't the fainting or hysterical sort and surely there'd been little feeling left between her husband and her Yet ...

He said to Dake· 'How long will it take us to catch up with the regiment?'

'Three days Mebbe four We will slant northwest till we cut their trail Got to allow they have moved on ahead the while, though I hazard not very fast.'

They were three days overtaking the slow moving cara-van During that time, they ran out of corn and jerky, but finding food for only five people was no problem to the plains wise Dake shot a wild turkey and several rabbits; Ona found wild turnips to roast with the meat. Something less than an epicure's delight, but it filled the belly Toward the end of the third day, they overtook the Dragoons and it was like coming home

Dodge, oppressed by a burden of worry, brightened to a surprised brief pleasure He hadn't expected to see any of them again; he hoped their return might be an augur of

132

improving fortune. For the regiment was almost on its last legs.

The fever seemed to have run its infectious course; no more men had fallen ill. But the aftermath of fever had continued to wither the regimental ranks. Men had died daily. Wagons creaked with burdens of groaning sufferers. Hardly any of the remaining horses outside of the team animals were capable of carrying riders. Men still able to walk plodded on foot, leading their gaunted mounts. Above all, a specter of starvation dogged the caravan. Dodge had counted on help from the Comanches who had moved on, no telling where; without that help, their situation was truly serious.

Looking down a scarecrow column of men and animals, Stennis felt more of the uneasy doubts that had begun to plague him since MacPherson's death He thought of the ways in which so much blundering might easily have been avoided. Pyramided down through a military structure, even sensible propositions seemed to filter out as monumental, purblind stupidity. . . .

Mrs Sherrod was placed in the care of Dr Haile, who was somewhat recovered He confirmed Ona's assurance that Mrs Sherrod had suffered no real physical harm, but he couldn't diagnose what was wrong except to observe that he'd seen people react thus to a great shock or bereave ment Obviously her husband's death was the cause. The two girls could tend her needs until, hopefully, she came out of it. All they could do was wait.

Shortly after they made camp that night, there was a shot in the slow dusk. Stennis converged with others toward a corner of the camp. Dodge was already there, listening to a sentry explain that he'd spotted a figure skulking near the picket line. He had challenged, and when no countersign was given, had fired. And had obviously missed.

The cause of the excitement was a lank figure of an Indian who sat crouched on his haunches, fingers touching the ground ahead of his feet. He sat like an animal, he had an animal's bright eyes and an imbecilic grin He was ribby and emaciated, his skin like raddled rawhide. He wore much-patched old buckskins.

'After horses, no doubt,' Dodge grunted.

'A feed, more like,' said Ben Poore. 'Looks like a loonie

t' me, Cunnel.' He tried a plains dialect on the Indian, who answered readily. 'Says he's Crazy Dog, a Comanch', Poor devil sort o' Injun. People turned him out 'cause he is odd in the head, full o' bad spirits. Very holy now, but they're all scared of him. Much bad luck to kill.'

'Ha!' Dodge said 'Good thing you missed, Adams. What does he want with us, did he say?'

Poore nodded soberly 'Been watching us. Says he likes white men. Says we're even crazier'n him.'

Dodge smiled grimly. 'Comanche, eh? Ask him if he knows of the band that lived in the town five suns to the east.'

Poore spoke and translated the reply: 'Says the white chief is truly crazy. It is two suns, Injun measure, Cunnel Says yes, those was his people and they're in a place one sun from here. Ast him if he'd take us there. Says yes.'

'He pointed north.'

'That's our way if we go with him.'

'A day or two days or even more out of our way,' Dodge muttered. 'Could be as much as our lives are worth, trusting an addled redskin.'

'Cunnel, I 'low we couldn't be no wuss off. We need hosses and fresh meat and that damn quick Otherwise we ain't got a beggar's chance to make the Wichitas. I say take him up.'

Dodge's shaggy head tipped up and down. 'Very well, Ben. I'll put him in your charge....'

The outcast proved his value at once. Addled or not, he was an unerring mine of information about the country. Before noon the next day, he had led the hunters to buffalo More important, in this region where even dry streambeds were rare. Crazy Dog could pinpoint the scarce waterholes or dig up water where it seemed none should be And so the troops rode exhaustedly northwest July was savaging toward August and the heat and drought were at a lashing peak. The sun leaked like bitter white flame between men's half-shuttered eyelids. Pale brittle grass crumpled under boot and hoof. Hot wind blew; impalpable dust billowed.

On the third day Crazy Dog, who had disappeared shortly before the noon stop, came into camp at his soft languid lope that was like a wolf's or coyote's. He gave his lolling dog's grin and held his right forearm across his chest, play-fully moving his hand in a wriggling motion.

'What the devil?' said Dodge.

'Sign of the snake,' Poore explained. 'Some tribes call the Comanch' "Snakes." '

Unasked, Crazy Dog jabbered the answer. Poore trans-lated 'Says you will see the Snakes before the sun is highest.'

Dodge didn't wait till noon. By late morning they were crossing the broad flank of a ridge and here he halted the column. Accompanied by Poore, Crazy Dog and several officers, he climbed to the top and swept the plains with his spyglass.

'Dust,' he muttered. 'Riders ... about a hundred, I should say What do you think, Ben?'

The chief scout took the proffered glass. 'Hunting or war party's my guess. They got us scouted already, I'd reckon.'

Dodge's orders were crisp and incisive. All firearms were to be checked, each man equipped with powder and shot to twenty rounds. His officers caught some of the colonel's fiery mettle as they moved among their companies, barking commands. Columns which had worn down to shuffling straggles reformed smartly, awaiting orders

Dodge wheeled his roan out at the head, gloved fist cocked on his hip. He ran his eyes over the cavalcade, whose lack of horses was balanced by human casualties and the sick list A gritty wind stiffened the pennons. 'All right – bugler!'

Advance was sounded. Proud and sweltering, the 1st Regiment of U.S. Dragoons moved forward, feeling the quick high sweat of excitement. Few of them, aside from the officers, had ever tasted the possibility of battle.

Shortly an advanced unit topped an undulant rise and faced the party of Comanches from not a hundred yard's distance. They had stopped in a feathered and beribboned. line that bristled with shining lancepoints. The brave's faces glistened with oily color.

Dodge signaled a halt. He shifted in his saddle, his brows lifting. 'From the show of weapons,' he muttered, 'I wonder if we shouldn't out sabers'

'Sit easy, Cunnel,' Poore said. 'They're painted up for

greeting strangers. Comanch' custom. I'd hazard the rest is just for show.'

'You wait. Let 'em make the move. They seen our dust a good spell back and readied for us, you can bet.'

A single gaudily arrayed warrior on a milky-white pony broke from the line and rode toward the Dragoons, tacking his mount from left to right in show off fashion. Around his neck he wore a heavy cross; he carried a strip of snowy fur on the point of his lance.

'Hide of white buffler,' Poore said, 'Very sacred. Means peaceful intent. Best hit 'em with yours.'

'By George, I believe the fellow's a Christian.'

'That cross? Don't you believe it, Cunnel. She's a sign of military rank, much as them eagles on our shoulders.'

Dodge and some officers, accompanied by Poore and an ensign bearing a white flag, rode out to meet the spokesman. Dodge offered the warrior his hand. After a puzzled moment he grasped it, a grin breaking his dark cheerfully pugnacious face. The whole line of Comanches surged forward with shrill yelps. The next few moments were precarious ones as the Indians swirled around the Dragoons, brandishing their oval, feather trailing shields and waving their fourteen-foot lances, panicking the fine worn thoroughbreds and trying the men's patience.

'Steady,' called their officers. 'Stand steady!'

Luckily, all did. A threatening gesture, not to say a gunshot, might wipe out the truce.

The Comanches were a hunting party of the Kotsoteka band, the 'Buffalo Eaters.' The leader confirmed that they were not far from the main town; he and his braves would provide an escort His name, His oo-son chees, was rendered by Poore as 'Little Spaniard.' He had an aura of dash and glamour and was obviously a half-breed He must have surpassed himself in the qualities of a warrior and leader, Poore commented, for generally the Comanches despised half breeds.

The cavorting warriors led and flanked them the whole distance to the Comanche town, performing all sorts of breakneck stunts on horseback. Even the Kentuckians in the command, hailing from a country where fine horsemanship was taken for granted, were amazed by their centaurlike grace. They had heard, but seeing was believing The Com-

136

anche brave on horseback was an incomparable sight to behold.

It was late afternoon when they came in sight of the village. It sprawled on a well grassed meadow between shouldering hills about two hundred conical tipis covered with tanned buffalo hides. Horses were grazing everywhere His oo son chees requested that the regiment halt while his party went ahead to apprise the people of the white men's coming. Dodge agreed, and the warriors dashed away toward the village. In a few minutes there was great activity on the meadow, horses being rounded up and driven in and people running excitedly about.

Worriedly, Dodge ordered the Dragoons drawn up in three compact columns. When a mass of mounted, screeching warriors came boiling out of the town, Dodge firmly ordered the columns to advance, but slowly. Ahead of them moved a lone Dragoon standard bearer with a white flag. Quite suddenly the approaching Indians fell into a uniform line, dressing out as disciplined cavalry. Again His oo-son chees rode out ahead with his lace held emblem of albino buffalo hide. Drawing abreast of the standard bearer, he planted his lancebutt in the earth beside the white flag. Now the Dragoons saw that all the warriors had ridden out without weapons of any kind, token of trust and friendship.

The columns were escorted into the village. A horde of dogs and naked children went wild with fear or excitement at sight of the soldiers. The adults, particularly the women, seemed friendly and curious. Dismounted, the breechclouted braves looked surprisingly graceless. They were thickly built men of medium stature with oversize heads, their skins a rick copper hue. They wore their hair in braids with gaudy bunches of feathers and their broad faces hinted that their mood could turn malevolent in an instant. The women wore two-piece camp dresses of buckskin and ornamented their long hair with beads and silver. Contacts with the Spanish showed in skirts and leggings of red and blue stroud as well as the evidence of mirrors, metal pots and gimcracks, ancient muskets and iron bladed knives

The head chief was an enormous man named To-wahque nah, which translated as 'Mountain of Rocks.' More accurately, he was a mountain of fat; he was jolly, two chinned and sported a scraggly beard. But his small eyes

137

were shrewd and stony as he waddled to meet them. Poore told Dodge how the chief had won his name · once when enemies had cornered his warriors against a cliff, To wah que nah had led them to safety through a subterranean passage of which only he'd known.

Stiff and sweating, the Dragoons held ranks while Dodge went into consultations with the chief. The Grandfather of the Americans, Dodge explained through Poore, had sent his white children to greet his red children with open hearts. They had brought gifts, useful gifts of cloth and tools, to seal the bonds of peace and friendship.

To wah que nah's sleepy gaze moved to Ona and Buffalo Calf Girl, who had moved up from their wagon and were standing off a little distance. He wondered whether the white chief had brought these women as personal gifts for his brother.

Dodge firmly indicated that the women were Kiowa and Pawnee and would be returned to their own peoples.

In his tipi, the chief said agreeably, he had a Spanish woman he had captured, the daughter of a *haciendado*. She was quite skinny, but it was said white men favored skinny women. Perhaps his brother would like to trade.

Dodge indicated that this was impossible.

To wah que nah found the reply quite amusing. He laughed loudly. Then raised his old brass bound fusee above his head and shouted an order to a dozen or so young braves standing expectantly nearby. They promptly vaulted onto their ponies and streaked away, making a broad swing around the village at full gallop.

Douglas moved slowly back and spoke in a controlled tone to Captain Mulady. An equal number of soldiers were quickly formed in a line ahead of the column, muskets at the ready. Nervously they watched the warriors circle back to the tipis at a dead run, bodies flattened to their ponies' withers. At the same time, as if by signal they let their bodies slip down their mounts' far flanks so that each was screened from the soldiers' view except for a leg flexed over his pony's back. Shielded on the gallop, they unslung their sinew-backed bows and strung arrows to them.

'Steady, men,' Dodge said clearly.

Off from the tipis stood an isolated post chewed to splinters by long bow practice. In loose unison now, the braves released a flight of arrows. Ten of them bristled in the post; two struck lightly and dropped off. Then the braves whipped back beside the soldiers and dropped from their animals, whooping and laughing. The exhibition was completed To-wha que nah held his sides with laughter

'Now the old hyena's put hisself in high humor,' Poore murmured, 'is the time to fetch and skin him, Cunnel.'

While the soldiers mingled and bartered with the villagers, trading tobacco, trinkets and spare pieces of clothing for bone whistles, claw necklaces and other souvenirs, Dodge and his staff smoked pipe and held council with To wah que nah and his headmen. Pleased with the white man's generous gifts, the chief agreed to provide his brother with as many horses as he needed.

Dodge explained the Grandfather's desire that the roving bands of his plains children be called to a great council whereat delegates should be chosen and sent to Fort Gibson with emissaries from Washington. Useful gifts would be exchanged for the tribes' agreement to let American wagon trains pass unmolested through their lands. Would the Comanches sit in council with the Kiowa and the Pawnee? The Kiowa were their brothers, To wah que nah replied, and he did not object to sitting with the Pawnee. More, if his brother wished, runners would be sent to other bands of the western Comanches: the Penetakas, the Nokoni, the Kawhadi and the Yamparikas. Whether their chiefs would come to such a council, he could not say. The Grandfather whose tongue he was would be pleased, Dodge said. One thing more. Did his brother know anything of a small white boy captured by the Pawnee ten moons ago? Of this, Mountain of Rocks knew nothing. . . .

Jubilant at the success of his first peaceful overture to a warlike people, Dodge curbed his impatience to press on to the Wichitas at once. The men needed at least several days' rest. Camp was set up beside a clear stream a half mile from the village and sentries posted around it. Dodge wanted to keep the good opinion of his host and the best way to ensure it was to avoid letting his soldiers overmingle with the high-spirited braves and the friendly Comanche ladies. An untoward incident could bring disaster at the moment when prospects for a successful mission had sharply brightened.

Nevertheless conditions in the Dragoon camp that evening were generally in a state of pleasant confusion. The soldiers filled their bellies with roast buffalo and a variety of edibles bartered from the villagers, including fresh greens. Spirits were running higher than they had since the outset of the journey; the worst of the ordeal seemed past and the men were proud and pleased with themselves. Those who had survived were. How easily men forgot or at least discounted a heavy cost if their satisfactions were achieved, Stennis thought. For Dodge, a rung of ambition scaled; for his men, the pride of personal attainment.

Taps had blown, the camp was settled down for the night, when Stennis finished a last round of duties and, stumbling with weariness, headed for his blankets. Funny how such postures as duty and patriotism seemed to boil down one way or the other, to forms of self serving. But had it ever been any different? Probably not Nothing had really changed except some of his cherished illusions. Maybe ideals were just perspective and ...

Hell with it. He was damned tired, that was all He'd stowed his plunder off in a hollow behind a big rock where he might catch a night's uninterrupted sleep. He fumbled his way the last few yards, the firelight barely reaching here, and was feeling in the dark for his blankets when it occurred to him to shake them out for snakes.

Something moved under his groping hand. Stennis leaped backward a good three feet. 'What in holy hell!'

Now somebody was sitting up in his blankets; he could just discern the bronze oval of Ona's face. Ah, my God, he groaned inwardly....

'Might's well face it, Loot,' said Dake Satterlee. 'This twist o' brown calico has got you staked for her own.'

'Like hell she has!'

'Curb your choler, Lieutenant,' Dodge said crisply. 'The girl can hear you.'

Stennis's teeth clenched. 'I can assure you, sir, that she's heard a good deal already'

Dodge nodded, thoughtfully stroking his jaw with a
140

finger. 'I don't doubt it. But being excitable won't solve anything, Fry. Let's try to pursue the matter calmly.'

Calmly! Stennis tightened his hands over his drawn up knees. He looked at Dodge sitting on the other side of the fire, at Satterlee crouched between them, and finally at Ona standing a demure distance away. She looked very grave Stennis was still badly rattled by her unexpected usurpation of his sleeping space and even more by the potential complications.

Ona spoke quietly now.

'What's that?' Stennis said edgily.

'Says if she ain't your woman now, why'd you foller Skinned Ear all that way to get her back?'

'What the hell kind of reasoning is that!'

Dake shrugged and grinned. 'Sounds like as any. Least to her it does.'

Stennis groaned softly. He hadn't failed to notice how Ona had been eying him the past few days. In almost a proprietary way, he'd thought. He had made an effort to avoid her whenever his duties had taken him into her vicinity. Tonight's general disorganization and his locating his blankets strategically off from the others had given her the chance to implement her notions. Now he had brought his problem to Dodge, hoping to dump it in the colonel's lap in a private discussion. It was private enough, only Satterlee being on hand to interpret, but the colonel's attitude had him worried.

'You understand,' Dodge said low voiced, 'It's not as simple as just telling the girl she's overstepping bounds of ordinary propriety A reasoned solution is indicated '

'Sir,' Stennis said desperately, 'What's to reason? The whole business is . . .'

'Listen, Fry. The whole outcome of our mission could hinge on maintaining this girl's good opinion She is the granddaughter of the big Toyash chief and I believe that says it all. For the present, you'll have to play along with whatever her heart desires.'

'Sir,' Stennis grated, 'I will not marry the girl! Not if my head rolls for it. I'll resign my commission first, I'll –'

'Now calm yourself, mister. It's no doubt a whim on her part, a casual savage whim that will pass directly she's among her own people.'

141

'But God, sir! If it doesn't?'

'Let's cross our bridges as we come to them, boy. You'll not have to wed her. I give you my word.'

'Meantime she is *not* to share my blankets. It's out of the question!'

'Just as you wish, Fry.' Dodge waved a vague hand. 'Better explain that to her, Satterlee. Uh ... tell her white men have different customs. Different ways of doing things.'

'Yeh,' Dake said dryly. 'Growing up on the Lovely Purchase watching white lads visit her red sisters, she musta got her lights full o' how different.'

He spoke to Ona; she replied. Stennis caught his own name among the soft syllables.

'What?' he said. '*What?*'

Dake winked ribaldly. 'Says you need not feel troubled. She has kept herself a maiden for the man she chooses.'

'*She* chooses? Damn you, Satterlee, you think this is funny, don't you?'

'Me? Perish the thought, Loot. I am fair sweating blood on your account.'

CHAPTER FOURTEEN

Dodge had broken ticklish ground in a historic milestone: the establishment of a first treaty between the United States and the far tribes of the western plains. His instructions from the War Department were explicit. He was to make direct overtures to all the leaders of the puissant Comanches and Pawnees. Unless these powerful bands were won over, negotiations with other plains tribes would be futile. A hundred miles east of the Comanche village lay the main town of Pawnee Picts Dodge believed that the key to final success lay in delivering Ona safely to her family. And the political relatives of the Martin boy, nine-year old Matthew, had rallied enough voices in Washington City to make his recovery from the Pawnee a must.

The rampant fever had faded, but it had left Dodge's command broken and wasted. Even after several days' rest, 39 more men were too sick to continue If he went on with the rest, more would die. He knew it. Just as he knew that his spent column had little force or glitter left with which to impress Indians. If he did go on, all that had been endured would be for nothing. To Henry Dodge, this was no argument. It was an answer.

Leaving Lieutenant James Izard and some volunteers to care for the stricken, he gathered up his remaining 183 Dragoons and pushed out across the early August furnace of the Great Plains. Somewhat recovered from early vicissitudes, they made good time the first day. Until now, the jagged blue sweep of the Wichitas had seemed to retreat implacably. Almost miraculously they were growing nearer. . . .

At the noon halt, Dake rode to where the wagons were drawn up. He grimly told himself he was a goddam fool, but what the hell He had to see how she was faring, anyway. He had deliberately avoided Alexandra Sherrod since their return to the caravan and was beginning to feel a mite silly Sight of him wouldn't do her any harm and Doc Haile had told him she was perking up some. Starting to do for herself again, even if she still lapsed into odd trances. Flesh and spirit were strange, Doc had said. Tied together in ways he didn't rightly understand. But time usually did the trick; time was the healer.

Oshel Callicutt an his two sons were squatting in the shade of their wagon. He passed them with hardly a glance, though aware of their muddy looks. Hell with them. They still had a lot of mean locked into their craws about him, even if he'd done his best to save Asa from his just deserts. That Tute boy's arm, though. Sooner or later, he supposed, they'd try to level the score. It was the way with their kind A sight brighter men than the Callicutts lived by that old code. Same as in the deep hill country of his Carolina boyhood. One wrong way nudge to the scales, then it was an eye for an eye.

Ahead was the girls' wagon. Ona and Buffalo Calf Girl had a little fire built and were fixing tea and grub. Watching the graceful Ona, Dake almost grinned. That pert little hunk surely had old Loot Fry treed and sweating. Knew what she wanted and went after it pure eyed as a dove, not giving a damn for the odds. Tan velvet outside, iron underneath.

Dake halted, swung down and greeted her in the Pawnee tongue. She answered readily Her ma must have grounded her in the ways of her own people, despite her Cherokee upbringing. He asked where the Fire Hair was and she pointed with her chin at the end of the wagon. Dake stepped around it.

Alexandra sat in the wagon by the open pucker, the sun on her face. Her eyes seemed faraway and he said, 'Miz Sherrod,' before she looked at him.

'Oh ... Mr. Satterlee.' She blinked and smiled. 'Where have you been keeping yourself?'

'Busy, sort of.' Dake leaned an arm on the wagon box. 'You are looking more pert than you was.'

'I believe so.' She gazed across the brown prairie. 'Do you know what I was thinking?'

'No'm '

'Something strange, I guess. That I love this country. It is harsh and terrible, but I can't think of a time when I've felt so alive as I have during this journey '

Dake said bluntly: 'Spite of what happened?'

Her eyes shadowed, but she nodded. 'Yes, in spite of everything.' She looked straight at him. 'Dake.'

'Yes'm.'

'There is something you should know. Randall was not all to blame. I was not a good wife to him . . . not as I should have been.'

Dake shuffled his feet. 'Hadn't ought to let yourself get thinking that way.'

'It's true I should have made allowances for his nature. I'd stayed with him out of duty, yes – but only that. A man needs more. Understanding –' She bent her face, running a palm over her skirt 'That day . . . before the Indians took us off, he came to me. He was sober and honest as I couldn't remember seeing him. I think he had changed. He tried to tell me that. I wouldn't listen. I turned him away.'

Dake chose his words carefully. 'Ain't that a sight too easy to get thinking, now your husband is dead? People can change, but it don't come overnight.'

'Dr. Haile said that,' she murmured 'He said I am giving myself excuses to feel guilty about Randall because I no longer had a feeling for him.'

'Doc sounds right. Folks get set up in curious ways about things. Do that, it is best to stop thinking about 'em.'

'I can't help thinking about them I can't forget.'

Her eyes turned inward on her thoughts and she gazed past him again. Dake stood there a moment longer, then dropped his arm and quietly moved away There was no more to be said now But enough had been said, he thought. Just enough A kind of hope that he hadn't even voiced to himself thickened his throat.

Time, Doc had said. Well, there was still plenty of that.

The prairie swells grew steeper and more irregular as the column advanced into the foothills. The terrain was slashed by deep sudden gullies that forced them to make sweeping detours. As the country grew rougher, horses went lame on strewings of sharp rocks. At last they were climbing into the Wichitas, tediously infiltrating them through defiles whose tall cramped red granite walls blocked out the sun The abruptness of sheer drops and monolithic crags almost baffled their progress. From an elevation, a man could see the column broken and straggled out below

145

like files of blue ants, working roughly west through the range by a half dozen passages that twisted and intersected. Satterlee scouted out a trail that would accommodate the wagons; squads of men half-lifted them over the roughest places.

Soon smoke of Indian signal fire began talking back and forth from the heights of land. Satterlee said they were less than a day's ride from the Toyash village. The smokes were signaling their approach, but whether with peaceful intent or hostile, he couldn't tell yet. The Comanche runners had gone ahead; the Pawnees had been apprised of the soldiers' purpose. To wah que nah had sent his personal blessings to the council proposed by the white chief.

High in the peaks, as the swift mountain night rushed down, Dodge called a halt and ordered the sentry watch doubled. When dawn tinged the peaks to old copper, the command was already on its feet and moving out, scouts flung well out to front and flanks.

As full sunrise broke, the column debouched on a rocky, gully sashed plateau. It halted, waiting for stragglers to come up, while Dodge listened to his scouts report that they had found the Pawnee Pict village. They had not gone too close and they had seen and heard nothing, no sign of people. Dodge took council with Poore and Satterlee. Should they proceed without some sign from the Pawnee? Dake allowed they might as well. Pawnee knew the soldiers had come in peace; if they had withdrawn from their town, it was likely a precautionary move. They'd show themselves when ready and in their own way.

The Dragoons had proceeded nearly two miles when the advance scouts turned their horses and raced back toward the column. Not waiting to learn what was ahead, Dodge ordered the caravan stopped and ranks formed defensively.

The companies were still in movement when half a hundred Indians came streaming into view on the gallop, whooping, brandishing bows and muskets. At the fringe of good rifle range, they sheered off and began cutting wild capers with their mustangs.

Poore clucked his tongue. 'Friendly.'

Moments later the Pawnee braves, big sinewy fellows whose heads were cropped to long central roaches, were surging around the soldiers, mocking them with taunts and

146

gestures. It seemed all in good fun, and soon the colonel was in movement again. By now, the feathery bronze dawn light had fanned across the whole sky The rocky terrain had given way to smooth meadowed slopes and well culti vated fields of maize and beans, also plantings of wild plum trees and watermelon vines. Beyond these clustered the lodges of the Toyash, about six hundred wigwams made of tall prairie grass thatched over a frame of poles bent inward at the tops, resembling beehives of straw.

Scenting water, the horses were given their heads. The Dragoons came clattering in among the grass lodges at the half lope As with the Comanches, the soldiers provoked great excitement and curiosity Some boys swarmed out of hiding, twanging their small bows and pointing toy muskets, their faces daubed with soot in a fierce and obvious mimicry.

'Jeez,' a private muttered 'Give 'em a few more years.'

Apparently the Pawnee lived well on the fertile upper plateau. They ate well and dressed well, like the Comanches they supplemented the products of their native crafts with goods obtained from Spanish traders They 'were a hand some and healthy race, Stennis Fry thought, cleaner than many white frontiersmen in person and habit, and a far cut above members of their own race who had quickly degenerated from a touch of Anglo Saxon culture.

Again the Dragoon ranks held firm while the ceremony of greeting and welcome was concluded Chief Wa ter ra sha ro emerged from his earthlodge, a huge domelike structure roofed entirely over by squares of sod and set in the middle of the village He was an old man, but big and oak solid in bright figured togalike robe and a scarlet Mexican blanket. Ona's grandfather · Stennis studied him with par ticular care and wasn't reassured Wa-ter ra shah ro had the glummest face he'd ever seen and damned near the ugliest

However his greeting of the white chief was stately and courteous He remembered Dake Satterlee and called him 'brother ' He bade the white chief enter his earthlodge, where they and their wise men might consult. Dodge chose a half dozen officers, including Stennis to accompany him, along with Poore and Satterlee He gave orders for the dis position of a camp near the village and the troops were given an hour's liberty to trade with the villagers.

147

They followed the chief and his elders into the earth-lodge, entering through a passage covered at each end by a skin curtain. A heavy taint of grease and smoke that suffused the interior almost choked them, but they restrained all reaction to a quiet curiosity as they gazed about the giant lodge. Its roof consisted of bent poles supported by four central logs; a thatching of willow branches and grass in turn supported the sod shingles Along the curving wall were ranged rows of beds, some curtained off for married couples. Platforms were heaped with food and household implements. In all, the chief's earthlodge should accommodate forty to fifty of his clan Set below a smoke vent between the central poles was a fireplace and a leaping blaze that washed the rude home with a foggy yellow glow. Wa-ter-ra shah ro seated himself on a regal seat of buffalo hide and motioned his advisors and guests to the pole benches that stood at opposite side of the fireplace.

When Dodge thought that preliminaries had been sufficiently observed, he gave the Toyash chief the message he had given To wah que-nah of the Comanches. The Grandfather's heart was good toward his red children, he desired that old wounds be healed and forgotten. In token of his good heart, he had sent many gifts for his children. Dodge then broached the matter of which his brother To wah que nah had already sent word to the Pawnee· a great council whereat the Americans and plains people might speak together. But he didn't speak yet of the girl Ona.

'Don't trot out them two gals right away,' Dake Satterlee had advised him. 'Hold 'em in reserve a bit, Cunnel. I know that old man. He'll hoss trade you out o' your brass buttons, give him a chance.' So the girls were to remain out of sight in their wagon till the time was right.

Now they awaited Wa ter ra shah ro's response.

He hacked loudly in his throat and gave his women some orders. An iron kettle was taken from the fire, stew ladled into clay bowls and handed around. The Indians fell to with gusto, dipping up chunks of meat with their fingers While the officers hesitated, exchanging glances, Dake sampled the stew.

'Buffler yearlings,' he grunted 'Prime too.'

The whites smiled and pitched in.

148

Dake grinned and gave Stennis, who sat at his left, a nudge. 'That wa'n't all, but don't see no odds sp'iling any-one's appetite some'at.'

'I'm honored, naturally, that you have no qualms about spoiling mine,' Stennis muttered. He dug into his portion with little enthusiasm.

It seemed to augur well when, the meal concluded, Wa-ter ra shah ro passed around the pipe of peace. Then he spoke. The words of his brother were fair words and would be weighed by his wise men. The discussion went on for a couple of hours, Dake translating the gist of what was said. Questions were put to Dodge; he answered readily. Polite little agreements and concessions were made. The Pawnees would accept the gifts of their friends and would make gifts of their own · corn, beans and buffalo meat.

As to the great council, they were divided several ways: for it, against it and undecided. It might be a useful thing, said the dissenters, but how could they know? If bad things came of it, the bad would fall on the heads of those who called it. Dodge quiety observed that the council would be a most prestigious thing for those who called it and that this fact should be weighed first of all Next, he said, was the question of good faith He, as the tongue of the Grandfather, would be held as much to account by his people as would the Toyash by theirs, should things go awry.

It would be seemly, therefore, if both he and the Toyash yielded tokens of their good hearts to one another. There was among them a white boy of nine summers whose family carried sick hearts because of his absence from their lodge Dodge did not assume; he flatly stated The boy should be brought forth, he said, and made to stand beside one whom he, the white chief, had brought with him Let the Pawnee look at both and say whether the exchange of tokens was fair.

It picqued the Pawnees' curiosity; they took hasty coun-cil. Wa ter ra-shah ro hacked on his throat and said there were several in his town in whom the white blood had once flowed, all or in part. They came generally of the tribe who lived in Mexico. Perhaps there *was* such a boy of the Ameri cans among the Toyash. If so, who did the white chief have who might stand beside him?

Let the boy be brought here, Dodge repeated. His own

offering would be fair to Toyash eyes. This was the truth. Let them test it.

That did it. Wa ter ra shah ro gave his assent.

'Bring the girl here, Mr. Satterlee,' Dodge said.

'Just the Pawnee?'

'Just her. We might need another bargaining card later.' Dodge smiled. 'No strings, of course, on a token of friendship. But we want to get as we give.'

Dake gave an approving nod and left the earthlodge. So did one of the Pawnee men. In a minute the latter returned, accompanied by a boy of nine or ten. The lad was breechclouted and moccasined, deeply browned by the sun but unmistakably white.

'What's your name, son?' Dodge asked.

The boy glared at him.

'Speak up, boy!'

'Matthew Wright Martin.' Sullenly.

Poore chuckled. 'Don't want to leave. They never do.'

Any man who had been a boy would understand why, Stennis thought. When famine, disease and other perils of primitive living were conspicuously absent, as with the Toyash, the Indian way must be a boy's dream life.

Dake came silently out of the passage and stood aside, holding the hide covering open. It lent a dramatic touch to Ona's entrance. As she walked forward, the Pawnees were silent, all eyes on her. Grunts that sounded disdainful rumbled from a couple of warriors. This to denigrate the sexual status of the white chief's token, Stennis supposed. But the rest waited unspeaking, as if sensing something portentous.

Wa-ter ra-shah ro rose from his seat, his glumly lined face not changing. But his eyes were intent. He spoke.

' "Who is this woman?" ' Dake translated.

'The daughter of his daughter,' said Dodge. 'Tell him in your best style, Mr. Satterlee. And don't fail to grease the axle all you can.'

CHAPTER FIFTEEN

Many questions were put to Ona; she answered them all to the Pawnees' satisfaction. What her mother had told her about her tribe, her family and her own immediate past had clung like burrs to her young mind. She described in detail her life with the Cherokees and stressed her good treatment by the soldiers. The Pawnee councilors pronounced themselves satisfied as to her identity and agreed that the white chief had made an act of good faith.

Wa ter ra shah ro said that arrangements would be made at once for the council desired by the white chief. Runners would be sent to all Comanche, Kiowa and Pawnee bands. Meantime the hearts and lodges of the Pawnee were open to the white men; whatever they desired would be theirs.

However Dodge, with success in his grasp, wasn't about to see it jeopardized by a chance rift between Dragoons and Pawnees. He gave his soldiers orders that restricted concourse with their hosts to certain hours and close supervision The men grumbled, but nobody breached the rules. If ony had harbored doubts when the journey began of who was running things, they no longer held them. Anyway it was enough, after so grueling a journey, to recuperate in the relative cool of the plateau and, having established facilities for care of their sick, to idle away pleasant days as they waited for the council to convene.

'Yep,' said Ben Poore, 'I wouldn't be surprised they's truth to the talk we are getting set to take an underholt on Texas. All nice 'n' legal seeming, o' course Get American settlers there t' declare 'emselves a separate state, like.'

'Rubbish,' Stennis said without enthusiasm 'Suppose the American Government intervened in such an instance. We'd be obliged to send troops to protect our own. That would mean war with Mexico '

Poore puffed a stream of pipesmoke 'Sure enough, boy. There's high-placed augurs figure Texas is worth that price.'

'Rubbish,' Stennis muttered

He felt curiously detached, squatting beside Poore in the shade of a wagon and watching currents of life in the camp, men resting and talking, going about small duties, plying needle and thread to repair their dilapidated clothing For all that they'd endured, morale was good. One couldn't fail to be stirred by their collective pride. But did anything justify the suffering and dying that was the cost of such pride?

The whole trend of his thinking lately had Stennis depressed and uneasy. Was he wrong for the Army – or vice versa? More and more his feelings pointed to a negative answer he hated to face. Men of his family had traditionally chosen careers in law, banking or the military. Since childhood he'd set his heart on a soldierly future, his father had pulled strings to get him a congressional recommendation to West Point. What could the old man say? But that wasn't really the question. The governor and the whole family would have to accept what he decided ...

'Yep,' Poore ruminated around his pipe, 'Get an underholt on Texas, the Mex Army will be just half your problem. Rest'll be all the Injuns on the Llano Estacado.'

'What's that?'

'Texas tableland, buffler grass, Injuns and plenty canyons for 'em to hide in. Mexes got more sense'n to push in there. Us – hah Once all them Comanche, Kiowa, Wacos, Caddoes, Wichitas, Lipans and Tonks see the handwriting, they will catch a pure itch to lift white man hair.'

'I might like to see Texas,' Stennis said moodily.

'Yeh? Lemme tell you, this child tramped a good piece of her once after he jumped old Jean Lafitte's buccaneer vessel *Pride* off Galvez Island They say all Texas is wanting for is water and a good drink o' whiskey. That's all Hell is wanting for too.' Poore gazed across the trampled stretch of meadow between the camp and the Indian lodges. 'Here comes Dake.'

Satterlee tramped straight up to them, grinning. 'How, hosses. Dodge sent me to find you, Loot. Him and the old man been palavering.'

'The chief?'

'Yeh. I been translating 'most all day. Wa ter-ra-shah ro got a powerful hankering for a better look at the apple o' his granddaughter's eye.'

'Damn you, Satterlee.' Stennis got to his feet. 'I suppose you . . .'

'Loot, I ain't done a thing but turn that ole boy's palaver into good English Ona musta bent his ear 'bout you. You coming?'

Stennis headed for the tipis, Dake in step beside him. His mouth was dry with worry; he'd been dreading the worst sort of development where Ona was concerned. Just how far would Dodge press him to carry the charade?

They entered the earthlodge. Wa-ter ra shah ro was seated on his buffalo throne, Dodge on the pole bench at his right. Stennis looked around, but saw nothing of Ona. He and Dake seated themselves and Wa ter-ra shah-ro spoke.

'Wants you t' take off your bonnet,' Dake said.

Stennis grated his teeth and removed his battered shako The chief gazed intently at his head, then hacked violently and spoke again.

'Says he was told truth. The sun has entered your head and made you his own. You are touched by a tall medicine.'

Stennis muttered an expletive. Dodge sent him a warning look. Wa ter ra shah ro spoke on and Dake rendered the gist of his words. It was clear that the Americans were a powerful tribe. It would be a good thing if his bloodline were joined with an American chief's and it was said that the young chief's father stood high in the councils of his people. Since the woman was good in the young chief's eyes, he had no objections to his pursuing a courtship.

Stennis sat rigid with alarm. 'Colonel, this is preposterous! And where did he get that about my father?'

'Quiet,' Dodge said, his lips smiling. 'Look pleased and keep your mouth shut and listen. I didn't suggest a thing, Frv. Obviously the girl's doing.'

'But surely you've made it clear –!'

'Shut up and listen. We must make the best of the situation. There is too much riding on this council to risk his enmity over so trivial a matter. You will have to play along *for the time*'

Stennis swallowed, his throat squeezed with desperation. The blood drumming in his ears almost eclipsed Wa-ter ra-shah-ro's speech. Dake gravely translated. 'Wants to know how many hosses young chief can give.'

Dodge cleared his throat. 'Tell him, ah, the young chief has many horses and great wealth in his own country, but that is many suns away. Tell him there are other considerations. White men do not court in the Pawnee way. The white man must speak alone with his beloved many times before gifts are made and vows spoken.'

Dake rendered the chief's response. 'Says he sees for himself Americans are a people with strange ways. Let the young chief court the woman as he will, not forgetting she is of a chief's line and her worth is high. Meaning don't forget about them gifts.'

The caucus concluded amiably with Dodge and the chief exchanging pleasantries. The three white men left the earthlodge. Stennis was inwardly seething. When they were a distance from the tipis, he came to a halt and said determinedly: 'Colonel, I will not go through with it. I don't give a damn how important this council is or what measures you may choose to take against me.'

Dodge smiled 'Let's not build mountains out of anthills, Fry. Why did you think I stressed that you be allowed to court the girl in our way?'

'I wish you'd tell me, sir.'

'To give you time, of course. She wasn't raised by the Pawnees and is not deeply instilled with Injun customs. She knows our ways far better She has fastened her sights on you precisely as might a civilized girl. Though I confess there's precious little difference in how ladies anywhere fix on certain goals. And pursue them by whatever means are in their grasp. I grant that by civilized standards her method may seem blatant and crude. Yet direct and innocent too Which is refreshing, don't you think?'

'No,' Stennis said between his teeth.

'In any case you'll have plenty of chance to work a fray in Ona's interest. Naturally it'll require tact and diplomacy of a high order. It would be *damned* unfortunate if our plans went awry because you gave the girl offense.'

'You've made that eminently clear, sir. But what in hell do I tell her?'

Dodge gave him a roguish poke in the arm 'Come on, man. Don't tell me that a young blood of your background hasn't pursued his rakish amours. Surely you've adequate practice in working the gentle arts of persuasion and dissuasion on the ladies.'

Stennis said: 'Well. Uh.' Why was it so devilishly hard to admit that a lifelong shyness had hampered you into your mid twenties?

'There you are,' Dodge said heartily. 'You'll have time and leisure to mull and explore small subterfuges. Or large ones. And I'm herewith relieving you of all other duties so you can apply yourself unstintingly to this one. What could be simpler?'

'Nothing,' Stennis said, 'sir.'

'The possibilities are really unlimited. For example, you might show her what a *dull* clod you can be when you set your mind to it.'

That, Stennis thought, should be no problem at all.

The stream coursed out of the peaks, fed by little rivulets till it dashed downward in chasms of creaming spray. Here and there it swirled into deep pools overhung by plum brush and willow wands. Stennis sat in one of the pools, scrubbing his lank white body

The water was icy and the sun did not reach past the tall shoulders of rock that hid the place. Stennis's teeth chattered; he shivered and shifted his backside against the sharp-pebbled streambed. Not a comfortable bath by any means, but clean and refreshing. He congratulated himself on finding this secluded pocket in the cliffs south of the plateau. It was good to be alone and think about nothing in particular while enjoying a spot of sylvan solitude for its own sake.

In the two days since Dodge had relieved him of his duties, Stennis had more or less shunned the camp and village, getting off by himself as often as he could. He'd given his problems an occasional worried nudge of thought, but mainly had avoided confronting them. Just as he'd avoided confrontation with the source of one problem, Ona.

He couldn't put it off much longer. Both Dodge and the old chief would wonder what ailed him He was beginning to wonder himself Shy or not, he surely wasn't so abysmal a fool that he couldn't tactfully put off one Indian girl.

155

Trouble was, she was a terrifyingly determined one. Knew exactly what she wanted while he vacillated between uncertainties Well . . .

Brush rustled faintly up the draw. Stennis froze. He twisted his head, craning it to see above the brush. Good God. Ona. Picking her way easily along the boulder strewn bank between cliff and stream. Damn it! One thing sure, she hadn't found her way here by accident.

Stennis measured with his eye the distance to his pile of clothes on the bank. He could reach them in seconds, but couldn't possibly get them on before Ona was close. He scrambled down in the water, hugging his shoulders. The water hid him nearly to his chest, his knees knobbing up into sight. Somehow that really discomfited him; he straightened his legs to pull his knees under.

Ona reached the bank above his piled clothes. She stood gazing at him mercilessly.

'Hello,' he said weakly.

She said· 'I come wash.' And still watching him, sat down on the bank and began pulling off her long moccasins.

'That's fine,' he said through chattering teeth. 'But would you mind? I'd like to climb out of here and get dressed.'

'Nobody stop you.'

She stood up, reaching for the waist of her skirt. Good God! Hot-cold with embarrassment, he lowered his face. Kept his eyes tightly shut until, moments later, he heard the water softly break to her entrance. He tipped open one eye. Ona was a few yards away, also sitting in the water. It covered her small body to the shoulders; a twisty gold outline showed below water. She smiled pleasantly, an isn't this nice smile, then raised her arms and began to undo the tight bun of her hair.

'See here,' Stennis got out, 'this won't do at all! Your people must have rules about this sort of thing.'

She shrugged. 'Nobody here but you, me. You no mind, I no mind'

'But I damned well do mind! This is highly improper and if anyone found out . . .'

'Nobody find. We alone' Her teeth flashed. 'Is nice here, eh?'

'You followed me,' he said with bitter accusation.

She nodded, shaking the mass of hair to her shoulders. It fanned like a glossy shawl on the water. 'All day, every day.'

'By God, you ought to be spanked!'

'You mean beat, eh?'

'You're damned right I do!'

'My chief may beat me if he pleases –'

Ona said it in good, perfectly clear English, at the same time starting to her feet.

'Don't! For God's sake!'

Stennis frantically jerked his knees up and ducked his face against them. Water wrinkled to her movements, then subsided. He heard her say softly: 'I am ugly to look on?'

'Oh no, no, I'm sure you're not.' He kept his eyes straight downward, his heart pounding wildly. 'See here,' he said desperately, 'if you will look the other way and let me get dressed, we can uh, talk. How would that be?'

'Promise?'

'God, yes! I promise.'

Silence. Stennis lifted his face warily. Again she was down shoulder-level in the water, her head bowed modestly. Very slowly he eased to his feet. She giggled softly. He cried, 'Don't look!' And floundered hastily to shore, scrambling out of the water. Turning his back to her, he began whipping on his clothes.

He nearly had his pants on when water made a cascading splash behind him. He stumbled partly around, almost tripping in his half-on trousers. He gaped.

God, why had he turned? Knowing already what he would see. Ona standing in water midthigh deep. A golden slim naiad polished by wet-silver highlights.

She moved toward him, water rustling lower along her legs.

He stood jaw agape, hands frozen, blood dinning in his ears. As she reached the bank, he summoned enough presence of mind to yank his pants up to his waist. But that was all he was capable of. Just standing immobile then as Ona stepped from the water and came up to him. Her sleek arms lifting to him made the gold-velvet cones of her little breasts tip up, brown-pointed. He could not move, could not even start to back away, he was thinking in a panic

157

before he ceased thinking altogether. Knowing nothing then but the wet cool skinned closeness of her that, arching to him, melded swiftly to a pounding warmth. That and the young strength of her arms, her fiercely eager mouth. Then his hands crushed her closer.

The heated bow of her body relaxed; she stirred away and he let his arms fall. She stepped back a bit, eyes half-lidded like a sleepy child's, high color straining her tilted cheeks. Desire thickened his brain; the fire in his blood coursed to the far ends of his nerves. He followed her glance to the heavy thickets along the cliff's base, shaped bower-like as if to invite seclusion.

'Come,' she whispered, taking his hand.

To one side of them, the overhanging wall dipped inward, concave at its base. To their other side, plum brush flourished, heavy-leaded above and bare-stemmed below. They lay curtained in a natural hollow, cool sand beneath their backs, her dark head pillowed on his arm.

Stennis still felt faintly stunned. Accepting now, but not quite believing. Lord ... Lord! Could women be born with such sensual wisdom? For she'd received him in that swift pure pain that presaged an ecstasy never tasted, as unknown to her as it was to him. *I tell you I am maiden,* she had whispered.

Yes – truly. But Lord!

She stirred lightly. The sun was higher now, topping the far cliff wall, percolating down through the leaves. It dappled her honey hued skin to a still warmer glow. How delightfully the darks and lights of her mixed heritage had crossed, he thought. Not in sharp contrasts but in one tawny blend of beauty, body and spirit, that was uniquely Ona. Even her name, lovely on the tongue, seemed neither white nor Indian, yet could derive from either side.

'I am wondering,' he murmured, 'where you got your name?'

She seemed not to hear him. She whispered, running a finger over his chest: 'You are so white '

Somehow it was a half question. He did not know how to answer it. Her hands slipped up to his hair. 'And here the sun himself has entered into you.'

'Into you too, I think,' he said awkwardly.

'The sun doesn't shine at night. I think you are like the day And I. .'

'No, see He's entered your skin as he has my hair' He turned on his side, holding out his sun coppered hand. 'Here he's entered me and turned me black as a Pawnee. Nowhere are you so dark as my hand.'

Gravely she laid her hand over his and gazed at them together. 'That is so. But –' Her mouth curved at the corners '– he has made your hair so beautiful.'

He laughed. 'And finding you lovely, he has entered all of you and made you lovelier, my lady. My darling –'

Suddenly, as if a knot had burst, the words were coming easily. He had many more words for her. He would say them all. But not now. Not with her eyes widening soft dark on his eyes and the laughter dying in his chest. Her arms reached up and drew him down. . . .

CHAPTER SIXTEEN

The Indian delegates began arriving within a week. How they were able to cover the long hot distance in so short a time and arrive seemingly no worse for it was a mystery. Braves from more than a score of bands thronged the town. They made a primitive pageant in their ceremonial costumes of white buckskin, dyed strouding and flamboyant blankets; their headdresses ranged from roaches to braids, feathers to turbans. A raucous tinkle and shrill and boom of bells, skin drums, nose flutes and bone whistles mingled with the racket of horses and dogs.

After several days of feasting, drinking and studying the whites, the delegated chiefs settled down to business in the great earthlodge. The ceremonial ice was hardly broken when thirty Kiowa came streaming into the village, calling taunts and threats at the Dragoons. They belligerently declared that the Americans had made alliance with their hated enemies the Osage. Also they had learned that the Americans were holding a Kiowa girl prisoner Dodge's explanation that they were returning the girl to her people cooled their fury; they even subjected him to a barrage of greasy embraces.

The council opened with angry, impassioned avowals by some that the Americans intended to seize their lands as they had those of the eastern peoples. When the hot heads had been heard and their remarks indirectly rebuked by more conciliatory chiefs, a mood of careful, tentative bargaining began. All shared a common worry about the white man's territorial ambitions, but the prevailing wish – at present – was to avoid trouble with the Americans.

Dodge was at pains to point out that not only was his mission peaceful, the United States was at peace with all the white nations. Nations that would not tempt American wrath by molesting tribes who had agreements with the United States. More, if Americans were permitted to build trading posts among the tribes, they need no longer be dependent on the Spanish at Taos and Santa Fe for

160

such civilized goods as they desired. Finally, if the bands represented here would choose delegates from those present to return with the Dragoons, treaties could be drawn up.

They would speak at length of these things and consider them, said the chiefs.

Dake Satterlee was predictably pessimistic about the council's outcome. He told Stennis Fry as much.

'I'm familiar with your cheery prognostications,' Stennis said dourly. 'They are right not quite half the time. You predicted that none of us would reach the Wichitas alive. Also that we'd be mincemeat for a horde of savages if we did.'

Dake grunted. 'Half's right enough. You lost pret' near half a hunderd men we know of. They's more at the sick camps along the way that ain't never gonna see home again. Neither are some who are still with us. You got again the distance to cover going back and your command's in miserable shape already. Good third o' your regiment are dead men by my reckoning. Plenty o' them as do make it back won't be fitten for service no more.'

'I know. Dammit, I know!'

'This council ain't cinched up neither. Wrong nudge to the scales, the lot o' us could still be mincemeat. Yeh. I'd say half's a right plenty.'

'The council has gone smoothly thus far,' Stennis snapped.

'Some fancy-fine consolation that be. Jee-zus! Don't you see all these Injuns keer about is keeping things like they was? Means raiding and making war agin each other like always, only keeping outen trouble with the Americans. Hell! It'll work that way awhile, but not for long. Happen some o' them butt-sprung wise men in Washington City get knuckling under to some stinking pack of investors who want to grab off treaty lands for one reason or t'other, the gov'ment'll sick you bluecoats on these people and tell 'em to move where they say. That or fight. Hell, I seen it all before. Only these plains Injuns'll fight you like them eastern 'uns never done. Take fifty, a hundred year to lick 'em all.'

They were sitting on the ground at the edge of a meadow, watching the young braves play stickball. Goal posts had

161

been set up at opposite ends of the field; two masses of warriors were pitted against each other in the bloodiest rough and tumble mêlée Stennis had ever witnessed Each man was armed with two sticks for securing the wooden ball which was being urged back and forth by the opposing sides. Rarely did anyone score a goal. The players, unidentified as to any designation of teams, used sticks, feet and butting heads on one another as freely as on the ball. Broken noses, cracked jaws, and streaming wounds were plentiful; several men had already been carried from the field unconscious.

The savagery of the play was unbelievable. But no more so than the mood prevailing on the sidelines. Stennis had heard that Indians were inveterate gamblers, but he hadn't conceived of that fact applying most vigorously to the women. Half the ladies of the village were present. From their excited jabber and the heaps of goods around them, they were betting everything they and their hapless mates owned on the game's outcome. Goods and chattels, pots and kettles, cloth and blankets, guns and knives, horses and dogs.

George Catlin had set up his folding chair and easel. He was painting a panorama of the scene, his swift furious brushstrokes capturing the action with a vivid power. How, Stennis wondered, did Catlin manage it? Nearly incapacitated by sieges of recurring fever, he was constantly at work sketching or painting aspects of Indian life. He'd ingratiated and awed their hosts by whipping off portrait after portrait of individuals, producing quite passable likenesses in a few minutes. The warriors insisted on posing in full regalia, sometimes on horseback, capering about and spurring the animals' flanks bloody against Catlin's insistence that he could capture a motionless figure with more fidelity. His averred interest was to record everyday aboriginal life as well as the many ceremonies and games that attended this gathering of the tribes. Something was going on every minute in and around the village: dances, horse races, foot races and ball games.

Stennis said: 'Don't you ever rest, George?'

Catlin gave him a quizzical look. 'No time for it. In a few years all this will be changed, perhaps vanished forever. The culture of these people is a fragile thing ... quickly

162

enervated and destroyed wherever it's touched by white ways. At least I can record the shadow of it for posterity.'

A hard truth there, Stennis conceded. This mission was a mere spearhead of America's implacable, conquering thrust westward. He gazed glumly at his shako resting on his knee, fingering its frazzled orange pompon. That kind of thinking merely complicated his general dilemma.

He felt Dake's shrewd glance. 'Somep'n eating at you, Loot?'

'Not a thing,' he said absently.

Ona ... his personal problem. One that loomed larger by far than when he'd thought of her as a mere nuisance.

She could be his. His for a lifetime. All he had to do was to say the word. A word held in leash by all that he'd been taught was right and proper. To quit the service was one thing. To claim a half-breed girl as wife was another. What would it do to his whole future? She might be an Indian princess, deserving of the same respect that Poca hontas had been accorded in England after wedding John Rolfe. Interesting, he thought sardonically, to see how his family would react to that argument. Or any other he might offer.

An officer was coming toward them along the meadow's edge. Jeff Davis. There was urgency in his manner.

'So there you fellows are. Better get your tails back to camp on the double. Dodge has summoned all officers to an emergency pow-wow. He wants you there too, Satterlee.'

'What's up?' Dake drawled.

'A nasty piece of business. Our Kiowa wench, Buffalo Calf Girl, has been shot. Doc Haile thinks she may not live.'

They stared at him.

'Shot!' Stennis exclaimed. 'What – who ...'

Davis shook his head. 'We don't know who did it or why. But the Kiowa delegates are irate as hell and things are looking ugly. If that girl dies, this council could turn into a disaster. One, in fact, that could turn squarely on all of us.'

Dodge consulted with his officers, aired all the pros and cons of the situation, and then put his troops on the alert.

163

The big council, which had been going well until now, was gripped by a sudden, hostile tension. At first the turnabout mood was confined to Chief Wa ter ra-shah ro's great earthlodge where, ostensibly, the delegates were hashing over the same issues as before. But the shooting of Buffalo Calf Girl had injected a growing heat into the proceedings. The Kiowas were in a particular fury, wrangling senselessly over points on which, a few hours earlier, they had been quite amenable. The whole atmosphere had sharply deteriorated and was worsening.

Some of it leaked outside the earthlodge and infected a number of young braves. In plain sight of the Dragoon camp, they heaped up a pile of goods that the soldiers had given in trade and rode their ponies back and forth, scattering and trampling it all into the earth. They continued to cavort about, shaking their lances and calling threats and challenges. The Dragoons watched and muttered, hands sweating around their muskets. One buck shook out a bolt of red trade calico and galloped past the regiment's picket line, the cloth flapping behind him. The horses went into a panic, rearing and tearing at their halters A Dragoon guard raised his musket but was restrained by one of his fellows. His oo-son-chees, Little Spaniard, stalked out and dragged the offending brave from his pony ...

The Callicutts were witness to the incident. They squatted by one of the wagons, rifles across their knees, passing a jug back and forth. Tute Callicutt cauterized his gut with a long pull and savored its sullen burn before passing the jug to Oshel.

'I think we bitten off a heap, Daddy,' Verl said worriedly.

Oshel swigged and smacked his lips, handing Verl the jug. 'Shet your tater hole and put some grit in you. Times I'd swear you ain't son o' mine at all.'

'Them Injuns is riled, Daddy They taken a real mad t' us, they will wipe up this here outfit like dog piddle.'

Oshel's beard parted with a snort. 'Ain't no ten Injuns I ever seen could stand up t' one good white man with a belly front o' his backbone You hold t' that now, and keep your fearful streak under your shirtback where it don't show I don't want to hear no more on't '

Tute shifted on his heels, glowering at the ground. He

had his own doubts about the wisdom of carrying out Daddy's scheme of revenge here and now. But they were on its course and would have to see it through, come what might. Way Daddy had put it, they'd bided their time long as they could. Pretty soon that Kiowa would be outside their reach. Time was ripe to take action.

Tute, though committed to the triple revenge Daddy had in mind, had felt downright skittish about the girl. That didn't faze Daddy any. Injuns wa'n't people, they was pure wolf. Follered that a squaw wa'n't a woman, just a wolf-bitch to be shot or pizen baited as a man pleased. All that was wanting was a likely place to fetch her. Oshel hadn't been long finding it. When the Kiowa had gone to a spring a ways from the village to fetch water, he'd followed. Other Injun women were at the spring too, but Daddy had simply laid up under some thornbush, taken the Kiowa in his sights and pinked her square. He'd thought for keeps, but turned out she was still alive, though maybe not for long. Leastways Doc Haile had concluded so before the angry Kiowas had taken her off to their own camp to work Injun medicine.

Tute wiped a finger across his sweat beaded upper lip. Jesus. Happen that female died, ther'd be hell to pay sure. Might be anyways, from the look. Dodge had gone to the earthlodge and sworn to the assembled chiefs that he'd do all in his power to find and punish the man who had committed the dastardly act. But that wasn't like to hold off those crazy young bucks much longer.

Then – suppose it was discovered who had fired the shot?

'Daddy,' Tute ventured, 'I surely hope you covered your sign good.'

'Don't you fret none 'bout that, son. I laid up in prime cover a good ways from them squaws afore I fired. They scattered a-screeching; ain't a one caught sight o' me.'

'Dodge had his scouts a looking for track.'

'Teach your granny to suck eggs,' Oshel growled. 'I wa'n't born yestiday. Scuffed out my sign whilst I was skinning outa there.'

'That's good, Daddy, but could be Dodge'll figure out t'was one o' us, he gets thinking on't.'

'Yeh, well, leave him prove it then. Only he ain't gonna have a deal o' time t'think on't. Gimme that jug, Verl.'

'You looking t' fetch Dodge next, Daddy?' Verl asked. Bright-eyed with whiskey now, he was unwinding some.

Oshel tipped up the jug, beard bobbing. He lowered it and wiped his mouth. 'Naw,' he said quietly. 'I am saving that fine haired bastard for last. There is another matter to settle and it will take some figuring to set up.'

'Satterlee?'

'I given a promise. His two hands for Tute's one. Now is our time, whilst everyone is tight assed about this council uproar.' Oshel's bloodshot gaze moved to a wagon some hundred yards away. A woman was standing beside it, her hair coppery under the noon sun. 'Won't be no easy mark, the buckskin man. But I fancy he can be got to, all right. That Sherrod woman. She is the way.'

Verl's heavy brows puckered. 'How's 't, Daddy?'

'Goddammit, don't you never keep your eyes open? Satterlee is sweet on her. We got to do our figuring after that fact.'

Dake decided to go over the ground once more. Not that he figured it was much use He and the other regimental scouts had had no difficulty locating the spot fifty yards north of the spring where the assassin had laid up. The earth under the brush had been freshly scuffed all to hell. The man hadn't attempted to hide his sign; he'd merely dragged his feet so as to erase any clue to his identity Not a clear print in the lot. Sharp sole-edge marks had shown only that he was wearing boots, not moccasins, ruling out any Indian or Dragoon scout A fact which hadn't escaped the angry Kiowas· the man was white.

The scuffed prints led from and back to a stretch of solid rock that left no sign at all. Any further conclusion about the boot wearing assassin had to be a guess. And Dake could make a pretty fair one· the Callicutts. Revenge for their son and brother, Asa. But how to prove it?

Hell, suppose'n they could prove it, Dake dourly reflected as he tramped back toward the Dragoon camp. What difference would it make? The older chiefs and headmen had counseled patience Wait, they had said, and see what the white chief's word counted for. But nothing had been said as to the would-be killer's fate if he were found. Dodge might order the man shot, might even kill him with his own hand. But Dake couldn't see the colonel just handing a white man over to angry Indians; it wasn't his style. And it was highly doubtful that the Kiowas would be satisfied by anything less than meting out punishment themselves.

A gang of young bucks raced their ponies across the trampled meadow, veering toward Dake with savage howls. He came to a halt and faced them, not flinching a muscle as they rushed at him full gallop. At the last moment the bunch split to either side of him, the nearest of them missing him by a foot. They dashed away with derisive yelps. Dake moved on through the settling dust and passed the cordon of Dragoon sentries.

He went to the water wagon. Sergeant Bohannon was squatted nearby, scribbling industriously in his journal, as Dake filled a dipper and drank from it.

'Make 'er shine, Sarge. Could be your last entry.'

'Agh,' Bohannon said. 'I'm thinking the same.' He slapped the little book shut and shoved it in his pocket. 'There's a fine irony in the thing if you can see it.'

'Whatever'n hell that means.'

'Why, only that the colonel's dearest wish was to deliver our little Kiowa darling untouched to the bosom of her own. To ensure as much, he had poor Jack Tevis whipped bloody and the Callicutt lad shot. That he kept her safe and well till now has fired back on him with a vengeance.'

Dake chuckled sardonically. 'Anyone who got a notion 'bout keeping that Kiowa untouched shoulda started 'bout six year ago.'

He dipped up more water, rinsed his mouth and spat it out. Then, feeling someone watching him, he turned. Verl Callicutt was standing about twenty paces away. Dake said flatly: 'You looking for some'un, ridge runner?'

'You,' Verl said. 'Got some'un to tell you.'

He glanced pointedly at Bohannon. Dake walked over to Verl who led him off a few steps further, then said in a low voice: 'That Sherrod widder lady. Daddy says you are sweet on her.'

'Daddy got a big mouth he ain't too old to get curbed,' Dake said. 'That all?'

167

Verl's black beard divided in an arrogant grin. 'Not by a far throw, Buckskin. You wants keep that widder lady fitten to look on, you hark to what I say.'

Dake's eyes pinched at the corners. 'You best make sense o' that,' he said quietly.

'We got yer lady. Taken 'er out o' here clean as a whistle. Iffen you don't believe it, you just –'

'Got her where?' Dake's hands shot out and doubled a fistful of the bigger man's dirty shirtfront. 'Speak up, goddam you! Where's she at?'

'In a place I know of.' Verl's grin was unruffled. 'Can take you there straightway, Buckskin. But iffen I do, you come alone. That is the bargain.'

'*Bargain* –' Dake tightened his fist. 'Bargain as to what?'

'Her for you. You come along like I said and she gets set loose.'

'Jesus, If you Callicutt bastards done her harm.'

'It is up to you. She ain't come to none. Won't if you foller me like I said. Now, straightway and alone.'

Dake let his hand drop. He looked at Bohannon who was watching the two of them with narrow-eyed curiosity. Dake walked over to him. 'Sarge, I be going off awhile. Would take it friendly you didn't tell a soul what you just seen.'

Bohannon frowned. 'Is it with that spalpeen you're going off?'

'Can't give you no answers, Sarge.'

Bohannon nodded slowly. 'All right, laddie buck. As you say. But there's something here I don't fancy the smell of.' His gaze flicked to Verl. 'I'll keep silence for an hour. If you ain't back then, I'll remember it's a Callicutt you went off with.'

'I'll be back, don't you fret.' Dake clapped him on the shoulder, then returned to where Verl Callicutt stood. 'Lead the way,' Dake said.

'What you tell that sojer boy?'

'To mind his business.'

Verl didn't move. 'You gotta leave your gun here,' he said. 'Daddy says so.'

Dake was standing four feet from Verl and now he raised his rifle till the muzzle touched Verl's belly 'You got Miz Sherrod,' he murmured. 'That's what you said.'

Verl grinned confidently. 'That's it, Mister Buckskin.'

'And I got you,' Dake said gently. 'I wonder what sort o' trade that is good for.'

Verl's grin vanished. His eyes tipped down to the rifle and up again. 'You are taking one helluva long chance.'

'Not half the chance I be taking going to meet Callicutts whilst under a Callicutt gun.' Dake reached out, lifted Verl's rifle from his hands and tucked it under his own arm. Then appropriated a long knife from Verl's belt. 'Get moving.'

Verl's face had a greasy shine. 'Maybe you wanta get your widder lady killed. Maybe that is it.'

Dake shook his head 'Your daddy is already shy one o' his pups Rather'n lose another 'un, he will make a trade-off There's something you had oughta keep in mind too. Which is that anything happens to her happens to you likewise. So you don't do nothing but what I tell you.' He gave Verl a savage prod with the rifle. 'Move!'

CHAPTER SEVENTEEN

Tute Callicutt prowled the little clearing in a restless circle, his fingers closing and unclosing around the rifle in his left fist. Now and then, unthinkingly, he would swing his right arm up to grasp at the weapon with a hand that wasn't there Each time he did so, his face would go tight and ugly with his thoughts.

Raging and dangerous thoughts, Alexandra guessed. Gaining intensity with each brooding, bitter, painwracked day. Focusing finally on one solitary goal: revenge against Dake Satterlee.

Lying on her side in dense oak shade, she again carefully tested the rawhide thongs that bound her wrists They were quite unbreakable and the knots quite secure ... no question of that. But a very slight, stretchy slickness and give in their tight loops touched her with a faint stubborn hope The rawhide was green and new, lacking the flinty toughness of cured hide For some minutes, ignoring the tearing pain in her wrists, she had been twisting against the greasy strands with a careful, desperate pressure She quickly desisted whenever either of the Callicutts looked her way.

'Goddammit!' Tute burst out. 'This goddam arm o' mine...'

Oshel, sitting patiently on his haunches with his rifle across his thighs, glanced at his son. 'Quit bellyaching,' he rumbled. 'You been practicing steady since your hand got took off Just a bracing that piece across your right arm, you have learned to shoot well as ever. That's all you got to keep in mind.'

'Ain't same as drawing bead on a stump or rock,' Tute muttered. 'Body misses a stump or rock, he can allus shoot again. I get my sights on Satterlee, won't be no such allowing'

'You hark to me, boy. We taken no shot at Satterlee less'n he makes us His two hands is what we're after and a man shot dead couldn't keer less.'

Alexandra felt a cold ripple on her flesh. His hands!

Dear God, they must be crazy. At least the old man must be. She saw, or thought she saw, a repugnance color Tute's expression. But he said nothing. Even if he preferred a straight-out revenge on Dake Satterlee, his father was still the leader.

Tute said heavily: 'Think he's gonna walk right up and leave us just whack off his hands?'

Oshel tilted his shaggy head toward Alexandra. 'We got the one argyment he can't answer but one way. We got his woman. Yeh, boy. That is what he will do.'

His woman, Alexandra thought. She wondered if many now thought of her that way. Dake Satterlee's woman. Not long ago she'd have laughed at the idea. Not that it had seemed displeasing, merely unlikely. The difference between them might be one of background only, yet it was real enough. Since then she'd seen past all surfaces to Dake Satterlee's inner worth, part of her mind wholly accepting the fact. Her reservations stemmed less from reluctance than from simple caution. The mistake she'd made long ago with Randall Sherrod had resulted from an immature weakness for his superficial charm. Whereas Dake's genuine qualities attracted her as much as his lusty manhood did. But she still wasn't entirely sure of her feelings. . . .

It was, in fact, a preoccupation with this dilemma that had caused her to stroll by herself awhile ago. The guilt she had felt following Randall's death had by now faded to a small occasional twinge. If she were in some small measure responsible for his fate, it was too late to change what had happened. Randall had pursued his own selfmade course too long and unswervingly for her to justly accept more than a mote of blame. She still had her life to live and a right to live it as best she might. Quite naturally, and almost with relief, her thoughts had swung fully, for the first time, to Dake Satterlee.

Needing to think alone, Alexandra had wandered away from the cordon of wagons and up a tree-fringed creek close by. One of the sentries, spotting her, had warned her not to walk beyond sight of the camp. She'd said she wouldn't, but musing unconsciously along, she was deep in the trees when brush had rustled sharply at her back. Before she could turn her head, much less cry out, a rough hand had been clamped over her mouth. Big, powerful

171

Verl Callicutt had held her as easily as he would a baby while his father and brother had tied her hands and forced a filthy gag into her mouth. They had marched her up stream for some distance, crossing the lower meadows to an arm of heavily wooded hills that stretched to the rocky bases of flanking peaks. Halting in this clearing, they'd tied her feet as well. Then Verl had been dispatched back to camp with a message for Dake Satterlee.

Dake would come, Alexandra thought. Would walk knowingly into the trap. Even if he should guess what Oshel Callicutt had in store for him, he would do so.

Oshel Callicutt got to his feet and tramped to the edge of the clearing. They were on the crown of a low hill, one of five or so that formed a loose horseshoe enclosing a humpy stretch of meadow. The upper slopes were covered with stands of young oak irregularly broken by small glades like this one, from whose south edge a watcher could scrutinize through half-screening leaves the meadow below.

After taking a long look, Oshel said: 'Tute, you keep a watch over here. Soon's you catch a sight of anyone, say so.' He returned to his patch of shade and squatted down again. Briefly glancing at Alexandra, he said 'I got naught agin you. Long as your man don't try no foolishment, you will be set free.'

Alexandra wanted to say that her fate shouldn't present any great qualms to one of Oshel's bargaining style, but the foul tasting rag bunched in her mouth effectively prevented speech. When he looked away, she silently strained her wrists apart, fighting the thongs again. Her eyes followed Tute as he crossed to the clearing's edge and peered down through the trees. His shoulders stiffened.

'Daddy. Looks like them a coming.'

Oshel moved swiftly to his side. 'My eyes ain't up to such a piece o' distance, son. Tell me what you see.'

'Cain't tell much yet. But ... by God, it looks like Saterlee is trailing behind Verl. Now that shouldn't be.'

'Is Verl toting a gun?'

'Daddy, I can't make out yet. Can only tell 'em apart by the clothes.'

Alexandra felt one of the greasy loops slip a little on her wrists. If she could pull a hand free. But even if she succeeded, she must still free her feet. And then? She did

172

not know. Ignoring the pain and slick wetness of her wrists, she tugged strongly against the thongs.

''Y God, Daddy,' Tute exclaimed, 'that Satterlee is got two rifles, his 'n' Verl's. And he got one stuck right in Verl's back.'

'That mountain pup has got some smarts,' Oshel said quietly. 'It did not occur to me he 'ud think that far, bargaining Verl off for the woman. But it is clear that is what the son of a bitch means to try.'

'Jesus, Daddy. We can't take no chance on him killing Verl!'

Oshel scratched his beard. 'There is still a way. We got to taken a chance on Verl getting hurt. But I be goddam if I let that buckskin bastard get away. Won't be another such chance to fetch him. You hark close now. . . .'

Dake ordered Verl Callicutt to halt. He didn't like the lay of the situation at all. Verl was leading him straight up a wide meadow between the open prongs of a wooded horseshoe of hills. Enclosing them on three sides, that horseshoe would provide a beautiful lay-up for an ambush. Squarely in the center of the meadow now, they were not close to any cover, and Dake didn't like that either. At the same time anyone taking a bead on him from the hill cover would have to do some fine shooting.

Yeh. Damned good place to stop.

Dake poked Verl's backbone with his rifle muzzle. 'How much farther?'

'Tain't much.' Reluctantly, Verl pointed. 'Right atop that hill yonder. There is a clearing where Daddy and Tute is waiting. Widder lady too.'

'Call to 'em. Tell 'em to get down here and bring Miz Sherrod along.'

'I don't reckon –'

'Call 'em!'

'Daddy!' Verl bawled it at the top of his voice. 'He says come down and bring the woman. He is got my gun, Daddy. Do like he says!'

Silence. The cricket-keening afternoon seemed to pause as if all nature were deliberating the answer. None came. Dake rammed the rifle harder against Verl's back. 'Say it again. Louder!'

173

Verl turned a sweating face. 'Mister, you might's well throw down them pieces and come along. You got your answer. Daddy ain't gonna give you up. You wanta get the woman killed?'

'Thing is, does he wanta give you up? Sing out, damn you!'

'Daddy!' Verl's voice quavered toward cracking. 'He says it's me for the woman. Daddy, he means it!'

Dake could feel sweat crawling under his buckskins. What was Oshel up to? If he had Alexandra, he wouldn't simply throw away a bargaining card; he'd parley first. Therefore she was in no immediate danger, Dake was sure. But why didn't Oshel reply?

Then his stentorian voice boomed from the hill top. 'I heard you. What's your offer, Buckskin?'

'He said it,' Dake called. 'Him for Miz Sherrod. No other deal.'

'You ain't in some'at position to name terms, boy. I tell you, now. You hand Verl both them guns and march straightway up here. She goes loose. That is the only deal I will talk.'

Dake blinked his eyes clear of sweat-sting at their corners. He knew Oshel's rough position from his voice. And he, Dake, was covered in front by Verl's body. But where in hell was Tute? Dake swung a swift look at the side prongs of the horseshoe. Tute might be anywhere up there. Was that Oshel's idea? String him out with talk whilst Tute eased over to the side for a shot at him?

Suddenly Dake dropped both rifles, at the same time whipping his knife out and up. He reached, snaked an arm around Verl's neck and dragged Verl tight against him. Now they were a single target and his knifeblade was laid against Verl's throat.

'Hear me, old man!' Dake shouted. 'Whatever you got stuck up your craw, forget it. Your stick is floating wrongway. You ain't just taking a chance with his life. You try anything atall, even if you get me, your son is gone to glory sure. One flick o' this blade'll do it.'

'We got your woman, Satterlee!' Oshel's voice was hoarse with rage. 'You harm Verl and she will die with a bullet through her head. You hear me, Satterlee?'

174

A threat. But the voice shook. He'd pressed his own terms to success, Dake was sure then. Odds tipped his way and Oshel would accept a trade-off. Nail it down fast, Dake thought.

'You step out where I can see you clear,' he yelled. 'Tute likewise. Bring her out with you. I want to see her in plain sight and no harm done her. Then you leave her go, I leave Verl go. They both of 'em start walking slow. We will all be under the guns, so there will be no tricks. You try any' — he paused emphatically — 'and I will shoot Verl square in the back.'

'You have got a deal, Buckskin.'

Oshel's too calm tone put Dake on his guard. He had something in mind for sure. A desperation move.

After a minute brush stirred on the hilltop; Oshel pushed out to view, gripping Alexandra Sherrod by the arm. Her hands were tied at her back. 'Tute, come out!' Oshel bellowed. Another movement up on a flanking hill and Tute stepped out. Sure enough, the son of a bitch had sneaked almost up on his side.

Oshel released Alexandra. Quickly Dake lowered his knife and gave Verl a shove forward, simultaneously bending over to seize up his rifle. Verl stopped. 'Gimme my gun.'

'You move on,' Dake snarled, 'or I'll feed this 'un down your gullet. Walk slow.'

Verl hesitated, then started walking. From the other direction Alexandra began to descend the hill, stumbling a little, moving awkwardly with her hands bound. Her dress was torn at the shoulder, but she looked fine otherwise. Both Oshel and Tute gripped their rifles tensely, watching. And waiting, Dake was sure, for Verl to come a distance from him before making their move. Just so Alexandra was equally distant from them and not in line. But Dake, not she, would be their target.

Verl was about halfway to the hill now and Alexandra had nearly reached its base.

'*Giddown, Verl!*' Oshel roared, at the same time swinging up his rifle.

Verl threw himself flat in the grass. Dake dropped to the ground simultaneously, yelling at Alexandra to do the same. Oshel fired. Dake heard the ball whistle close. He

175

squirmed around on his belly to line on Tute, but Tute had already faded back into cover to wait his chance.

Dake raised his head. His thudding heart locked in his chest. Alexandra had ignored his warning; she was running straight toward him. She had the presence of mind to veer wide of where Verl was sprawled, but came close enough that he couldn't resist lunging to his feet and running to intercept her.

Dake fired from the ground, too quickly. A miss. He dropped his piece and grabbed up Verl's rifle.

Too late. Verl gave a triumphant laugh as he cut side-on across Alexandra's path. She tried to twist past him, but he seized her around the waist. God – he had her! Dake dropped his sights, unable to fire.

'I got 'er, Daddy!' Verl crowed. 'Now we –'

Both Alexandra's hands shot up – suddenly free, and raked across Verl's face. He screeched with pain and surprise and let go of her, staggering back. Dake came up on one knee as Verl, his face contorted, bulled after her again. Dake hesitated just an instant, steadying the unfamiliar piece, then sinking his sights a fraction.

Verl's big hand was reaching for her as Dake squeezed off the shot. Verl spun, his jaw flapping open, and plunged down in the grass.

Alexandra wheeled and ran toward Dake, her rippling skirts caught up in her hands. Frantically he motioned her down. Changing his mind then, he grabbed up both rifles, leaped to his feet and ran toward her. The meadow offered no real shelter except for a few shallow hummocks.

A rifle's sharp report was followed by a smashing blow in Dake's right leg. His feet crossed and tripped him in a bruising somersault. He rolled instantly to his feet, still clinging to the rifles, and had a glimpse of Tute high on the hillside, his gun up and a cloud of powdersmoke fraying around him. Then Dake plunged on, pain streaking hotly up his leg.

He met Alexandra in mid-run, caught her around the shoulders and whirled them both off their feet as he flung his weight sideways. The two tumbled on the hard earth and rolled into a small depression behind a hummock. Alexandra lay crushed against him; he felt the wild pounding of her heart. Even in a moment of pain and danger, he was

176

conscious of a violent and unheeding desire for her. She shuddered and stirred, and he let her move back. Her eyes were wide, her mouth trembling, with unspoken feeling.

'You ain't hurt?'

'No . . . but you –'

'Scratch. Best get these rifles loaded afore anything.'

Dake quickly loaded both weapons, awkwardly trying to avoid movements that would expose his arms or head. Sprawled in the grass-edged depression, they were barely hidden from the Callicutts. But Oshel and Tute could easily shift positions to any point on the horseshoe. The hummock sheltered the depression fairly well on the north side, but what about east and west? The Callicutts could cover each side of the prong and take them in a crossfire. It would be over quickly. Unless.

When he had primed the rifles, Dake squirmed close to Alexandra. 'We are going to have to run for it and that right sudden. Get to them trees –' he pointed at the western prong '– we'll be on an equal footing with 'em. Oshel will work over to this side now, but Tute is already in place on the east hill. Waiting his daddy's move. We'll be under Tute's gun, but we got no choice. Understand?'

She jerked her head affirmatively.

'When I shoot, you run. Run to where them trees bend in nearest us.'

'But what of you? Your leg –'

'I'll make it. Be right behind you. Get ready.'

Dake raised his piece and discharged it at the east hill. In the covering shroud of powdersmoke, Alexandra scrambled up and began running. Dake leaped after her, intending to shield her in her run. A knot of pain wrenched at his right calf; he stumbled and nearly fell. Already Alexandra was well ahead of him as he lurched after her, trying to keep his body between her and Tute. But he was limping too badly, his leg threatening to cave under him.

Suddenly hauling up, Dake whirled to face the east hill. Sure enough, Tute had sprung out to sight again, his rifle coming up. Dake dropped his empty gun and brought the other sweeping level.

The high piercing reports of the rifles beat down each other's echoes. Tute staggered and fell, but almost immediately got to his knees. Scooping up the rifle he'd dropped,

177

Dake hobbled after Alexandra, who had reached the fringe of forest. A few yards from it, his leg collapsed and he fell. She ran out, helped him to his feet and supported him till they were deep inside the trees.

Dake sank down against an oak trunk, holding his leg. 'You got to get out of here,' he said. 'Cut through these trees back to the stream and foller it to the camp.'

'And just leave you?'

'I ain't alone.' He patted the two rifles. 'Tute is out o' it and I got two guns to Oshel's one. You can fetch back some sojers to he'p me. Snap to, now!'

Her loosened hair swung to a quick shake of her head. 'He will be on you in a minute or so ... and it's no equal contest, whatever you say. Can you move?'

'If need be.'

'Hardly at all, with that leg.' Alexandra dropped on her knees beside him. 'I will look at it.'

Blood was puddling in Dake's moccasin, a dark stain widening on his leather legging. 'Ain't nothing much. Anyways there is no time.'

'There is for this. Unless you prefer to bleed to death while you're waiting.'

'I'll take keer of it. You get going.'

'May I have your knife?' She held out her hand.

Dake sighed and unsheathed his hunting knife. She thrust it through the bullet tear in his legging and ripped it wider, exposing the big muscle of his calf. The hole was bluish-bruised around the edge and leaking plenty. 'The ball is still in there, but we can check the bleeding somewhat.' She ripped off the hem of a petticoat. Strong-handed and sure, not scared a mite. Not so a man could see it.

While she twisted many tight turns of cloth around his leg, Dake reloaded the empty rifle, his eyes continually questing the dappled woods. Particularly he scanned the area to the north, for Oshel would work toward them from that direction. Also Dake could make out the vestiges of an old game trail winding through the trees from the north. It curved close past where he and Alexandra were. Oshel might follow that trail, but he would work offside of it so as not to expose himself. And being hillbred, he would come quiet and careful. . . .

'Something I would like you to know,' Dake said.

178

'I had me a Pawnee wife a few years back. I had figured to settle down with these people for good before she died in childbirth. Her and the baby both.'

Alexandra knotted the cloth firmly, then raised her eyes. 'That was when you left the Pawnee?'

'That's when. I had been pretty wild before she come along and afterward I went wild again, only wuss'n before. Been that way since. Had no reason not to be. Not till now. She was a damned fine woman.'

'I think she wed a fine man, Dake. Do you have a reason again?'

'I have been hoping so.'

'So have I.' Her strong smooth hand moved and closed tight on his.

It was good to know, but he wished it had come to light at a better time. A better place too. Again he started to tell her to get clear of here while there was time. Then, as he continued to study the old trail and the heavy verdure all around, an idea came to him.

Oshel would be coming slow and watchful. But slow, that was the thing. So there ought to be time enough.

Oshel Callicutt was bear-big, but moving at a stealthy pace in heavy cover was nothing new for him. He made only slight stirrings as he pressed slowly through the thickets, gently parting them with the outheld barrel of his rifle. Constantly on the watch, he paused every few yards to make sure of his bearings and to ascertain that he wasn't blundering into a trap. Which would be damned easy to do in this massed brush.

The red rage that scoured Oshel's mind made it hard to restrain himself from plowing blindly ahead in search of his prey, heedless of everything except getting his hands around Satterlee's throat. Verl was done, of that Oshel was sure. The way he'd dropped at the bullet's impact. Oshel had seen mortally hit game drop the same way. Tute? Maybe he wasn't bad hit, but he was out of the fight.

Up to their daddy now. No more fooferaw about taking off Satterlee's hands. Man tripped himself up with fancy ideas. Get Satterlee, get him dead, was all that mattered.

Oshel was moving roughly south alongside the game

179

trail, keeping it always in sight but never showing himself. He couldn't fail to flush his prey soon, for he was nearing the spot where Satterlee and the woman had ducked into the trees. Hurt and badly limping, Satterlee couldn't have gotten far away; he'd be close by.

Cautiously prodding aside a last screen of brush, Oshel found himself peering across a large glen through which the trail passed. He froze where he was, letting his eyes circle the mottled walls of foliage.

The *tu-whu* of an owl, close by, startled him. His eyes narrowed. An owl ... here and now? Or maybe a damned good imitation of one. Sounded like ...

He caught a distinct rustle of bushes. His eyes pounced on a slight but definite tremor of leaves. There ... far end of the glen. He watched intently, his rifle snugged against his shoulder but not yet raised. Sure as hell. Someone had laid up in those bushes by the trail. Let the son of a bitch move just once more. . . .

The leaves shook.

Oshel's rifle sprang level and roared. In the pale burst of smoke he saw the thicket jerk and sway as if from a sagging weight inside. Ripping out an exultant growl, he plunged into the open and charged across the glen, clubbing his upswung rifle in both fists.

A gun bellowed close at hand.

Even as the sound filled his ears, he knew he was hit. Something smacked Oshel Callicutt's leg like a bludgeon and he went down in a twisting fall.

Still aware only of a crushing numbness, he swung quickly to a sitting position, his rifle up. And found himself facing a man limping from the brush.

'Put it down, old man,' Satterlee said quietly. 'You have fired your charge and I got another rifle'

Sure enough. He had Verl's in hand. Savagely, Oshel threw his useless gun at Satterlee's legs; it fell short.

What in hell had happened? Oshel scowlingly fixed on the thicket he'd fired at. Suddenly the branches had straightened up as if a holding pressure had been released And now Alexandra Sherrod was crawling out of a thicket flush beside it. She was holding one end of a short twisted rope made of what looked like strands of torn petticoat tied together. The other end led, by God, into the thicket he'd

180

shot at. She'd fastened the improvised rope to the inner stems and, at Satterlee's own signal, had given it a couple of tugs to pull Oshel's fire, afterward dragging it sideways to simulate a body falling.

'Ain't hard to figure,' said Satterlee. 'Is it?'

A full and tearing pain flooded Oshel's wounded thigh. Squeezing both hands around it, he blinked his squinting eyes clear. When he could manage words, he husked: 'You ain't quits with me, mountain man.'

Satterlee shook his head with slow disbelief. 'Old man, if you ain't a caution for sure. You ain't got a thing left to fight with. Your game is played out and you don't even see it. Well, we will see what Dodge has to say on't,'

CHAPTER EIGHTEEN

Verl was dead and Oshel was unable to walk. Tute was leaking from a hole in his right side, but it didn't appear to be serious. Dake plugged his and Oshel's wounds with wads of torn petticoat, then tied up Tute to keep him where he was. Afterward Dake and Alexandra started back to the Dragoon camp, he leaning on her as they walked. His wounded calf hurt like hell and he stopped twice to rest.

On the second stop, he heard noises from the trees ahead and then a squad of soldiers came into sight, Lieutenant Fry and Sergeant Bohannon leading them.

'Hour wa'n't up,' Dake observed. 'You busted your word, Sarge.'

'A good thing he did, from the look of matters,' Stennis said curtly. 'What the devil happened? Where are the Callicutts?'

Dake told it briefly, saying then: 'Wa'n't no other way I could see to do it, Loot. I gone after these yahoos with a bunch o' sojers, could o' got Miz Sherrod killed '

'Perhaps. You took a big chance, nevertheless. By the way, Buffalo Calf Girl will live . . . a deputation of Kiowas brought Dodge the word a little while ago. But they still demand the life of the man who shot her.'

Dake sighed 'Well, we got a dead man to show 'em. Verl Callicutt. That ought to satisfy 'em.'

'Let's hope so We'll fetch his body in and bring along his father and brother Can you make it all right?'

Dake smiled 'I got help enough, don't you fret '

Stennis smiled too and touched his cap to Alexandra, and he and his soldiers moved on toward the horseshoe hill.

Dake and Alexandra continued on their slow way, he with an arm around her shoulders, she holding him around the waist Their holds were a bit tighter than necessary; it couldn't have seemed more right or natural Again they halted to rest.

'Listen,' Dake said, 'I want to say this better than I done before '

'There is plenty of time.'

'There's time now. You said you'd come to care for this country. Did you mean that?'

'Of course I meant it.'

'Well, then. Something I got in mind. Was farm-raised and I feel a hankering to get back to farming.'

It was her turn to say it: 'Do you, Dake? Are you sure?'

'Sure as God made apples green. With you I'm sure.' They were sitting close; his arm tightened around her. 'There is choice land in the valley of the Arkansas River. It will take time to build us up a good farm. No such fancy-fine place as your family had, but . . .'

'It sounds fine.'

'No. It ain't. Not for you. It ain't enough. But it's what I got to offer.'

'It is more than enough. For me it is. As for time, I said it before. We'll have plenty. The rest of our lives . . .'

Henry Dodge sat in a folding chair in the privacy of his tent, arms folded behind his head, legs outstretched and boots propped on a crate that served him as writing desk. His buckskin blouse was off against the heat; no draft coasted through the open flap of his tent and his red flannel shirt, seam-strained by his raised arms and thick trunk, was blotched with perspiration. But Dodge was oblivious to heat and sweat; a smile played on the lips pursed around his cigar. He puffed occasional rolls of smoke at the tent wall, his speculative gaze resting on the inkpot and clean sheet of paper on the crate top by his crossed boots.

The report he must write would contain (he thought) more good than bad. Just a question of how to phrase it, and Dodge was in no hurry.

He wondered how many key events of history had turned on the littlest things? Many – or all. A lead bullet weighed only an ounce. But the one that wounded Buffalo Calf Girl had nearly wrecked the mission. Another ball, the one that killed Verl Callicutt, had as sure saved it.

Dodge couldn't have surrendered a live white man to Indian vengeance All to the good, therefore, that Satter-lee's bullet had disposed of the problem. Of course since the real murderer was Oshel, not one of his sons, Dodge had had to dissemble a bit to the Kiowas. He'd merely

183

shown their deputation Verl's body and told them, through Poore, that retribution had been meted out. Since Buffalo Calf Girl would live, the blood debt was more than paid. Satisfied, the Kiowas had returned to the council, which now, with the white chief's good faith confirmed, should go ahead smoothly. Oshel and Tute would return to Fort Gibson chained in a wagon; they would face trial in a territorial court. So much for that business . . .

What next? Dodge's mind dwelled pleasantly on the possibilities. Let a successful mission write its own ticket. If Andy-Jackson had a reputation for dealing harshly with failure, he was also known to reward generously for success Dodge's mouth straightened. Hardly an unequivocal success, with close to a third of his regiment wiped out. Not in a battle whose outcome might excuse the cost, but to ravaging fever which had taken its toll to no purpose.

Someone touched the tent flap.

'Sir?'

Dodge looked up, rousing himself with an effort. 'Ah, Fry. Come in . . . come in.'

Stennis Fry stepped inside and stood almost at attention, his hair brushing the tent peak. His cap was held in the crook of one arm; sweat beaded his face.

'At ease, man. Something troubling you?'

'No, sir. That is . . . I hardly know how to say it. I know you didn't anticipate any development of this sort.'

'Of what sort?' Dodge swung his boots to the ground. 'Make it clear, Mister.'

Stennis did, in remarkably few words. Dodge listened with amazement, slowly shaking his head as Stennis finished. 'You're right, Fry. I never expected you to carry the game this far.'

'I haven't decided anything for sure, sir. I am still wrestling with the question. . . .'

'Of whether you'll marry her? That's sense, anyway. You'll want time to be sure you've not merely been overwhelmed by the lady's warm golden beauty.'

Stennis flushed. 'I don't think I am, sir.'

Dodge smiled faintly. 'And your family – how would they take the news?'

'I think you know the answer to that, Colonel.'

'Hm. Well it's hardly in my own interests to discourage

you. No denying the union of a Dragoon officer and the granddaughter of a leading Pawnee chief would have a highly salutary effect on this whole mission. But I can't forebear pointing out that so far as your career-to come is concerned, such action could only be termed disastrous.'

'It would be, if that consideration entered into the matter. It won't because I plan to resign from the service.'

'Oh? May I ask your reasons?'

'I'm afraid, sir, that I just haven't enough son of a bitch in me.'

Dodge's brows quivered upward; he cracked his palm on his knee with a roar of laughter. 'I've suspected that for some time, Mr. Fry. As a much-resented presidential appointee myself, I can sympathize with the decision, if not the reason. Tell me, what judgment do you think history will render on this mission?'

'Frankly, sir, I think that this expedition has been one of the most tragic and costly fiascos in peacetime military history. I think it should be remembered as such.'

'And how many of the top brass do you think will be willing to accommodate such thinking ... should the mission wholly succeed in its original purpose?'

'I should say none.'

'Bravo. You've learned despite yourself. Your upbringing drummed you full of pious catch-all cant; you sincerely desire to live by those precepts. Well and good. But a fellow as fervent in his ideals as you are would always be plagued by the holes in the Army contract. The ambitions, subterfuges, downright stupidities of your peers, their scramblings for citation and advancement, would always revolt you. Yes, Fry, you're wise to bow out and keep the substance of your ideals. Just remember: ideals are nothing but gilded tinpots till they've been chipped around the edges a little. What's left will stand if it's worth a damn. End of speech. Your lady love is welcome to return with us, unless her relatives object – is that what you're here to ask?'

'Yes, sir. Wa ter ra-shah-ro has indicated that he'll abide by whatever Ona decides, and she is quite willing to go back with me.'

Dodge steepled his fingers, nodding. 'Not being particularly idealistic myself, I think that to pair with your dusky
185

maiden on a permanent basis would be a stupid goddamned mistake. But whatever you decide, I wish you luck, my boy.'

'Thank you, sir.'

'None of my business, but I'm curious to know if you've any long range plans for your future.'

'Yes, sir.' Promptly and crisply. 'Dake Satterlee and I plan to farm in the Arkansas Valley. Cotton. He has the experience, I the financial means, to get us off to a good start.'

Dodge leaned back in his chair, eying the younger man with a fresh interest. From the first, he had felt an uncertainty in Fry. An untried strength that was searching for direction. He seemed to have found it.

'I know something of farming myself,' Dodge said then, 'and you couldn't be making a better investment. Nor, if I know men, a better choice in partners.' He rose, extending his hand. 'All best of luck, Mr. Fry.' This time saying it with heartfelt belief.

Stennis shook hands, saluted and walked smartly out.

Standing in the tent opening, Dodge watched him cross the camp compound to where Ona was waiting. Coming to join them now were Dake Satterlee and Mrs. Sherrod. Dodge, looking at these four young people together, smiled and shook his head.

Maybe that was what this land, this America, was really all about. Not another mere contrivance of a conquering race. Not, certainly, at its best. And that best was a human closeness, a giving and a sharing. Strangers coming together for a purpose. An acceptance by men and women for what each one was, not for what he or she had been born.

Dodge was smiling as he turned back to his chair. He pulled it up to his improvised desk and sat, then dipped his pen and began to write.

AFTERWORD

After a week of parleying, the big council was brought to a semi successful end. Fifteen Kiowa, three Pawnee and one Comanche chief agreed to return to Fort Gibson with the Dragoons. Negotiations would be held to lay a ground work for future treaty agreements. Somewhat recuperated, the 1st Regiment of U.S. Dragoons turned their faces homeward.

Their troubles weren't finished. At the sick camps they'd left along their trail, they found that most of the stricken men had died. The casualty list continued to climb as they moved on, wagons and horseborne litters conveying the sick. At Dean's camp on the Washita, they learned of General Henry Leavenworth's death. When he had failed to show improvement, the ailing general had been placed in an ambulance and started for Fort Gibson, only to succumb within a few miles.

It was the sorry and broken remnant of a 'regiment that finally limped into Gibson on August 24, 1834. The mission had cost ninety lives, of which all but a few had been lost not to bullet or arrow but to rampant fever. Yet costly or not, the immediate results of the expedition seemed like spectacular gains. Eight days after the Dragoons' return, emissaries of the Kiowas and Osages arrived to sue for peace. Long standing quarrels between the plains tribes were at last temporarily healed.

Henry Dodge reaped a reward for services well-performed when, in 1836, President Jackson appointed him first governor of the newly formed Territory of Wisconsin. Stephen Watts Kearny, assuming full command of the 1st Dragoons, inaugurated tough and practical measures that rebuilt the shattered regiment into a veteran hardened outfit that was smooth functioning and stripped to essentials.

Gradually the pony soldiers learned to cope with the harsh conditions of the western plains. In the decades that followed, the horse army whose designation evolved from 'dragoons' to 'mounted rifles' to 'cavalry' would forge a major role in the winning of the West, in America's Mexican and Civil wars, and finally in the making of a nation.

BREAK THE YOUNG LAND

T. V. OLSEN

Winner of the Golden Spur Award

Borg Vikstrom and his fellow Norwegian farmers are captivated when they see freedom's beacon shining from the untamed prairies near a Kansas town called Liberty. In order to stake their claim for the American dream they will risk their lives and cross an angry ocean. But in the cattle barons' kingdom, sodbusters seldom get a second chance...before being plowed under. With a power-hungry politico ready to ignite a bloody range-war, it is all the stalwart emigrant can do to keep the peace...and dodge the price that has been tacked on his head.

_4226-6 $4.50 US/$5.50 CAN

BONNER'S STALLION
T. V. OLSEN

Winner of the Golden Spur Award

Bonner's life is the kind that makes a man hard, makes him love the high country, and makes him fear nothing but being limited by another man's fenceposts. Suddenly it looks as if his life is going to get even harder. He has already lost his woman. Now he is about to lose his son and his mountain ranch to a rich and powerful enemy—a man who hates to see any living thing breathing free. That is when El Diablo Rojo, the feared and hated rogue stallion, comes back into Bonner's life. He and Bonner have one thing in common...they are survivors.

___4276-2 $4.50 US/$5.50 CAN